****

A Prelude to World War III:
The Rise of the Islamic Republic and the Rebirth of America

Book One of the World War III Series

By James Rosone & Miranda Watson
****

Published in conjunction with Front Line Publishing, Inc.

Copyright Information

ISBN: 978-1-957634-20-3
Sun City Center, Florida, USA
Library of Congress Control Number: 2022904137

Disclaimer

This book is fictional in nature. Any resemblance to persons or events in actual existence is merely coincidental. The views expressed in the book are the views held by the characters and are not reflective of the authors' personal views.

Table of Contents

Chapter 1
The Stage is Set

Some news creeps over time. It may not steal headlines because of its slow progress, but its significance can come to overshadow all other events in the world.

Beginning in the 1960s, the border between India and Pakistan became one of the most heavily militarized regions in the world. Tensions over who would ultimately control the resources and water flow of the Kashmir Province were compounded by a natural distaste of each group for one another along religious lines. The more radical Muslims of Pakistan found the idea of hundreds of Hindu gods in India to be disgraceful and repulsive on a level that inspired widespread hatred.

For decades, the only thing that kept these countries from engaging in all-out warfare was the knowledge that each country possessed nuclear weapons. However, this standoff was bound to end eventually. There was simply too much loathing and abhorrence between the two parties for peace to really be successful. By 2024, both sides had deployed numerous intelligence assets into each other's countries to try and detect weak points in security. It was only a matter of time until one was found and then exploited.

During the late 2010s and early 2020s, the various Islamic extremist groups steadily united under one banner and organization, the Islamic State. This merging of groups and resources strengthened their ability to influence politics, policies, and various regimes throughout the world. Then their strategy of violent and continuous conflict shifted to education, spreading extremist teachings and infiltrating various political offices in Europe and North America to further their agendas. This dramatically increased their support base and political influence across the globe. Like the mafia, they enforced their rules and positions within their organization, and like the mob, they had a front man with the true leader hiding in the shadows.

Their leader was a man named Mohammed Abbas, a man who hid in plain sight. He was a distinguished Saudi prince in his late fifties, responsible for diversifying the Saudi Arabian economy so it would not be solely dependent on oil. In his younger years, Mohammed had fought with Al Qaeda forces in Iraq and then later in Afghanistan before he was wounded and forced to return to Saudi Arabia.

After surviving his participation in the global jihad, Mohammed maintained his allegiance with Al Qaeda, albeit secretly. He knew being a foot soldier would ultimately get him killed, so he opted to pursue the leadership track. He smartly leveraged his position in the royal family to pursue a PhD in economics from the London School of Economics. Upon completion of his education, he returned to Saudi Arabia and worked his way through the ranks of the Ministry of Industry and Science. Meanwhile, in his secret life, he became very influential within the Islamic State and led the change in strategies within the organization.

After a decade of planning, the Islamic State was preparing for their first major military operation in Pakistan. The next few weeks would set in motion a series of events that would change the world. The air was rife with anticipation. If things went according to plan, then the ensuing war between Pakistan and India would be the first pawn to fall in this global game of chess.
****

Mohammed woke up early one morning, shortly before it all began, and opened the laptop in his apartment bedroom for a video chat with the Director of Pakistani Inter-Services Intelligence, or ISI, Zaheer Akthar. As the chat window opened, Mohammed watched his ally take a seat in his office chair, a fancy leather number that was a little too expensive for his position. Influence could be gained in many ways—Zaheer liked the finer things in life and was willing to do quite a bit in order to take a shortcut to prosperity. Mohammed was more than happy to oblige Zaheer's tastes to buy his undying loyalty.

"As-Salaam Alaikum," began Mohammed. The greeting had all the fervor of a truly devoted man.

"Alaikum As-Salaam," replied Zaheer.

"Are your operatives in India ready for the big day?"

"Yes, Mohammed. My most trusted commanders have ensured the assets are in place throughout India. The weapons are in place, and everything is ready for the coming operation."

Mohammed leaned in to the video camera. "Zaheer, it is imperative that this operation goes according to the plan. This is the first domino of many that needs to fall for our strategy to work."

"My men understand, Mohammed, as do I. Once the shooting starts, this conflict will turn nuclear quickly. When this happens, I will ensure the President launches our nuclear weapons in retaliation. I have guaranteed that enough evidence will be found to directly link these attacks to the ISI, which will force the Indians to respond," said Zaheer confidently.

Letting out a sigh of relief, Mohammed nodded. "Just make sure you are at your safe location when this starts. I'll need you here in Saudi Arabia for the next phase."

"As you wish, my Caliph. Peace be upon you, and Allahu Akbar."
****

Through the years, the ISI had smuggled hundreds of Islamic State and ISI operatives into India to prepare for the day when they would decapitate the Indian government. During the 2030 opening session of the Indian parliament, their terrorist plan was finally put into motion. Fifty operatives dressed as security personnel successfully snuck high-grade explosives into the parliament building, strategically placing them within the ornate meeting hall to achieve maximum carnage.

While the country was watching their versions of C-SPAN and CNN to see the newly elected officials sworn in, they had no idea they would be watching the murders of hundreds of people. The ceremony began with its usual pomp and circumstance, droning on without anything to set it apart from any other government formality. However, as soon as the prime minister took the stage, one of the ISI operatives who was disguised as security began to sweat profusely. From his vantage point in one of the second-floor porticos, he would be able to see the man he hated most die before he met his own end. Before anyone could stop him, the nervous terrorist pressed the detonator button, beginning a chain reaction of destruction. At least the prime minister's death would be swift.

Explosions ripped through the structures supporting the building, causing large portions of it to implode in on itself. Pieces of the walls and ceiling continued to crack and crumble down for several minutes. As surviving and stunned members of parliament fled the building, the militants executed them, firing their machine guns into the crowd and using knives on those who happened to be at close range. Those who were smartest among the group tried to appear as lifeless as possible, hoping this would save them from certain death. Sirens wailed, and alarms sounded all across the government buildings and the city. As help began to arrive, first responders and military members were met with a barrage of small-arms fire from the militants.

Meanwhile, on the other side of the capital, a separate group of five suicide bombers set out on their own mission of chaos and destruction. Knowing thousands of people were injured at the parliament building and many more would be wounded before the day was out, these five suicide bombers each drove an ambulance packed with 3,000 pounds of explosives towards their intended targets—the five largest hospitals in New Delhi. Upon reaching their destinations, all five successfully detonated their cargo, effectively destroying the hospitals in the capital and causing thousands of additional casualties.

Over the next several hours, Islamic State militants and ISI operatives conducted coordinated terrorist attacks all across India in what would be known as Bloody Monday. They attacked all types of political leaders, religious leaders, business owners, and companies. Throughout the rest of the day, malls, train stations, bus stops and open-air markets were all attacked with indiscriminate gunfire. There was no apparent rhyme or reason to the attacks other than to just kill as many innocent people as possible.

By the end of this horrible day in human history, over 53,000 people were killed. In the following days, additional attacks took place, this time directed at police and other security personnel who were trying to restore order. Then, for some unknown reason, the men and women who had carried out the worst terrorist attacks in world history dropped their weapons and simply disappeared into India's sea of humanity.

What was left of the Indian government gathered in underground bunkers and began to piece together the information to determine who was responsible for these dastardly attacks. Fortunately for them, during one of the terrorist attacks, an Islamic State member had been successfully captured. In the course of his tortured interrogation, he admitted to receiving training and assistance from the ISI. The prisoner then divulged a treasure trove of information about other terrorists' cells and the ISI handlers who were providing them with the weapons and explosives to carry out their attacks. It became clear that this attack had been planned for years by the ISI. With this newly obtained information, it left the remnants of the Indian government with some tough choices, chief among them how to respond to this brazen attack by the Pakistani ISI and Islamic State.

****

Horrifying and shocking as these attacks were, they were only the beginning. In every catastrophe, there is always an opportunist, looking to take advantage of the situation. The attacks on India were no exception. Throughout the past several decades, Mohammed Abbas had mentored, recruited, and manipulated hundreds of individuals in key positions across the Middle East and Asia as he looked to build an Islamic Caliphate. Now it was time for those pawns to move on the giant chess board he had created.

In Indonesia, Ismail, the regional spiritual figurehead for the Islamic State, had been following the news closely. He watched every second of twenty-four-hour news coverage that he could stay awake for. Weeks of being holed up in a dirty warehouse, changing safe houses, and avoiding the government's counterterrorism sweeps were about to pay off.

He startled briefly as he heard one of the building doors open but breathed a sigh of relief when he recognized his military commander, Mohammed Jamal. Ismail waved him over, eager to tie up any loose ends. He grabbed a dusty seat, brushed it off, and sat down across a dilapidated table from his partner in this grand scheme to discuss their plans.

"Ismail, it is time for us to begin our phase of the operation," said Mohammed Jamal. He lit a cigar and took a giant puff. Mohammed knew Ismail hated it when he smoked, but it was his way of making sure Ismail understood that he was his own man and not beholden to Ismail and the laborious readings of the Koran.

Ismail predictably crinkled his nose in disdain at the foul smell of the cigar, letting out a soft cough in protest. "We have worked long and hard to enable our people to infiltrate the various key positions within the government and military. Now that our brothers in arms in India have successfully conducted their attack, we must hold up our end so that Mohammed can initiate his plan and bring in the new Caliphate."

"Is there anything I should worry about? Are all the pieces in place?" questioned Mohammed Jamal. He knew he had the military side of the operation under control, but he was a bit unsure of Ismail's followers.

"Inshallah, there is nothing that has not been prepared for," replied Ismail confidently.

"Then, Inshallah, the next time we meet, we shall have a true celebration, my brother."

****

On Thursday of the same week, with the world still reeling from the massacre in India, Ismail's group of Islamic State militants broke through the security detail surrounding the president of Indonesia. Their attack was so swift and well-coordinated that none of the security guards knew what was happening until it was too late. While their motorcade traveled to an event in Jakarta, an IED blew up right in front of the lead car, sending it rolling end over end. The president's driver was unable to respond quickly enough to evade the flying hunk of metal, and their car was quickly smashed as the lead car landed on the hood. Armed men rushed in before anyone could react, killing the guards and dragging the president and his family from their vehicles.

While this was taking place, several cameramen were videoing what was happening and live-streaming it to social media. Minutes after the capture of the president and his family, signs that read "Infidel" were placed around each of their necks as they were strung up by ropes to a lamppost. While they dangled from their restraints, someone read off a list of charges against them, detailing their crimes against Islam. Then their bodies were riddled with bullets.

Within minutes of this gruesome attack, other key military figures all over Indonesia were assassinated by Mohammed's trusted military officers and were quickly replaced by trusted men who had been prepared for this moment in history.

Days after the bloody coup, Ismail appeared on the main news station in Indonesia. He announced to the world that he had taken over as the new Caliph of the Islamic Republic of Indonesia and had assigned Mohammed Jamal as the new head of the Islamic Revolutionary Guard of Indonesia. Fearing deadly retaliation, the majority of the Indonesian military quickly backed the leader of the coup, and martial law was imposed across the country. Panic, however, had spread rapidly throughout the countryside. Most of the opposition was smart enough to stay silent during the transition, but those politicians and military members who did come to the aid of the former government were dealt with swiftly and made into public examples in a brutal show of force.

Still, various factions of the military and police fought against the army units that were supporting the coup and the Islamic State militants. Though they had the passion and spark of those who were fighting for their very survival, they lacked adequate firepower to combat Ismail's forces and quickly became outnumbered. The rebels were rapidly pushed into the backwoods of the remote parts of the country, unable to emerge for fear of annihilation. By Saturday, Ismail Mohammed was running the new Islamic Republic of Indonesia.

****

As Indonesia fell, the next piece on the chessboard was moved into position, and it was time for the Malaysian group to act. Islamic State militants waited until the dead of night to approach Kuala Lumpur, dressed in urban camouflage and hoisting large Islamic State flags on their vehicles. Dozens upon dozens of vehicles loaded with explosives carried militants towards their targets, full of zeal and confidence that their cause, like that of their brothers in Indonesia, would be successful. However, even after months of planning and with moles inside the inner circle of leadership of the Malaysian government and military, there was a wrench in their best-laid plans that had not been anticipated.

Two nights before the attack, the Commander in Chief of the Malaysian Armed Forces woke up in a cold sweat after a vivid nightmare. And since he held the dream world in high esteem for its power to inform, he quickly set a plan in motion to change patrol routes along the outside of the city. He doubled the size of the patrol units and pulled some strings to incorporate armored personnel carriers and infantry fighting vehicles.

The following evening, Islamic State militants, unaware of this recent change in military posture, started their assault on the capital. However, within minutes of the official go order, the lead column of militant vehicles drove right into a security checkpoint. With the element of surprise lost, the forces that had been going to raid the presidential palace were summarily defeated, and the coup collapsed.

The Malaysian Army and security forces quickly squashed any further uprising within their country, swiftly identifying the disloyal officers within their ranks and removing them. Several days of bloody

street battles and terrorist attacks stunned the nation, and the popular support for the Islamic State was crushed by the government. At least for the time being, Malaysia was prevented from becoming the next Islamic Republic to spring out this Militant Islamic Awakening.
****

Back in Saudi Arabia, Mohammed Abbas was watching the news about India and Indonesia on Al Jazeera with particular delight. As the unofficial leader of the Islamic State, nothing brought him greater joy than to see infidels lose their power and their lives. He stepped out on his balcony and smoked a cigarette, quietly looking out at the city. In the distance, he heard the evening call to prayer. With that, he pulled his prayer rug out and sought guidance, protection, and strength to carry through with the following day's plan. Following his evening prayer, he got a surprisingly restful night's sleep.

Mohammed woke up the next morning to his usual routine. It had taken him decades to build an intricate network of loyal workers across the country and throughout the Arabian Peninsula who shared his same religious goals. Each day at his day job, he managed to maintain the façade of loyalty towards the royal family. But secretly, in his spare time, his only focus was fomenting anger and insurrection against the various monarchs that ruled the Middle East and preaching the need for a new Caliph and Caliphate that would unite the nations of Islam under one banner and one religious cause. Despite his secret private life, he had slowly worked his way into the upper echelons of the royal family's inner circle through his economic modernization plans.

Before Mohammed left for the royal palace for his monthly meeting with the king, he drafted an email and saved it to his special account. Across the city and country, other members of his cell were logging in and looking at his message. Because it was never sent to a recipient, it could avoid security checks and monitoring, which was critical to the secrecy of their group and future operations. Mohammed's plan was on schedule, and the world was about to change forever.

At the palace that morning, the first few hours did not differ in any noticeable fashion from any other day. Appointments were made, mail was sorted, cleaning personnel managed, and a feast that was called breakfast was brought to the king and Mohammed while they discussed the modernization of the Saudi economy.

As the meal was being cleaned up, one of the staff members received a phone call that the new yacht the king had ordered was going to be made with oak cabinets instead of mahogany. The man quickly left to personally see to the "fixing" of this situation. Following breakfast, the King and Mohammed drank their coffee before going over the redevelopment plans for a new manufacturing plant near Jidda.

The King was not accustomed to having coffee without a cigarette, and he made a motion to Mohammed to join him and light his cigarette. Of course, Mohammed obliged and opened a fresh pack of Marlboros for the King, pulling one out and igniting the end with the gem-encrusted twenty-four-karat lighter the King had given him as a gift several years back. However, as the King of Saudi Arabia took that first drag, he would be making his final move. As the trail of smoke emerged from his mouth, Mohammed slipped his right hand into his suit jacket and pulled out the knife that had been hidden in the inside pocket by a janitor earlier that morning while Mohammed had been eating breakfast with the King. In one seamless motion, he slit the infidel pig's throat.

In that moment, a shockwave hit the room. The guards, who had not been paying particular attention, suddenly gasped in genuine disbelief that this could have occurred on their watch. The surprise caused a momentary delay in response. What seemed like a minute went by in silence, but five seconds later, three guards had pulled out their guns and aimed them at Mohammed.

Just as they were about to shoot him, men loyal to Mohammed, who had been secretly planted in order to be in the room at this time, killed the body guards with knives. A butler, a housekeeper, and two bodyguards loyal to Mohammed made short work of the other guards. All the routine actions of the day had been carefully orchestrated to ensure a maximum number of men loyal to Mohammed's cause would be in the room or nearby when the King was to be assassinated. The Saudi royals never saw it coming as he had been one of them for so long.

Once the guards had been killed, one of Mohammed Abbas's men pulled out his smartphone and recorded a short message from their fearless leader while proudly displaying the dead body of the King. Soon the group was sending out a broadcast showing their victory to all television channels across the region and signaling for the other attacks to take place. In between declarations of "Allahu Akbar," it became clear that this day would end with the death of more than one Saudi royal.

Across the country, selected members of the Saudi military, who were secret Islamic State members, hunted down and killed members of the royal family wherever they could find them.

Mohammed Abbas proudly proclaimed the following day that he had assumed control of Saudi Arabia as the new Caliph. He sat in the King's chair, sending out a broadcast to the world. Taking a deep breath, he smiled, turned to the camera, and boldly declared, "At long last, the land of the Prophet will once again return to Sharia law and be ruled by a true and just Caliph. This nation will no longer be occupied or used as a puppet by the West and their influences. All US forces must leave the Kingdom within three months. They are no longer welcome in our new nation."

****

May of 2030 was a bloody month of revolution and change across the Middle East and Asia. Despite the West's best attempts to try to stabilize the regions, many feared that a clash of civilizations between the West and Islam was looming on the horizon.

President de Blasio and his administration were caught completely flatfooted by the events. There had been no intelligence reporting to indicate something like this happening, and they were left with no real choice but to accept the changes being made in Saudi Arabia. The American president called for calm and dialogue between the various factions vying for power but refused to directly involve America or the military. In compliance with the new Caliph's request, President de Blasio ordered all US forces to withdraw from Saudi Arabia, Qatar, Bahrain, and Kuwait, relocating the majority of them to newly leased land and facilities in Israel.

Many Americans saw this as a capitulation by the President to Islamic extremists now that the Islamic State had announced they were responsible for the regime change in Saudi Arabia. However, even many of the more moderate Muslim Americans supported the President's move to recognize Mohammed Abbas as the Caliph of Saudi Arabia.

****

With the loss of infrastructure and key leaders, it took India a full three weeks to determine how they would respond to the horrific attack on their country and to position divisions and aircraft accordingly.

Without consultation with his allies in the West, the newly sworn-in prime minister of India launched an all-out attack against Pakistan in retaliation. Within the first four days of the India-Pakistan war, an Indian armored division had penetrated the Pakistani defensive line at the border and was driving fast and hard, rolling up the Pakistani defensive positions.

With an Indian Army bent on revenge, once they had broken through their line of defense, the Pakistanis saw no other alternative than to do the unthinkable and consider the use of tactical nuclear weapons. At first, this decision had been ruled out. However, Zaheer Akthar, the Director of the Pakistani Intelligence Service and Mohammed Abbas's right-hand man, had persuaded the prime minister that this must be done or Indian forces could be on the streets of the capital within weeks. The prime minister, believing that it was Al Qaeda militants responsible for the attacks in India and not his own intelligence service, felt India was using these terrorist attacks as an excuse to invade Pakistan. Reluctantly, the use of tactical nukes was authorized.

On June 3 at 1835 hours, the Pakistanis deployed the first of five 30-kiloton tactical nuclear weapons against the Indian Army. The attack was devastating, wiping out multiple Indian divisions and air force units. The Indian military was severely crippled. Initially stunned, the Indian forces quickly scattered and dispersed to minimize the chance of being hit with another nuclear strike.
****

Throughout the decades of tension between the two countries, the Indian prime ministers had warned that if Pakistan ever used nuclear weapons against India, they would respond, and their response would be unequivocal in nature. It was time for this threat to become a fulfilled promise.

Less than eight hours later, at 0132 in the morning, India launched ten 300 kiloton nuclear missiles and thirty tactical nuclear weapons at suspected Pakistani nuclear missile locations, four military installations, and their six largest and most strategic cities. Within an hour, mushroom clouds filled the skies of Pakistan with the fiery glow of their destruction, visible for dozens of miles in every direction.

Deep below the earth's surface, some Pakistanis were safe in their bunkers. From the comfort of their cots and sleeping bags, they still possessed the power to respond to the attacks. Mobile launchers had been dispersed across the country for some time, and they were finally put to use.

Forty-five nuclear missiles were launched at Indian cities within range of those weapons' capabilities. Being mobile missiles, the largest of the warheads was 200 kilotons—the "city killers" that the Indians feared.

The Indians responded with a second launch of thirty more 300-kiloton missiles and fifty smaller 20-kiloton nuclear weapons at their remaining military bases, while the "city killer" nukes were heading towards the remaining large cities of Pakistan. By 0257 on the morning of June 4, a combined 160 nuclear weapons had detonated across Pakistan and India, killing over 600 million people. The carnage was grotesque and extensive.

By sunrise, Pakistan as a nation ceased to exist. However, the Islamic State had just sacrificed their last chess piece for the greater good. The vast majority of the Pakistani people had been killed during the nuclear exchange; what few remained were left to die of radiation poisoning and starvation.

During the nuclear exchange, twenty-eight Indian cities were seriously damaged, and three were destroyed outright. The nuclear weapons hit across the north and northwestern portions of the country, sparing the lower half of the nation from the destructive power that had just been unleashed. While the south of India had been spared Pakistani nukes, over a third of India had been devastated by the nuclear attack.

Following the nuclear exchange, Indian forces moved into what was left of Pakistan and absorbed the country into a greater India. It would take years, if not decades, to decontaminate and rebuild the areas that were hit, but India began work at once, determined to rebuild and restore what had been lost.

While the war between India and Pakistan had been brief, it had shaken the world to its core with the sheer devastation that had been wrought in that region. The global economies immediately felt the effects of the nuclear exchange as well as the massive political changes in the governments in Indonesia and Saudi Arabia. Within a couple of days, the price of oil had gone up to just over three hundred dollars a barrel as speculators swooped in to try and take advantage of the situation. Overall investor confidence was severely shaken in the wake of these global changes.

****

Throughout the 2020s, the United States and the European Union became bogged down with a severe sovereign debt crisis and were struggling to provide basic services to their ever-growing and aging populations. The US had to begin a series of tough austerity programs to try and balance the budget. By the end of the 2020s, the US had borrowed nearly $45 trillion, and there just wasn't any more money left to borrow. The European Union was in the same shape, with many members having defaulted on their debts by the end of the decade.

The new leader of Saudi Arabia, Mohammed Abbas, and the Mullahs of Iran, saw this as an opportunity to squeeze the West further by cutting the production of oil. This caused the price of oil to remain over three hundred dollars a barrel for an extended period of time. The United States and the European Union began a massive shift in consumption from oil to natural gas, of which the United States had an immense reserve. Converting power plants, semitrucks, and trains to run on natural gas as an alternative to diesel was going to take a long, sustained effort, but the people and their leadership were all in agreement that they must make that goal a reality.

The economies of the West suffered even further in the wake of the nuclear devastation of India. With the explosions came not only political stability in the region, destruction of infrastructure and loss of life, but also the devastation of numerous technology research centers, manufacturing cities, software development companies, and numerous research and development departments for many major global corporations. India had been an economic and intellectual powerhouse prior to the attacks. The conflict had brought them backward more than a few decades as they began the process of rebuilding and caring for the tens of millions injured.

When the affected corporations announced their losses, the economic tragedy of the situation truly began to unfold. The stock markets had already been shaky due to the political climate, and with these corporate disasters, markets began a steep decline. The US even closed trading on several days when runoffs were initiated because of immense single-day losses. With the steep oil prices staying steady, shipment costs increased exponentially, and so did the cost of goods and services, making everyday shopping excruciatingly painful. All unnecessary consumer spending came to a halt. Unemployment rose, GDP plummeted, and the income tax revenue of all major nations fell dramatically.

President de Blasio instructed the Treasury Secretary to do whatever was necessary to restore confidence in the market and to stabilize the American economy. The US began a series of continuous quantitative easing policies to improve liquidity in the market. The problem that arose was that no governments or private financial institutions were buying the US bonds because the interest rates were at zero, and the Treasury kept printing more money. This forced the Federal Reserve to buy the very bonds the Treasury was issuing. At first, sovereign debts began to default across the third world nations. Those defaults soon spread to Eastern Europe and the European Union. By the winter of 2026, when things didn't look like they could get any worse, people across Europe and the United States lost confidence in the banks' and the governments' ability to keep things under control. Fearing the worst, the public pulled their money out of the banks and the stock markets.

During the first few weeks of the financial scare, the bank withdrawals were kept to a minimum, but somewhere along the line, a panic set in, and within a week there was a full-blown run at banks all across the United States, the likes of which had not been seen since 1929. Within a week, Bank of America, Wells Fargo, Bank of the West and CitiBank had to close their doors and stop people from withdrawing their money. They simply did not have the reserves to cover everyone's accounts, and given the current economic climate, there was little faith in the FDIC to return cash to the average account holder.

As the banks across the US and Europe started to fail, the global economy began a tailspin that no one could have envisioned. By the spring of 2027, the world had fallen into a global depression. The Great Collapse caused the price of food to skyrocket along with other commodities, while precious metals soared to unseen heights. Gold had risen to over twelve thousand dollars an ounce. The costs of transportation, manufacturing and even farming had risen with the cost of fuel and with the devaluation of the US dollar. People simply could not afford the basic necessities of life.

Glaciation as a result of the massive use of nuclear weapons in Asia also started to take its toll as once-fertile farmlands were now susceptible to late-winter thaws and early freezing, reducing the growing seasons and diminishing the amount of food that could be grown.

The loss of crops caused by the environmental issues was just the beginning of the world famine. While bananas had once been shipped from Central America to the United States, the cost of fuel made them too expensive to export. Grain that had been grown in the US was no longer being sent to Asia and China. People across the world had to begin coping with eating only the food that could be sourced locally.

As transportation systems broke down, nations had to turn inward to provide for themselves. As a last dig at Saudi Arabia and Iran, the US ensured that any food or commercial exports that could have been sold to the Middle East were diverted to other markets, causing Saudi Arabia and Iran to suffer immense food shortages. They might have made enormous profits from keeping oil above three hundred dollars a barrel, but they were paying the price for it as the US and the EU refused to sell them any food.

While the crisis continued to escalate, hundreds of millions of people around the world starved to death. The global population shrank. Entire nations were simply famished, lacking the basic necessities to provide for their people. This caused immense amounts of civil unrest all across the world but was particularly felt in the "previously developing world," which had fewer resources on which to draw. Rather than large population centers migrating to areas in the country that could support them, most people continued to stay in areas that could not sustain the population without outside help.

As the only group to really profit from all this chaos, radical Islam continued to spread across the rest of the Middle East, and then the philosophy became much more popular in Europe and Africa as well. Young people were disenfranchised by their governments and felt a sense of hopelessness. The Caliph, Mohammed Abbas of Saudi Arabia, was using this restlessness to his full advantage. On many of the remaining functional television stations with a global presence, Mohammed appeared on a continual loop, preaching his message.

"Let us overthrow these nonbelieving governments! These nations must turn to Islam, the one true religion, and ask for Allah's divine help and guidance through these tough times. Only through turning to Islam will the world begin to right itself and prosper once again."

Had he been preaching a message of peace and nonviolence instead of a violent overthrow of their governments, Mohammed's plea to turn to Islam might have worked on many more people. As it was, most European and Western powers, and also China, saw his message as nothing more than a direct threat to their own power and way of life. Slowly and steadily, the world powers were headed on a collision course due to religious differences and conflicts over how to manage what resources of the world remained.

During the height of the crisis, Mohammed's message of radical Islam led to the overthrow of the King of Jordan as well as the presidents of Egypt, Syria, Yemen, and Iraq. Throughout this turmoil, Saudi Arabia fomented hatred and infighting against Shia Islam and united these countries under a new country and banner, the Islamic Republic, or IR for short. Shortly following the formation of the IR, several non-Middle Eastern countries—Sudan, Somalia, Libya, Tunisia, Algeria, Morocco and Indonesia—were quick to align themselves with this new coalition of nations. The unification of these countries would allow them to pool their resources to survive the Global Depression and emerge a much stronger country.

While the US had been focused internally on its own struggles, the rapid change in the Middle East and the formation of the Islamic Republic caught the de Blasio Administration ill prepared to respond. The challenge the US then faced was how to support their traditional allies in the Middle East: Kuwait, Oman, United Arab Emirates, Bahrain, and Turkey. After some consideration, President de Blasio ordered the repositioning of the US Fifth Fleet to Eilat, Israel. With the economic conditions in the US on the brink of disaster, de Blasio didn't feel America should continue to protect the Middle East or the rest of the world. He began a series of military withdrawals, leaving a power vacuum in a number of global hotspots.
****

While not every country was ready to submit to the leadership of radical Islam, the entire world was feeling the pinch of the Global Depression. By the spring of 2027, tensions between nations over livestock and agriculture were commonplace. On the border of Russia, the provinces of the South Caucasus were growing more and more isolated and disconnected from Moscow. The citizens of that region were practically being forced into slave labor to grow food for the greater Russian Federation while being allowed to keep very little for their own use. With every bead of sweat that ran down their foreheads while tilling heavy soil on an empty stomach, the farmers' hatred for Moscow grew. This anger burned, becoming the only fuel that would awaken them in the mornings. Allegiances to Moscow were shifting quickly.

During the spring of 2027, a Russian convoy of vehicles that was transporting food was ambushed near the border of Kazakhstan, the drivers and other support staff mangled and left to die on the side of the road. At first, this was treated like an isolated incident. Hunger had certainly caused an increase in violence across the globe. However, over the next couple of months, it became clear that this attack was not the act of a rogue group of thieves. Insurgent forces from Kazakhstan and the South Caucasus began regularly interdicting food supplies on their way to southern Russia and rerouting them to their own people. Perhaps they were a little careless about drawing attention to themselves; however, when the same groups siphoned off larger and larger portions of Caspian Sea oil for their own use, Moscow became more heavily involved.

After this supreme miscalculation of stealing oil from the oligarchy of Russia, the insurgent rebels would not have such an easy time. The Russian government produced a military show of force, moving tens of thousands of soldiers and Special Forces to the border regions. The political dissidents that were caught were tortured and publicly humiliated. To ensure everyone knew the government was firmly in control, they used social media and prime-time news coverage to increase the "shock and awe" factor and remind the people not to test the will of the Russian president.

Unfortunately for the Russian government, this strong response was the wrong play on their part. Their actions spurred even more anger, and pretty soon the situation spiraled out of control until the entire southern half of Russia was in a full-blown revolt against the heavy-handed government. Within a month, no trucks could transport food from the South Caucasus or near Kazakhstan to Russia without being robbed. As food supplies were further disrupted and the one resource that was producing income for the government—oil—continued to be

interrupted, the government crackdown became even more severe and urgent.
****

United States

The winter of 2030 came with a blistering, brutal chill that had not been seen in decades. For seventy plus years, environmentalists had claimed world temperatures were increasing, until the 2030s, when it became clear the world was going to be facing a period of global cooling, not associated with carbon emissions. Arctic vortexes from the North Pole became commonplace across North America, bringing subzero temperatures and blizzards that struck remarkably far south. People in Florida were caught completely off guard by the first serious snow they had ever seen. Around the globe, there were fuel shortages and food was in short supply. The frost and ice killed crops with a vengeance but didn't hesitate to kill the old, weak or sick among humankind as well. The global cooling also affected the rest of the world, causing a decline in global food production and further extending the global famine.

Russia was beginning to splinter as a nation. More and more provinces were revolting against the central government. While tensions were high in Russia, Europe was struggling with the massive influx of refugees fleeing Eastern Europe and Africa, all looking for food, safety, and shelter. The European Union was beginning to buckle under the strain of both the human and economic suffering. The leaders of the EU shut down the borders with military troops, closing all entry into the EU and turning people away by the hundreds of thousands.

America was faring no better. The harsh winter had hit the northeast the hardest. Tens of thousands of people were reported dead, frozen to death in their homes because of fuel shortages and an inability to afford what little heating oil was available. Those people that could afford it had to contend with rationing, as well as desperate citizens knocking on their doors, begging to be let in. People were losing their patience with the government and their leaders.

It was during this time of despair and struggle that a new political party was formed in the United States. Its leader was a businessman from Florida named Henry Stein. He christened the new group the Freedom Party, or FP for short. In 2030, Stein won the governor's race as a third-party candidate, which drew more attention to the FP. Like most people during this turbulent era, he had lost faith in the political parties of America. Therefore, he decided to form his own party as a means of trying to save the once-great nation of the United States of America and leave behind the political parties of old.

Henry Stein had served in the US military and fought in the second Iraq War in the mid-2000s. Afterwards, he had become a successful businessman and self-made billionaire. Stein, like most Americans, had become disenfranchised by both parties and the level of corruption that seemed all too rampant in both factions, especially since the Global Depression had begun.

The Freedom Party began as a local political party in Florida, but by the summer of 2032, it had spread throughout Florida and was rapidly expanding across the United States. Over a million Americans had died from starvation and lack of basic services since the start of the Global Depression. Voters had become so distraught by the warring political parties and the state of the US economy that they searched for anything, anyone, that could provide them with hope for some kind of better future.

Henry Stein's group started out as a small statewide political party in Florida, funded mostly out of his own money. However, with a leader promising measurable change and a country that was rife with political discontent, the group soon turned into a nationwide movement. People wanted strong leadership. They wanted a leader who could turn things around and wasn't beholden to various political lobbyists and interest groups. While Stein might have had an unassuming appearance on the outside, he was a genius entrepreneur, and he had something that no one else really had at that time—a legitimate plan to restart the economy and the country.

Governor Stein studied the natural resources of Florida and the gaps in the state and national economies. During his first year as governor, he began to leverage the resources available in Florida to turn the economy around and provide jobs. He incentivized the construction of numerous offshore wind farms to provide cheap renewable energy to the state as well as create an economic demand for American steel and other resources needed to build this statewide project. In order to increase manufacturing jobs and help reduce fuel and energy costs for Floridians, Governor Stein started a statewide project to advance the development of sugarcane ethanol. Slowly and steadily, the Florida economy was starting to grow, and even the media was starting to notice that this politically independent governor was starting to make a difference.

In time, the media was fawning over Henry Stein like Barack Obama in 2008. Like Obama, and later Trump, he represented something different. Governor Stein began holding Freedom Party rallies across the country, attracting tens of thousands of supporters, waving signs and willing to plaster their entire neighborhoods with as much propaganda as they could get their hands on. After winning his second term as governor of Florida, it became inevitable that he should be a candidate for President of the United States in 2036.

Henry was a man of above-average intelligence, having graduate degrees from Harvard, Oxford and Wharton. He was an incredible organizer and extremely business-savvy. He was also an exceptional orator and a skilled communicator, not just with the average person, but with the media as well. He knew how to deliver his vision for America in layman's terms and could also present his message at a PhD level, depending on his audience.

As a student of organizational theory, Henry realized that he could not be an island unto himself. He spent a great deal of time recruiting and vetting likeminded candidates to run for Congress and Senate under the new Freedom Party banner. By the end of the 2036 elections, Henry Stein's Freedom Party had won control of not just the presidency but Congress as well. They also had a strong minority faction in the Senate, splitting the Democrat and Republican parties' influence and requiring the two parties to work with them in order to pass any legislation.

The Freedom Party's near-complete domination in the elections assured that their agenda was going to meet little opposition. Even before they were in office, all the FP candidates journeyed to a small resort in West Virginia to spend the week identifying the new party leaders, legislative priorities, political appointments, committee chairs and members based on their skill sets. They outlined a very detailed plan for delegating who within the party would be responsible for pushing specific items of the FP agenda through the various Congressional committees. These men and women were working together like no other Congress before them to try and craft legislation and executive orders. At a time when hope was at an all-time low, the Freedom Party was determined to restore optimism once again in America.

****

The winds of political change were also moving elsewhere. The EU elected a new Chancellor, Heinrich Lowden from Germany. Like President Stein, Lowden was a strong leader and an outsider. He pledged to keep Europe united and to take control of the dire situation that was facing the European Union. Despite the full political and fiscal union being less than six years old, Lowden was convinced a combined European government in close relationship with the US could succeed.

Lowden had a lot more to deal with than the first Chancellor, who had been elected in 2030, but he was not the kind of man to back down from a challenge. His main platform had been securing the European Union's borders against the massive influx of refugees who were trying to enter from Eastern Europe and Africa. There was simply not enough food and shelter to take in millions of new immigrants and refugees. The people of Europe, who had traditionally been rather involved in foreign aid to needy countries, knew that it was time to help themselves before they could be of any real value to anyone else.

Lowden's thoughts on a potential conflict with a militarized Russia were notably absent from public view during his campaign. While the main focus was certainly going to be on feeding the people of Europe and getting them back to work, the Chancellor knew he had to do whatever was necessary to prevent Russia from threatening the rest of the EU. After a series of harsh crackdowns throughout Russia, the Russian central government had consolidated power and was once again ruling with an iron fist. Russian nationalism was at an all-time high, and so too was their continued military modernization, which had continued virtually unabated since the early 2010s, despite the Global Depression. It was the one aspect of their economy that continued to provide jobs and helped to keep the country's manufacturing base alive. Though Lowden did not tout his furor against Russia publicly, he was constantly planning what his next move would be against them.

During this time, the British people elected Stannis Bedford as prime minister. Bedford knew Great Britain was facing a turning point in history—its demographics were heading in the wrong direction, and the great nanny state was no longer able to support the current system with its finances in the shape they were in.

Once President Stein, Chancellor Lowden, and PM Bedford had all been elected, they worked closely with each other to right their economies. All three governments started aggressive infrastructure and work programs aimed at improving and repairing roads, bridges, rail, and power networks. More importantly, these projects put people back to work.

****

Michael Montgomery, or "Monty" as most people called him, had been one of Henry Stein's closest friends for over thirty years. The two of them had worked together a number of times, and more recently, Monty had taken over as CEO of two of Stein's companies once he was elected governor. Now that Henry was President, there was no one else he would rather have at his side than Monty. He was a natural pick for Chief of Staff and senior advisor. Sparked by a sense of personal loyalty, Monty did not hesitate to accept the position.

After the first full week of Stein's administration, Monty strode into Henry's office with a sense of urgency. The Economic and Congressional Leadership meeting later that day was going to hold great significance for this administration. As he stepped into the Oval Office, he could not help but feel a sense of awe and excitement. Today they were going to change America.

"Mr. President, the Congressional leadership and your economic advisors are ready," he announced with a broad smile on his face. Monty had always known that Henry would one day become President, but he had no idea that he would one day become his Chief of Staff.

The President looked up and smiled at his friend. "Excellent, Monty. It's time to start putting people back to work."

Monty handed him a folder while they crossed the hall at a brisk speed, heading towards the Cabinet Room. The President glanced at the first two pages while they walked, then nodded to his friend. No other words were spoken. The two men had developed an almost telepathic form of communication that was nearly indiscernible by strangers who had not observed them during their long tenure together in the private sector.

Henry entered the meeting room, placing his folder in front of his chair. The idle chitchat that had filled the room suddenly ceased, and there was complete and total silence.

The president opened the meeting. "Ladies and gentlemen, thank you all for your hard work and determination in creating this economic plan. This strategy is going to be difficult and challenging for us to accomplish, but with your help, I feel we can do it."

Pivoting in his chair, the President said, "I've asked the Speaker of the House and the Senate Minority Leader to be here as well. What we have to discuss is important, and it is now time to begin the Congressional coordination aspect of this plan." Several of the economic advisors glared at the "intruders" in the room, but the president didn't seem to mind.

"Part of this plan is to put forth not just a new economic plan, but also a fundamental change in the way our country does business and how it runs. There will be no more compromises or endless arguing and debating for months while lobbying groups threaten to pull their support if politicians don't support or kill a proposal. The Freedom Party was elected to fix the problems that both the Republicans and Democrats were unwilling to fix, and fix them we will.

"Gentlemen, the first of these economic measures being enacted is a complete rewrite of the tax code. Let's face it—the country is bankrupt, and we need revenue. We need a fair system that promotes growth while still allowing the government to have the operating capital it needs to provide basic services and fund a military. Monty, will you please pass out the folders to everyone?"

The silence in the room was broken as each person received their packet and frantically rustled through the papers. This noise didn't bother Henry in the least, and he continued on undistracted.

"I want you all to look over this information and provide us with your thoughts on it." He tapped the file in front of him. "This folder contains the details of the economic plan and is going to be used as a rough template for putting the country back to work. It is by no means the complete answer to all of our problems, but I believe it will be part of the solution."

"Mr. President," interjected the Senate Majority Leader, Joyce Landrew, "I think you're trying to pursue too aggressive a program. This is only your first month in office, and frankly, I'm not sure there will be enough support in the Senate to take this forceful of an approach." The President restrained himself from shaking his head at Landrew. From his point of view, she was the quintessential idealistic California liberal who believed the government was the answer to all the people's problems, and that the ills of the poor could be solved if the rich would just pay their fair share. He couldn't relate to her worldview.

"Senator Landrew, if you feel the proposals I'm making are too radical, you are welcome to oppose them, but they will be pushed through in the Congress and you will either be with us and part of the solution or be a part of the problem. Either way, these changes are going to happen with or without your support. The American people are tired of politicking. They are tired of leaders who will not lead and who only say what needs to be said to be elected. The Freedom Party is different, and you are about to see that difference now that the new Congress has been sworn in."

Senator Landrew didn't reply out loud, but internally she was thinking, *Who does this guy think he is? If he thinks he can go around the Senate, he is in for one nasty surprise.*

President Stein continued, "As I stated before, the first step of the plan is to reform the tax code. We need to start generating income and start encouraging growth again. Unemployment is hovering near 23%, and that is intolerable. The first order the Congress will take up when they come into session on Monday is the tax code. We will effectively eliminate the existing code and restart it with a new one—a much simpler tax code that will bring in more taxes while leveling the playing field."

Tax reform had been discussed by previous presidential administrations and Congressional leaders, with little actual reform accomplished. The federal deficit had continued to climb at an exponential rate until it had surpassed forty trillion dollars. At this point, the money in the Social Security trust fund was now being used to buy government bonds in order to offset the record deficit spending.

"The plan calls for a 10% tax on all income earners and a 10% sales tax on all goods purchased, with the exception of food and medicine. Corporations will pay a flat 10% with no deductions, and any corporation caught not paying their 10% share will be fined by having to pay a 20% tax for the following three years. The days of corporations not paying their fair share are over. There will also be no further personal deductions; a flat tax of 10% on all income earners is fair to both the people and the government. There will also be a 5% debt reduction tax, which will be a part of the sin tax on alcohol, tobacco, marijuana and high-fructose corn syrup."

"Excuse me, Mr. President, did you just say corn syrup tax?" asked Senator Landrew. Even with her freshly Botoxed face, she could not hide her thoughts as her eyebrows raised incredulously.

"Yes, I did. As I said during my campaign, one of many issues I stumped on was the health problems associated with high-fructose corn syrup. Our people are becoming more and more obese, and this is caused in large part by the use of high-fructose corn syrup in virtually everything we eat. I'll never advocate banning it outright, but we will tax it in hopes we can start to change people's behavior and, in time, get the food industry to reduce its use and move back to a more natural sugar," said the President.

Well, at least he's keeping to one of his campaign promises. I know this will make a lot of people in my district happy, thought Senator Landrew.

"This new tax structure will allow the government to bring in more revenue and streamline things on businesses and people. The sin tax is going to be the big winner for people; the revenues used from this tax will be used solely for the purpose of paying off the national debt. We estimate that once we begin taxing high-fructose corn syrup, we will save billions of dollars a year in healthcare costs associated with poor health from this product while earning an extra $143 billion a year in new tax revenues. This will go a long way toward paying down the debt."

Other than the sound of shuffling papers, the room was quiet with rapt attention. "The simpler tax code will also eliminate immense amounts of waste at the IRS and allow for job creation. In addition, we will be eliminating numerous tax breaks that corporations and high wealth individuals are currently able to use. The reduction in the capital gains tax from 30% to 15% will also generate increased investment here at home, which is greatly needed."

Since the signing of the North American Free Trade Agreement by President Bill Clinton, America had been losing jobs, manufacturing capability and other advantages America had once held to subsequent "free trade" agreements. America, always playing by the rules, was being economically ripped off for decades by nations who did not value rules like America did. China and the rest of Asia had a particularly strong stranglehold on American manufacturing and the supply of rare earth minerals.

"The most controversial part of the tax plan is the tariffs. If a US corporation like Ford, Apple or GM choose to produce their final product abroad and bring it back into the US, they will pay a tariff equivalent to what it would have cost them to produce that same product in the US. Corporations are no longer going to be able to leverage free trade agreements to ship jobs overseas and then bring those products back into the US and pay no taxes on them. Corporations that also choose to establish their headquarters abroad are free to do so, but any money earned abroad has to be separated from money earned in the US and their US subsidiary if they want to avoid paying taxes. The cases of corporations like General Electric, Google, Apple, Facebook, Amazon, and others paying zero taxes will never happen again with this new tax code," the President said with conviction.

"You almost sound like a Democrat, Mr. President," said Speaker Fultz with a chuckle.

Congressman George Fultz was a retired Army colonel. He had joined the Freedom Party in 2029 after getting to know Henry Stein while he was running for Governor of Florida. Henry had recruited George to be one of the first party members to run for Congress, and upon being elected, he was made Vice Chairman of the FP. In concert with Stein, he would run the party and focus on recruiting likeminded people to run for political office under the FP banner. Several members of both the House and Senate also joined the FP, but with strings. They were required to back the party and not to accept any super PAC or special interest monies.

Speaker Fultz ran the party with an iron fist, carrying out Stein's vision and keeping members in line with the FP agenda. The FP was not for sale, and Fultz ensured its members stayed honest or they were out. George was six foot four and muscular, and he possessed a commanding presence when he walked into a room. As a young officer, he had served in the second Iraq War just as President Stein, so they had that shared experience in common.

President Stein continued, "I do not believe we need to raise taxes. We just need to set up a process that effectively collects the taxes due. That is what this new code will accomplish. The average person and corporation will pay less in taxes, but the government will bring in substantially more income, simply by ensuring corporations are not using an overly complicated process to cheat the system.

"If you all will grab the blue folder, we will move towards the jobs program. Monty, please walk us through this next initiative," said the President, nodding toward his Chief of Staff.

Monty smiled and stood up to give his brief. "Certainly. Moving towards the jobs program, we have a large workforce that is currently unemployed. We're going to start putting them to work. We have bridges that need to be repaired, we have an energy infrastructure that needs to be upgraded, and we have roads and schools that need to be serviced. We are also going to begin immediate work on establishing high-speed rail throughout the country. So, taking a page out of FDR's playbook, we are going to start government work gangs to put people back to work."

He paused just long enough to allow everyone to flip to the next page of the handouts to follow along. "There will be a government bid for one hundred American companies to manage these projects. The pay for these contractors will be set in line with the government pay grade system of WS-7s, WS-9s, WS-12s, and WS-13s. Let me also emphasize, these are not government positions—these are contractor positions with pay that is equivalent to those government pay bands. The President envisions this work plan having a ten-year shelf life, with positions gradually being eliminated as the program heads towards the ten-year mark and the projects are completed. The number of people employed will surge through the first six years with close to twenty-two million people, and then decline during the final four years until it ends at the end of the tenth year," Monty said as he guided the group towards the next section of the program.

The President interjected briefly to say, "While attending Oxford, I studied program management. This work program is going to be the largest program ever conceived and executed in our country's history, and perhaps the world. Because of the scope and size of this program, I have spoken with the director of the Oxford Center for Major Programme Management Studies, and they have agreed to assist in its management. I'm confident that, by bringing in a world-renowned outside group to head up this project, we will see tremendous success. Sorry for the interruption. Please continue, Monty."

"Yes, Mr. President. If the infrastructure projects are not completed, and the program needs to go beyond the ten-year mark, then it will have to be approved by the Congress and the President. This is not meant to be a new long-term government program or entitlement program. This is designed purely to put people to work on necessary infrastructure upgrades." Monty paused for a moment to take a drink of his coffee before he continued.

"Make no mistake, people in this program will work and work hard. The Army Corps of Engineers, along with the Oxford Group, will manage the overall program for the government. This program will help give people a reason to wake up in the morning and will be the first step in rebuilding this country and putting people back to work. As things begin to improve, more and more people will leave this work program to go to work for other businesses. The program will be paid for by shifting monies from personnel currently employed at the IRS and other government departments as we continue to trim the government down to become more efficient and lean. The American First Corporation's profits will also be incorporated into paying for this public works program." He held up a hand. "Before anyone asks me about that last part, we will discuss it shortly."

Monty paused long enough to look at the President and then continued. "Until such time as the long-term overarching goal of having people employed by the private sector can be realized, we need to do something to help stimulate the economy and put people to work."

The President interjected at this point. "I refuse to pay people welfare and not have them work. People will be fed and taken care of, but they will work for it. Our nation has unfortunately created a nanny state where people believe the government has all the answers and will take care of everyone. This ideology has been implemented and tested for the last seventy years, and it has failed. Particularly the last forty years…people do not know how to do basic tasks such as balance a budget, plan a meal or work a forty-hour work week. Twenty-five percent of the country can no longer support the other seventy-five percent—nor will it, under my watch. Under this plan, there will be jobs for people to be able to work—both through the public works program and through America First Corporation—and unless they are physically or mentally unable to do so, they will."

Senator Landrew cleared her throat, a little too loudly. "Excuse me, Mr. President, but it seems to me that you will be taking people in the welfare system and throwing them out onto the streets. I mean, seriously—giving them one hundred and twenty days to transition? How can you do that?"

The President had known Landrew would be difficult and could throw a lot of hurdles to hold up his reforms, but he also knew that she had concerns similar to his that she wanted to address. Because of this, he knew they could find common ground and work within those areas, giving her something her branch of the party wanted in exchange for something he needed.

The President had prepared for this response. "If you will go through to page twenty-three of the packet in front of you, you will notice that we will provide something which should have been nationalized a long time ago—education in basic job and life skills. People leaving the government subsidy system will know how to create a budget, plan a family menu that's not dependent on fast food, go to interviews, write resumes and perform the functions of being an employee with the basic consideration that most supervisors would consider to be a minimum standard of efficiency. People will not just be thrown into a different way of life without being taught the necessary skills to survive in the world. There will also be ample job opportunities for them through this new job-training and work program."

Ms. Landrew interjected, "—But, Sir, can you really expect a few months of education to change a lifetime of living under a broken system that has created entire generations who have never worked?"

The President paused for a minute before responding, collecting his thoughts. "I'm sure there will still be some problems with those who have been under the welfare system for multiple generations, and I do anticipate some violence in the beginning from those who feel they are entitled to a free lunch. However, it is time for people to wake up. There is no money for the country to keep paying those who are capable of working but choose not to do so. That said, we need to foster an environment where they can find work, and that is what we are intending to create through the new tax code and the America First Corporation.

"Simply put, if you don't work, you don't eat—simple as that. Those who voted for the FP are tired of people who have new smartphones and freshly lacquered manicures asking for government assistance while there are people who would be happy just to have enough food to eat and who are willing to put in labor for that privilege. They will be given the tools to survive in the working world, and it is up to them to walk through the open door," said the President, who at this point was clearly annoyed but still realized he needed Senator Landrew.

Stein sighed softly and softened his tone a bit. "I'm not ignoring the importance of what you're saying, Senator Landrew. However, we have a lot more ground to cover today. Do I have your permission to continue?"

With all eyes turning towards Senator Landrew she suddenly became very meek in her response. "Of course, Mr. President."

The President took a deep breath and slowly let it out. The meeting was going well, but he was definitely irritated with having to deal with a progressive liberal who just did not understand the financial situation these entitlement programs had placed the country in.

The President continued the briefing, moving on to the energy agenda. "Our economy is still dependent on fossil fuels, and so is the rest of the world. We have seen what three hundred plus dollars for a barrel of oil has done to the global economy. America has fared better than others because we have energy resources, but they are not enough. We need to become one hundred percent energy independent and lead the way in finding realistic alternative energy sources in order to ensure the world is never again held hostage by one country or region.

"Going forward, we are establishing a new energy plan and policy. Our new policy will be a multifaceted approach. We are going to move full speed ahead with ethanol-based fuel for vehicles. As a country. we can produce enough crops to convert into sufficient fuel for our domestic needs. This will increase demand in the farming sector and reduce our need for gasoline. Oil is too important to the rest of the economy for us to use such a large portion of it as fuel for vehicles when there are clean, renewable alternatives available.

"We will also expand the exploration and drilling for oil and natural gas in our own country. Petroleum is used in nearly every aspect of the economy. To ensure economic stability, further exploration needs to be done." The President stopped for a second to take a drink of water and turned towards the economic advisors and Congressional leadership before speaking again.

"The US has been sitting on an enormous surplus in oil and natural gas for the last couple of decades, yet we have never realized its full potential to increase our exports and revenue. Believe it or not, this industry is also a means to transform our economy into a greener economy. For the last one hundred fifty years, administration after administration has federalized immense amounts of public land to turn it into federal parks. At this point, over fifty percent of America has been turned into a federally protected park."

The President paused for a second, continuing to gauge the response of the Congressional leaders who were not part of the FP, since they had not been made aware of the forthcoming executive order. "With Executive Order 902, I am officially creating the America First Corporation, or AFC. The Congress will vote on this later in the year to make it a permanent organization beyond my administration. AFC will be run like a private enterprise, with the exception that sixty percent of the profits will be used to help fund the federal government. Ten percent of the profits will fund an internal R&D department with the sole purpose of creating new ways of capturing the sun's energy and will include space-based platforms. There are no shareholders or other special interest groups to interfere with this type of research, so I am confident we will see an alternative to fossil fuels within the next decade or two."

A few whistles came from some of the Republican representatives. Even Senator Landrew smiled at the thought of finally being able to move away from fossil-fuel-based energy.

Seeing approving looks so far, the President continued. "The remaining thirty percent will be used to develop organic growth, employee training, and community programs. AFC will initially be funded with fifteen billion dollars in start-up capital and will have exclusive rights to drill and mine for minerals and resources on all federal lands except for certain specific National Heritage Parks, which will remain as pristine treasures for our future generations. CEO pay for AFC will be capped at no higher than two hundred and fifty times the lowest paid employee. There will be no stock sold in AFC, and as there will be no investors, there will be no bonuses or dividends paid to banks or individuals. All internal CEO bonus pay is also capped at no more than fifty times the lowest bonus given. This will ensure that AFC will remain a corporation that serves the people of America and the government. There will be no excessive pay, yet it will still allow for merit pay and bonuses when warranted. We want the best and brightest to work for AFC.

"AFC's sole purpose is to earn money to help fund the federal government and entitlement programs—essentially a sovereign wealth fund. It will compete on the open market for materials and will receive no special privileges, with the exception of only being allowed to operate on existing federal lands. I'm also authorizing the construction of ten additional oil refineries, so as additional oil is brought into the market, we will have the refinery capacity to handle it and produce our own gasoline, diesel, and other petroleum products in the quantities needed to be completely self-sufficient."

America had trillions in unfunded liabilities, primarily Social Security and Medicare. If these programs were going to remain solvent, then a sovereign wealth fund solely dedicated to generating a profit to pay for them needed to be developed. The President also believed AFC would, in time, generate more than two hundred thousand new high-paying jobs, which was greatly needed in the wake of the Great Depression.

"During the campaign, I said I'd work to provide America with clean energy, and I plan on doing just that. As President, I am authorizing the construction of additional natural gas and nuclear power plants. As we build a new power plant, we will close down the dirtiest of coal plants, replacing them with natural gas and nuclear power. The goal is that over the next decade, we will replace virtually all coal plants with clean natural gas and nuclear power. Most of these new power plants and AFC facilities will also be located in coal-producing states and counties to help offset the job losses that will occur as we move away from coal.

"I have directed the Department of Energy to work on increasing America's generation of nuclear power by twenty-two percent to forty percent within the next ten years. Each of the new plants will have a built-in capacity to handle the nuclear waste they generate in a safe and guarded manner until scientists are able to find a better means of disposing of it."

Monty quickly interjected to point out, "—Older nuclear plants will be replaced by the new ones. As each new plant comes online, we will decommission an old facility."

After years of working together with Monty, President Stein was used to him bringing up important points during his presentations and continued completely unfazed. "As part of the Clean Energy Act, we are also going to begin construction of eight large-scale wind farms, both onshore and offshore. We will expand and build new solar farms in the southwest and geothermal plants as well. I'm also determined to put the devices that harvest wave energy on the market—this has been held up too long because of lack of funding. These initiatives will take time, but over the next decade, we will reduce America's carbon footprint and bring cheap inexpensive power to the marketplace through common sense energy policies, thus lowering the production cost of manufacturing and increasing job growth. This comprehensive approach will increase renewable energy generation by thirty percent, nuclear power by forty percent and natural gas power by thirty percent."

The President saw Senator Landrew looking as if she wanted to say something, so he gestured to her to invite her to speak.

"Mr. President, we may not agree on a lot of the issues we have been discussing. However, I'm surprised and excited to hear you speak so confidently about this renewable and clean energy plan and policy. I had figured all that talk on the campaign was just a way of drawing Democratic voters to your party," said Senator Landrew.

With the liberal Senator starting to come around to the FP's agenda, the President was more congenial in his response. "Senator, I was clear on how I'd run the country if elected. Expanding and building a clean, renewable energy plan is something America needs. It is not just a matter of financial security—it provides a way to protect ourselves from dependence on other nations. Likewise, we need oil and natural gas, not just for our vehicles but also for manufacturing, and unless we can bring down the price of oil and end our dependency on foreign oil, we will continue to be entangled in the affairs of those regions of the world. I want to bring a conclusion to our endless involvement in small conflicts over resources and make our country truly self-reliant. I hope that I can count on your support for all of these initiatives which will benefit our country?"

With a look that was neither approving nor disapproving, Ms. Landrew began a very measured political response. "Mr. President, it will be hard for me to gain support from the Democrats in the Senate on your oil drilling and the America First Corporation initiative. However, I do feel that if the legislation includes all these green energy projects you mentioned, I can get them to agree to support your legislative agenda. They would be hard-pressed to vote down legislation that includes some of their cornerstone ideas and projects."

The President knew that this was the closest thing he could expect to a glowing approval and show of support, and he smiled before responding, "Excellent. Then that is the approach we will take. These initiatives will be put into a single bill. It will provide your colleagues with a victory of their own and still allow us to move the country in a direction that will end our dependence on foreign powers for energy and resources."

The President surveyed the room for a minute, gauging the mood and response thus far to this extraordinary legislative agenda being discussed. For the first time in who knew how long, the leaders of America were talking civilly about how to address the problems facing the country and coming together with solutions to fix them.

"Monty will hand out the next set of folders...I would like to discuss the new monetary policy." He motioned to a new player in the room. "Joyce Gibbs, our new Treasury Secretary, will lead the next discussion and explain how we are going to restructure our debt and rebuild our currency. Before we begin, let's take a short thirty-minute break. We have some sandwiches and drinks being brought in as well." The President nodded towards an aide just outside the door. As the group stood to stretch, the President got up and walked into the hallway to talk briefly with Secretary Gibbs.

"Joyce, it's good to see you. Everything is still ready on your end, correct?" asked the President nervously.

"Yes, Mr. President. The markets will be closed tomorrow and will remain closed until Tuesday. This will be more than enough time for us to have the initial batches of the New American Dollar ready for circulation. Within two weeks, the banks will only have NADs for distribution to the general public. We anticipate it will take us about six months to fully convert all of the world's dollars to the NAD," Joyce said with excitement in her voice.

"Do we really have the needed gold to cover the currency? I heard that part might be a bit iffy," the President said hesitantly.

"We just secured the last order of gold from Canada and South Africa needed to cover everything. Short of several countries actively trying to convert all their NADs into gold and silver, we should be fine. Even if they tried that, we have sufficient rules in place to ensure they're not allowed to receive any new NADs unless they back their request with precious metals. Most people, even in the government, don't realize how immense the gold stashes held by the Federal Reserve are."

The President seemed to relax as he replied, "Excellent. When the break is over, I'll introduce you again to everyone, and then you can begin to inform them their world is about to completely change." Stein let out a slight chuckle.

"Yes, Mr. President."

Joyce Gibbs had been a long-term member of the Federal Reserve and was an outspoken critic of several of the previous administrations' continued use of quantitative easing and of the government printing money and then buying and issuing debt with that new currency. She had been a strong advocate for a return to a precious metals basket currency and a massive restructuring of America's debt and currency. When the Freedom Party had formed, Joyce had provided then-Governor Stein a lot of economic advice. So, when Stein became President, she was his obvious first choice for Treasury Secretary.

Once the break concluded, the President signaled for everyone to take their seats as he introduced the new Treasury Secretary again. "Joyce, if you could go over the new monetary policy for us," the President indicated as he took his seat at the center of the table.

"Thank you, Mr. President, for allowing me to address the senior leaders of the Congress in private. I feel this is important to discuss discreetly as these changes are going to have a profound effect on everyone and the economy."

Secretary Gibbs continued, "The US dollar, along with the other world currencies, has been in a race to the bottom for decades. As a consequence, they have been so devalued as a means of dealing with their sovereign debts and increasing their own domestic exports that drastic actions need to be taken to right the global currencies.

"Economists have warned in the past that we are on the verge of a hyperinflationary event. If that happens, I believe it will not only destroy the dollar but will cause the world currencies to completely collapse. The depression we have been experiencing—and still are—will become even worse as society will soon have no means to conduct commerce except through direct trade between parties. The proverbial 'can' may no longer be kicked down the road.

"This needs to be solved, and with the leadership of President Stein, we are going to solve it. However, what we are proposing is also going to cause certain short-term problems and have an enormous ripple effect in the market and around the world. If we are to right our financial house, then it is necessary."

Pausing for effect, and to collect her thoughts, Joyce looked at the President before letting the other shoe drop. "The Treasury is going to begin printing the New American Dollar, or NAD. The old US dollars will be converted to NADs at a price of five old US dollars for one NAD. As you can imagine, this will have a profound impact on people's savings accounts, debts and loans, 401ks, and investments, but it is also going to shore them up. The NAD will be pegged to the price of a basket of precious metals such as gold, silver, and platinum. We will initially set a NAD value against precious metals, but the currency will be allowed to fluctuate with changes in the market, which will ensure it is not being artificially propped up. The Federal Reserve has enough gold, silver, and platinum at the new NAD price to cover the currency that will be in circulation, and the Federal Reserve will have preferential buying power within the US to purchase these metals at the new NAD price and will do so on a continual basis to stabilize the NAD and increase its value."

Monty raised his hand to quickly interject, "—People will still be allowed to own and purchase precious metals. We don't want anyone to think this is like 1929 all over again, when the government required people to turn in their gold and made it illegal to own it. People can turn their gold in for NADs if they would like, but they will not be forced to do so."

Secretary Gibbs smiled at Monty and thanked him for clarifying a point she had forgotten to mention. "The Treasury will begin printing the NADs in enough quantities to absorb the number of US dollars in circulation and allow foreign governments to have ample time to convert the old currency over. I've also worked with the Federal Reserve, and they will reduce interest rates from 18% to 6% to lower the borrowing cost for people and businesses. This is an aggressive and radical approach. However, we believe it is time to start thinking unconventionally and try something altogether new," said Secretary Gibbs as she reached for a glass of water.

Seeing an opening to talk, the Speaker of the House interjected, "Madam Secretary, I've read your research papers on this idea when you proposed it while working at the Federal Reserve five years ago. Won't this cause some problems with our creditors abroad?"

Secretary Gibbs nodded in acknowledgment. "Mr. Speaker, this will cause some of our lenders to become angry, yes—but there is simply no way we can repay what we owe, and neither can they as long as we continue to operate on the old currency. A new balance needs to be struck to right the worlds' currencies. This endless circle of debt has finally caught up with the world. Through this currency revaluation and conversion, a sound fiscal policy for the world currencies can begin.

"I am not naïve enough to believe this will not cause problems in the global market, and I do foresee foreign governments not lending new money to the US for a while. In all reality, we can't borrow enough to keep up with the current inflation of our own debt payments. The creation of the AFC and the new tax code will help to balance our budgets, but it will take a couple of years before we see the full effect. At this moment, with the current financial situation we find ourselves in, we have to do this," Joyce concluded.

"When is the Treasury going to announce this change?" asked the Speaker.

"This evening, after the market closes—this is why it was imperative to speak with you all today. We couldn't inform you sooner for fear of it being leaked while the markets are still open. The US markets will remain closed tomorrow and will not reopen until next Tuesday. When they do, they will reopen with the new values displayed," she replied.

Clearly annoyed at this new information and drastic monetary change, Senator Landrew pouted. "I really wish you would have consulted us about this before you unilaterally made the decision to do this. I mean, this is the end of the first full month of your presidency, and already you are one-sidedly making a decision that is going to radically change the country."

Seeing that the conversation was about to get nasty, the President interceded for Secretary Gibbs and cut in. "Senator Landrew, in all reality, would informing you have made any difference? It only would have allowed for people to disclose the information to the media, and that would have further hurt the economy, if not crashed it. This had to be done in secrecy."

Considering that the Republican and Democratic Congressional leaders were clearly feeling blindsided by this new monetary policy, the President quickly moved to end the meeting and to incorporate them into the implementation of the various plans and policy directions discussed throughout the day.

"We've talked about a lot of information today, and we have a lot more details that need to be reviewed. I'm going to ask that you all stay into the evening tonight, so we can work as a team to begin putting these ideas into action. Senator Landrew, I would really appreciate it if you could help to lead the discussion and plan on how AFC can develop environmentally-friendly ways of drilling for oil and natural gas. I'd also like your input into the renewable energy aspect of this plan. Your insight would be greatly appreciated."

"Thank you for the offer, Mr. President. It would be an honor," said Senator Landrew, who still looked a bit angry over the financial news and not being able to spread the word to her contacts before the changes went into effect. She knew that her constituents and donors would make her pay for this transgression.

The President was clearly tired but excited that the plans had been disclosed and put into motion. "I'll return later in the evening to see what progress has been made before dismissing everyone for the evening. I will need you all back here again tomorrow for the entire day while we work out the rest of the details. We are radically changing our economy and financial system, so we need all hands on deck. I've asked the kitchen to prepare everyone some 'good brain food' for the next couple of days, so we won't have to worry about anyone's energy level," said the President, hoping to soften the blow of all the changes by diplomacy through good grub.

"Yes, Mr. President," responded the team.

Chapter 2
Kings and Pawns

It was no surprise that the introduction of the New American Dollar came as a complete shock to the world markets and governments when it was announced that evening. Over the weekend, the twenty-four-hour news cycle painfully dissected every ounce of the decision. The logic and reasoning for it was sound; however, the effect it was having on a number of countries was concerning. China had no choice but to accept the change, but they did call America's debt. This meant the US would now be making double payments in an attempt to meet their demands. As expected, no country in the world would extend credit to the US, and many countries insisted that America repay their debt in gold as they did not trust the NAD, despite it being backed by gold.

Countries that wanted their old US dollars converted into gold instead of NADs were allowed to do so but were not allowed to receive any new NADs without exchanging precious metals at the set price. Unlike the crisis with the Brenton Woods Gold Standard, during which a country could exchange their currency for USD and then exchange that USD for gold, in order to acquire NAD, countries now had to put up gold or other precious metals in exchange for it. This increased the value of the NAD and made it a viable and stable currency.
****

Riyadh, the Islamic Republic

Zaheer Akhatar loved being at the center of the decision-making process. Being the personal advisor to the Caliph was not just an honor, but a chance to have immense influence on the direction of the country. "Caliph Mohammed, the economic ministers are in the briefing room waiting to provide you with this past year's progress," he said, zeal and excitement in his voice.

"Excellent. We need to continue to retool and reeducate our people if Islam is to rule the world."

Mohammed Abbas had been the Caliph now for nearly a decade, and though a lot of progress had been made in unifying the Middle East and North Africa under one banner, there was still an immense amount of work that needed to be done. Mohammed was an economic wizard.

43

He had spent most of his life studying economics and worked tirelessly to convert the Saudi economy from an oil-focused financial system to a dominant manufacturing and banking center. After becoming Caliph, his major focuses were on economic expansion, manufacturing, and education across the Middle East and North Africa. He had secured numerous trade deals with China, Russia, the EU and South America and had garnered a lot of economic activity for the new republic despite most nations not agreeing with their political and religious beliefs.

Caliph Mohammed and Zaheer walked through the grand palace at the heart of the Islamic Republic as they made their way to the formal meeting room that had only been completed a year prior. The palace was made of the finest marble in the world and decorated with gold, gems, and other expensive and magnificent materials. It had taken five years to construct, and only the finest artisans were allowed to touch any part of the construction. The formal meeting room, the "council chambers" as it was starting to be called, was a fusion between the decorating sensibilities of the old world and the technologies of the current world. The Caliph walked past the long mahogany table to the golden chair intended especially for him. The other chairs in the room were made of silver and bronze, with comfortably padded seats and backrests.

The room had numerous 3-D media displays that showed either TV programs or computer-generated images and reports. Each media device was specially placed so every person at the table had the optimal view. In the center of the table was a small holographic interface. This allowed presenters to display their brief as a floating image, and it also could be used as a 3-D video phone.

Muhammad bin Aziz, the Minister of Industry, began the meeting once Mohammed and Zaheer had taken their seats. "Caliph, thank you for taking the time to meet with us. We have a lot of information to go over with you."

Nodding, Mohammed replied, "I hope you have good news to report. It has been five years since we took power, and we need to start showing more improvements."

"Yes, Caliph. I'd like to discuss our manufacturing improvements first. We have completed construction of the military manufacturing plants, along with the manufacturing facilities to build our new air-to-air and air-to-ground missiles systems. These new manufacturing industrial centers are spread throughout the provinces of Iraq, Saudi Arabia, Sudan and Indonesia. They will employ 330,000 people directly and engage another six million workers for supporting positions."

He paused for a second to gauge the Caliph's response and then continued, "With help from our Chinese and Russian advisors, we have been converting our manufacturing capabilities towards war production at a rapid pace. We also have numerous armament factories under construction, and the Chinese are in the process of assisting us in establishing our own ground-based antiballistic missile laser defense system. We believe we can have our first operational laser battery to cover Riyadh within the year," explained Muhammad bin Aziz.

"Excellent. And how has the modernization of our armed forces been going now that we have no prying eyes from the West?" asked Caliph Mohammed. His face did not hide the fact that he was clearly impressed with the economic progress being made.

"Caliph, as you know, a lot of our military equipment came from the US and Europe for many decades, so replacement parts are going to be a problem since they are no longer going to provide them to us. To get around this problem, we leveraged 3-D printing as a means to copy and replace the parts that are not readily available. With the help of our Chinese and Russian advisors, we have begun rebuilding our armored and mechanized infantry forces in line with theirs as well.

"I have been working with our Defense Minister to ensure we are producing the equipment he says they need as we continue to gear our entire military towards defending against and defeating those infidel pigs in Israel and the US. We have begun a full modernization of our air-defense capability with the most advanced Russian equipment available. Russia has also offered one hundred fighter pilot advisors to help train our air force to handle the Israeli and American Air Forces." Muhammad bin Aziz laid some papers down on the table in front of them. He knew the Caliph would be pleased to reaffirm that the economy was being shaped to confront their greatest enemies.

Clearly, Muhammad bin Aziz had things under control. It was good to see that he knew how to develop the industrial capability to take on their adversaries. "All right, gentlemen, continue with your current projects and report back to me at the end of next month. In the meantime, I have a meeting with Talal bin Abdulaziz, our Foreign Secretary," said the Caliph, indicating the meeting was over. The group stood up in deference to their leader as the Caliph got out of his chair and exited the room with Zaheer to walk down the hall to his next meeting.

Talal was a tall man, who stood about six foot one and weighed nearly two hundred and eighty pounds. He was also a wealthy businessman who knew how to work deals and get what he wanted. When Caliph Mohammad walked into the room, Talal stood up as a sign of respect. Caliph Mohammad nodded slightly to Talal and then sat down. He didn't need any pleasant niceties with his Foreign Secretary, so he just jumped right into business.

"How are the meetings going with the other foreign heads of state? Have the other Arab countries agreed to join our great Caliphate? Also, were you able to make any headway towards establishing our free trade agreement with China and our military defense pact?"

"Caliph Mohammed, let me address these questions individually. First, I have spoken with the leaders of Yemen, Qatar, Jordan, Syria, Egypt, Libya, Sudan, Lebanon, and Tunisia. They have all agreed to join the Caliphate, and the majority of their population agrees as well. They will move to make the transition over the next couple of months."

Mohammad Abbas nodded his acknowledgment.

"Moving to the trade agenda—the Chinese *are* ready for a free trade agreement with us. I'm working out the final details of when such an agreement will be finalized and signed."

"Excellent," responded Mohammad.

"As to the defense pact, the Chinese are more than willing to share technology and military equipment with us, as are the Russians, but neither country wants to enter into a military pact with us. Their representatives said that our intentions to destroy Israel and attack the West will draw them into a war they would like to avoid, or at least participate in at a time of their own choosing, not ours," said Talal, apprehensive at the thought of disappointing the Caliph.

However, despite the last bit of bad news, Mohammed was impressed with Talal. He was a real mover and shaker and could get things done. Some things were understandably still a little out of reach.

"In a way, that was to be expected, Talal. We may be able to approach the military alliance later on."

The two men then strategized on the tactics of their grand espionage plan to further support their foreign policy goals. With the proper information and money, anything could be accomplished.

****

The following two years, 2037 and 2038, saw tremendous growth in the US and a rebound of the global economy. Although numerous world governments and financial institutions were still angry about the new precious-metal-backed NAD, they could not refute the improved global economy. The $45 trillion US debt had just been reduced to nine trillion NAD with the conversion. However, it would still take more than a decade to pay off.

The America First Corporation was starting to post profits near sixty billion dollars a year and was growing fast. The profits were starting to offset a larger portion of the budget deficits with each month as profits were posted. The change in currency had also forced many other countries to back their own currencies with some sort of similar precious metals as the US had done.

With the world's reserve currency revalued, numerous governments around the world were forced to do the same. The US had remonetized its debt at the expense of its debtors, affecting virtually every other major government. This caused an increased strain between central governments and various financial institutions that had, up to this point, heavily influenced the lending and holding of government debts. The US-China relationship had already been shaky since their incorporation of Mongolia in 2034 at the height of the Great Global Depression. Now the revaluation of the debt owed to China further stretched the already-tense situation.

Despite the enormous challenges facing the US, there was an energetic sense in the air as people across America began to feel like things were finally turning around. Roads were being paved, bridges repaired, schools fixed and modernized, and tens of thousands of miles of high-speed rail were being laid. People had jobs, and though they weren't the highest-paying jobs, they had a way to put money in their pockets and support themselves again. People slowly began to spend extra cash, and demand for consumer products picked up again.

The tariffs on US firms importing products back into the US to sell tax-free finally forced US firms to repatriate their manufacturing back to America. Of course, the nationalization of American assets and facilities in China also forced a lot of US firms to cut their losses abroad. The Chinese government had seized nearly 375 billion NAD from US corporations in an attempt to collect on the US debt the Treasury Department had just remonetized. This had not gone over well with the business community, which demanded repayment from the government.

During the first two years of President Stein's tenure in office, America had increased its oil production by over one hundred percent and brought the price of oil down dramatically, to below one hundred dollars a barrel. New refineries were under construction and expected to be finished over the next four years. Sixty new natural gas plants and twenty nuclear power plants were under construction as well. The decommissioning of the dirtiest power plants was also well under way.

Five new solar farms, each covering twenty thousand acres of land, had been built in the southwest, lowering the price of energy. The refinement of ethanol from corn, sugarcane, potatoes, rice, and wheat had increased to three million barrels a day and was on pace to hit eight million within the next three years as more arable land was being sown.

Despite the improvement in the global economy, the situation in Russia was continuing to become unstable near their borders. The secessionist movements in Chechnya and Dagestan, along with the continued unrest in the "Stan" countries, were causing immense civil unrest across the various federated provinces. China's never-ending thirst for natural gas and oil, along with the free trade with Russia, was one of the few bright spots for Russia. Several high-speed rail networks had been built linking western Russia with greater China and were starting to pay dividends for both countries as trade and economic activity increased. Of course, the issues between Western Ukraine and Russia were also causing their own complications.

The Russian President, Viktor Zubkov, was using the civil unrest as an excuse to strengthen his control on the country and continue his modernization of the military. Military technology had changed a lot over the last twenty years. The use of unmanned aerial drones as fighters and ground attack drones had moved from science fiction to a new reality in modern warfare. Many countries had caught up to the US in drone technology. The use of drones had even made its way into light armored vehicles and tanks, changing the way future wars would be fought forever.

Western Ukraine had joined NATO and believed that this membership would allow them to get away with being more provocative with the Russians after their absorption of East Ukraine. Leveraging

NATO as a shield, Western Ukraine siphoned off natural gas and fuel shipments being sent to the rest of Europe. The situation was starting to spiral out of control as this action started to decrease the profits of Gazprom, and thus, the Russian Federation.

NATO, as an organization, had continued to decline in relevancy and capability throughout the 2010s and into the 2020s. In the early 2030s, during the de Blasio Administration, America continued to maintain the NATO headquarters in Brussels but had scaled down the military presence in Europe. By the mid-2030s, the US maintained less than ten thousand military personnel on continental Europe. NATO had become more of a European peacekeeping force than a real defensive deterrent against future Russian or Islamic Republic aggression.

Russia, on the other hand, continued to rebuild its military and began positioning more forces along their Ukrainian border and their secessionist provinces. Insurgent groups in the Caucasus were operating out of the Republic of Georgia and Azerbaijan, making it more difficult to conduct counterinsurgency operations without involving either of those countries.

****

June 2038
Washington, D.C.
Oval Office, White House

"Mr. President, Secretary Wise just arrived," announced Julie Wells, the President's personal secretary. Ms. Wells was in a rather unique position since she had also been the previous President's personal secretary. A new president typically would bring his own secretary into the White House, but in spite of her not voting for him, President Stein had chosen to keep Julie on because she was likeable and very proficient at her job.

"Excellent, Julie. Please have him brought in as soon as possible and inform the Chairman of the Joint Chiefs and the National Security Advisor. Please have coffee brought in too—this is going to be a long meeting."

"Yes, Mr. President."

The Secretary of State, a man who had been the head of the Kennedy School of International Studies at Harvard and had previously been an ambassador to the European Union, walked into the room.

President Stein walked over and warmly shook his hand. "Jim, it's good to see you again. Please, come sit down. I understand we have a lot to talk about today."

Mr. Wise did not mince words and cut to the point. "Unfortunately, Mr. President, we only have bad news and more bad news to talk about."

As soon as he finished his sentence, the National Security Advisor, Chairman of the Joint Chiefs, and the Secretary of Defense walked in and solemnly took their seats around the coffee table.

The President took his cue from their countenances and decided to skip any further niceties and get straight to business. "Gentlemen, we've called this meeting because it appears that matters in Russia may be getting worse, and the news coming from Iran and the Islamic Republic is not much better."

"Mr. President," interjected the NSA, Mike Williams, "Sir, the situation in the Middle East...I believe it is a bit more pressing. Our latest intelligence indicates that there is going to be a major announcement coming out of the Islamic Republic in the next couple of days—an announcement that will most certainly change the way we will have to deal with the Middle East."

What now? thought the President.

"Mike, please go ahead and tell us what your sources have discovered. I have a feeling that I know what it is, but the others should know." Mike hadn't known the President personally before his term in office; he had recently retired from the DIA Human Intelligence branch as a senior collector specializing in Middle East affairs. However, the two men had quickly formed a bond, and sometimes it was almost as if Stein could literally read Mike's mind.

"Yes, Mr. President," responded Mike. "As you all know, there has been some talk about a possible unification of additional Middle Eastern and North African countries into the Caliphate, the Islamic Republic. Unfortunately, these rumors appear to be true, and in the next couple of weeks, we expect an announcement is going to be made with the countries of North and South Sudan, Mauritania, Mali and Somalia all joining the IR. It would also appear that the IR, backed by their Russian and Chinese friends, is going to make a play for Iran." Grumbling emanated from the other officials as they digested this information.

Mike cleared his throat. "The situation gets worse. The countries of Algeria, Tunisia, Morocco, and to our dismay, Indonesia, will all likely become a part of this new Caliphate."

The President interjected, "Mike, can you please explain how the IR is going to acquire Iran, since they are a mostly Shia country?"

Mike pulled out his tablet and zoomed into an area of Iran annotated with markings indicating oil and gas fields. "The Chinese are going to acquire a hundred-year lease on these oil and natural gas fields in exchange for their help with the coup. The Russians are going to gain the port of Bandar Abbas to establish a new naval and air base. The Chinese will also gain the port of Chabahar, giving them an additional forward naval and air base.

"To ensure the military does not actively resist, the Russians, Chinese, and IR are paying nearly ten billion dollars in bribes across the government to key individuals, especially within the IRGC. Their goal is to make this coup and take over as bloodlessly as possible, and it looks like it will succeed," said Mike, clearly in awe of the complexity and reality of the deal.

Director Rubio of the CIA asserted, "Our intelligence assets agree with this assessment as well. A lot of the hardliners that would have opposed this have been either bought off or killed by the IR. When asked, the average Iranian citizen believes a merger with the IR would benefit them, which means there will probably be little in the way of popular resistance to such a move."

The President sat back in his chair and thought for a second. "What about our allies—Kuwait, UAE, Qatar, and Oman?"

"As of right now, they're not merging with the Islamic Republic. However, we're fairly certain that the IR will at some point make a move to occupy them and bring them into the fold. We have to ask ourselves what we want to do about it," asserted Eric Clarke, the Secretary of Defense.

President Stein replied quickly. "That is a good question, gentlemen. General Branson, do you feel our military forces would be adequate to defend our allies?"

"Sir, with the relocation of the Fifth Fleet to Israel, and with no viable bases in the region, there is little we could do unless we were to deploy all of our carrier fleets and an invasion force to secure additional ports and air bases once the campaign started. That said, our military forces have been seriously depleted over the last several decades. We frankly do not have the military strength to get involved. We also lost our air bases in Turkey when they joined the Caliphate," General Branson replied, sitting back in the chair with a sigh.

"Eric, I know you've only been Secretary of Defense for a year now, and I'm going to be asking a lot of you. Right now, we have a small budget surplus. I want to start putting more money back into the defense budget. We have, what—six carrier battle groups right now and about twelve brigade combat teams and another six more support brigades?"

"Yes, Mr. President. The Army stands at about active duty troops. The Air Force is down to 160,000, the Navy is at 210,000, and the Marines are at 62,000… Shells of what they used to be. We've moved most of our combat power into the National Guard and Reserve units because of funding issues," he replied glumly.

Eric Clarke had previously been the CEO of General Electric until the President had asked him to take over as the Secretary of Defense. Stein had chosen Clarke for the role because he intended to modernize the military while finding ways to reduce the military bureaucracy and waste. The US military was becoming outdated compared to the other global superpowers. Technology had changed so much since the introduction of drones, exoskeleton combat suits, and railguns.

"Gentlemen, given the intelligence and the events of the last twelve months, I think we need to do a rapid rebuild of our military. Yesterday, Mike was briefing us about the increase in the Chinese military, particularly in their ability to project power beyond just their territorial waters. They have fielded three new supercarriers and two smaller support carriers.

"In the past two years, Russia has increased defense spending by over four hundred percent with their renewed oil wealth. Russia, like the US, has been seeing their own resurgence in their economy—they are modernizing and growing their military at a rapid rate, and so are the Chinese. We cannot allow the United States to fall behind or be caught off guard."

The President had been worried about the ability of the American military to protect the country since receiving his first presidential briefing after taking office. The last twenty years had seen a real decline in the military while many other countries had been increasing their own capabilities.

Eric could see the President was concerned and knew he had doubts about the military. "Mr. President, our military force is small, but our capabilities are great. Our F-35 and F-22 aircraft are still unrivaled in the air, and our satellite and laser defenses are far above any other nation," he said.

"Eric, all that means is we can keep a possible enemy from our shores. It doesn't mean the US has the ability to project any serious force abroad or protect our allies if needed. We need to not just blindly spend money on defense but spend it on the right type of military force."

"What are you suggesting?" asked Mike.

"I believe we should move from six carrier battle groups to nine. I also want us to move from twelve BCTs to twenty-six, increase our mobile laser battery battalions, and add additional antiballistic missile laser batteries and airborne laser systems. I also want an increase in our cyber-offensive and defensive capabilities. The wars that may be coming are wars that are going to be fought and won with the ability to neutralize an opponent's ability to communicate globally and dominate the skies. We must make sure that America is able to meet that challenge."

"That's an ambitious goal, Mr. President, and also a very costly one. We would have to more than double the current defense spending, and it would take time to build up these forces," Eric said while tapping away at his tablet.

Henry knew if anyone could turn the military around, it would be Eric. He was a master at turnarounds in the business world, and reforming the DoD was going to be critical to transforming the military into the twenty-first-century fighting force it needed to become.

"Gentlemen, I will speak with the leaders in the Congress and the Senate. After this last election, we now firmly control both houses, so I don't foresee a problem with increasing the defense budget. I also want these defense contractors held accountable for their programs. No more cost overruns and no spending billions of dollars for them to develop the weapon systems *they* think we need. We will give them the requirements, and then we'll let them show us what they can do to meet those requirements."

"Sir, if you want to increase the budget, you certainly won't get any disagreement from me. I'll do my best to see that we meet your goals as soon as possible. I'd like to expand our drone program to include fighter and bomber drones and light drone tanks. They're far less costly than manned aircraft and heavy tanks and a whole lot faster to produce in the quantities needed," explained the SecDef.

"All right, with that settled, let's move on to Russia. Mike, we'll come back to the Middle East problem later. Can you please present us the situation in Russia?"

"Yes, Sir. As we all know, the situation on the Russian borders has been deteriorating rapidly, and it is our firm assessment that the Russians will probably escalate the situation in the Caucasus and along some of the 'Stan' countries as well," his national security advisor said.

"What do we anticipate the EU will say about this, or about the new Islamic Republic absorbing more African countries?" asked the President.

"As of right now, the EU will most likely put their forces on a high state of alert. The EU's main concern is that the Russians may decide to go further than their absorption of East Ukraine. As for the Islamic Republic, once they begin their unification process, they'll be quite busy merging their military and government forces. Presently, our military assessment is that the Russians will most likely look to absorb their formal satellite states and continue to retool their military before they would consider making a move against the EU, if they choose to. Right now, the EU is Russia's second-largest trading partner next to the Chinese, so, despite tensions being high, we believe trade will keep the tension from escalating further," Mike replied.

The President postulated, "Eric, I believe this further reinforces our need to begin a build-up of our forces. We are going to need to be able to project power if we are to have any say in preventing any of these countries from escalating their conflicts and their expansionist ideas. Of particular concern are some of the waterways in Asia and the Suez Canal, where so much of the world's shipping passes through."

"Sir, with your permission and with Congressional approval, we will slowly raise the Army to 550,000 troops over the next two years, and likewise push for similar percentage increases in the other services," responded the SecDef.

President Stein replied, "Again, I'll talk to the Speaker of the House, and we'll work on getting it pushed through Congress. I have a feeling that we're going to need to really step up our military buildup over the next few years, perhaps even higher than five hundred and fifty thousand. You should have your people put together a plan to increase the Army to two million if needed."

There was a small gulp before the response.

"Yes, Mr. President."

Chapter 3
Comrades

The Stein administration spent most of its first few years on domestic issues and the American economy. The tax code had been rewritten, and hundreds of thousands of regulations covering the entire economy had been revised, rewritten, or eliminated to streamline the regulatory environment in the US with an aim at improving the economy and making life simpler for the average citizen. Tort reform had taken place limiting the number of malpractice lawsuits and lowering the costs of healthcare. Unfortunately, world events continued to draw the administration into the complicated international web it sought desperately to stay away from.

Mike, the National Security Advisor, walked into the Oval Office suddenly one afternoon while the President was doing some paperwork. Stein looked up in surprise at his unannounced guest to see his secretary poke her head in and mouth, "It's important, Sir."

"Mr. President, we have a situation developing in Moscow right now," blurted Mike as he walked over and turned on the TV.

"What's going on, Mike?" asked the President.

"Sir, it would appear that President Zubkov was just assassinated. His motorcade was attacked with a car bomb, killing him instantly."

"Do we know who is responsible for the attack yet?"

"Yes, Sir, we do. We have very reliable intelligence that suggests the people involved in this attack originated from the Caucasus, the Dagestan-Georgian area to be exact."

"Great. So we can expect a heavy response from the Russians, then."

"Yes, Sir, I'd suspect the Russians will respond very quickly."

"Please send our condolences and offer any assistance we can. Perhaps we can help defuse the situation at least slightly, though I highly doubt it."

****

September 2038
Russia

After the death of the Russian president, the newly appointed president, Mikhail Fradkov, went on a tirade for the first couple of weeks, whipping up nationalistic anger over the death of President Zubkov. He appeared on a nearly endless loop on several major television networks, making speeches that could mostly be summarized as follows: "Russia will no longer tolerate these dastardly attacks by separatists from the Caucasus. Soon we will begin to bring the fight to the enemy."

President Mikhail Fradkov had been Zubkov's protégé before Zubkov's death. Fradkov had been groomed to take over Russia and lead it into the future once President Zubkov's term as president ended. Fradkov had served in the Russian Army and later with the FSB before being pulled into public office. He was young for a major world leader, late forties, and extremely aggressive. Now he was President and in charge of a country that was being attacked continually from its border regions.

Like the US, the Russian economy was starting to boom again as the Great Global Depression gave way to a global economic boom. The numerous high-speed rail networks connecting China and Russia were starting to have a real impact on both economies. The Islamic Republic was having their own economic renaissance, which was driving Russian exports through the roof, especially in the defense and manufacturing sectors.

Despite the economic improvements taking place in Russia, the Caucasus continued to fight against the government. The provinces of Dagestan and Chechnya were rich in oil and fertile farmlands, in addition to a burgeoning manufacturing base. Like Georgia, Azerbaijan, and Armenia, they wanted to become their own countries. After nearly fifty years of fighting against the central government, the situation had finally reached a precipice of violence that neither side was going to turn away from.

The republics of Georgia and Azerbaijan both had their disagreements with Moscow, and though neither country could directly stand up to President Zubkov, they could support, sponsor and train separatists from the region to fight against the central government. As tensions between Moscow and these two nations rose, so too did the support they provided to the separatists.

It was the end of September when the Russians began their "Red October" campaign, designed to root out and eliminate what they perceived as separatist safe havens and supporters. The Russians decided that if Georgia and Azerbaijan wanted to support the separatists, then they would need to be dealt with. Tens of thousands of troops poured into Dagestan and Chechnya to confront the separatists and to secure the region. Though some separatists chose to stay and fight the Russians, many fled the region into their safe havens in Georgia and Azerbaijan.

As it became clear that the separatists were fleeing into Georgia and Azerbaijan, the Russians quickly expanded their operation into those countries. In the twilight hours of the morning, over 6,500 Russian paratroopers attacked the Tbilisi and Baku airports in Georgia and Azerbaijan. At the same time, the Russian 2nd Shock Army invaded both countries as twenty thousand soldiers arrived in Dagestan and Chechnya. The most intense fighting took place at the Tbilisi airport, with Russian paratroopers having seriously underestimated the strength and determination of the Georgians.

Though the paratroopers caught the Georgians off guard, they quickly rallied and resecured the airport, forcing the paratroopers to take refuge in neighboring buildings and houses while they called in air support and waited for reinforcements. The Russians rapidly followed up the invasion with 30,000 additional mechanized and armored forces. The 2nd Shock Army separated into two prongs, one focused on securing Tbilisi and the other Baku.

The Georgian and Azeri armies were quickly being cut to pieces by not just a numerically superior Russian force, but by thousands of Russian light drone tanks and infantry fighting vehicles. Nearly one-third of the armored vehicles in the 2nd Shock Army were light and heavy drone tanks and fighting vehicles, which were proving extremely effective. As one vehicle was destroyed, the drone operator could quickly take control of another vehicle and continue the attack. With a second operator manning a separate machine gun or cannon, they were able to continuously attack the Georgian and Azeri soldiers, only stopping to rearm.

Despite the losses, Russian forces met heavy resistance from the Georgian military, who had been receiving training from the US Army for decades. However, the Georgians, though well trained and full of fury, were outnumbered and underequipped. The resistance collapsed after ninety-six hours of intense fighting and turned into all-out guerrilla warfare against the invaders. Within the first couple of days, Russian forces had advanced to the outskirts of Tbilisi and were pushing hard towards Baku, the Azerbaijan capital. Intense house-to-house fighting took place throughout Tbilisi and Baku as the Georgians, and Azeri turned their capitals into deathtraps for the invaders. Thousands of civilians were killed, but so too were soldiers on both sides.

While things were heating up in the Caucasus, the Russians launched an all-out offensive against Kazakhstan and the other "Stan" countries. The Russians were making their final move to secure their former satellite states, and more importantly, the minerals and resources held by those former allies. With another 230,000 troops and over one thousand T-14 Armata tanks racing across the "Stans," it was only a matter of time until the Russians would fully occupy their former republics.

By the end of October 2038, the Russians had fully dominated the countries of Georgia, Azerbaijan, and Armenia, along with the vast majority of the Stan countries of Kazakhstan, Uzbekistan, Tajikistan and Kirgizstan. This redrew the map along old Soviet Union lines and put Russian forces at the border of the Islamic Republic.

Russia deployed an additional 300,000 troops to these newly acquired regions and began a systematic purge of anything Islamic. General Anatoly Kulikov, the grandson of a former army general from the old Soviet Union days, was in charge of putting down the separatists and establishing the new occupation, just as his grandfather had done in the 1990s. Like his grandfather, he was a stone-cold killer and ruthless in his pursuit to crush the opposition, resorting to public executions and hostage taking until rebels turned themselves in. The Russians were intent on building a new and stronger country by restoring the former glory of the old Soviet Union.

It was estimated that over 200,000 civilians died in the first thirty days of the occupation. By the winter of 2038, things began to calm down with the realization that the Russians were not leaving, and they continued to consolidate their positions in the occupied territories. Hundreds of separatists and insurgent leaders had been captured or killed, and the Spetsnaz were relentless in their pursuit of insurgent cells and groups operating within the various cities and countryside. Continuous drone coverage and strikes throughout the region ensured around-the-clock surveillance and provided the Russians with the ability to attack anything that moved, if they chose to do so.

Chapter 4
Whole Grains

March 2039
Washington, D.C.
White House Situation Room

The President was having his national security team keep a close eye on military developments within the Islamic Republic. With Russia and China building their armies for war, it was imperative to keep tight surveillance on the IR to determine if perhaps the three countries were planning to initiate a war together. With those thoughts weighing on his mind, President Stein sat down in the Situation Room for a briefing with the National Security Advisor.

Mike Williams picked up a folder and opened it before beginning. "Now that the Russians have consolidated their gains during the Red October campaign, they are in a better position to help the Islamic Republic continue their military buildup. During the last six months, the IR has received a number of drone tank battalions from Russia and China.

"They are protecting the industrial belt of the Republic and their nuclear weapons capability with their new land-based laser antiballistic missile shield near Riyadh. They're also expanding that shield to Tehran, Baghdad, Amman, and Cairo. Once operational, it will make it virtually impossible for our cruise missiles to hit targets around those areas, and it will also make it impossible for our aircraft to conduct an air raid should that need ever arise.

"The most alarming report—and the main reason we have called this meeting—includes intelligence showing a massive troop movement by the Islamic Republic forces in Asia. As you have already been made aware, Sir, they've spent the last six months building up their military capability and troop levels. Well, last night, our satellites picked up a significant migration of troops in Indonesia towards several ports. When looking closer at the ports, we discovered over eighty large transport vessels anchored at the docks. Our only conclusion is that the Islamic Republic is moving a large number of troops from Southeast Asia to the Middle East," Mike said.

General Branson spoke up. "It may be nothing, but I get the sense that something greater is afoot, Mr. President. The Chinese, Russians and now the IR are all building massive militaries. Armies are expensive to maintain, and you don't create an army of this scale without having a purpose for it. These sizeable troops would simply be too expensive to maintain for peaceful purposes."

The President responded, "That's my thought as well. What we do know for sure is that Russia ultimately wants to overtake Europe, China wants to conquer Southeast Asia and dominate the Pacific, and the IR wants to destroy Israel and us. Given this development, we should start orchestrating war plans for how to deal with these known threats."

Stein turned to his Chief of Staff. "In the meantime, Monty, I want you to get in touch with the EU Chancellor and the British PM and let's see if we can arrange for a meeting between their defense ministers, national security advisors and ourselves. I also want the NATO EU leadership involved in the meetings. We need to go over some of these events with them and get our countries working together."

"Yes, Mr. President."

"All right, gentlemen. If you'll excuse us, Monty and I have to meet with our economic team to discuss some new initiatives and devise some new plans on how to speed up our own recovery." Stein stood up and walked out of the Situation Room. The other men in the room stood out of respect to their Commander in Chief.

Within a few minutes, Henry Stein was in the Oval Office, ready to face his next meeting. "Gentlemen, sorry for the delay. We were detained in the Situation Room. Now it's time for me and Monty to turn our attention towards the economy, so I'm hoping you all have some good news for me," said the President as he sat down.

Jeff Rogers, the White House Senior Economic Advisor, jumped right in. "Mr. President, we do have good news to report. As you know, tomorrow the GDP numbers will be released, and so will the jobs report. I'm proud to say that the economy grew at 5.6% during the third quarter, and unemployment dropped from 16.9% to 12.3%. More and more people have been getting hired into the jobs program, and the private sector has also recorded 653,000 new jobs added this month."

Prior to joining the administration, Jeff Rogers had been the CEO of Proctor & Gamble, and he brought with him years of experience in job creation and innovative ways of solving difficult economic problems as he guided P&G through the Depression. One of the hallmarks of the Stein presidency was his ability to surround himself with successful people from both the private and public sectors. There were no political appointments made based on political donations or to garner favor. The President was absolutely intent on appointing people who were subject matter experts in the area to which they were appointed. In several cases, individuals who had not performed well were asked to step down or were replaced. The best and brightest from the private sector were being poached to work for the Stein administration.

The President was very impressed so far with the changes Jeff had brought to the table. He acknowledged, "This is great news, gentlemen, great news indeed. We need more improvements like this, and we need to keep growing the economy. This should be the main focus in the media. We need to do everything we can to let people know things are getting better and help them to believe that there is hope. If people start to feel good about the country and our prospects, it will not only cement the Freedom Party as the party of growth and change but also inspire the rest of the nation."

The other people in the room nodded in agreement.

The President continued, "I also have an idea I'd like to float past you all to see what you think. As you all know, our country is still in massive debt—over thirty percent of our country's yearly income goes towards servicing our debt. The new sin tax has made some headway in paying it down, but I have two thoughts on how help to pay it down even further," he said with a smile.

"Mr. President, we're all ears. What do you have in mind?"

"I've given this a lot of thought, and there are two areas I'd like to discuss. The first is a national lottery system that would help to pay down the debt. For every NAD paid into the system, forty percent would go towards paying down the national debt, ten percent would support and sustain the national lottery system, and fifty percent would go towards the prize for the winning number. A drawing would be held every Tuesday and Friday.

"Lottery systems have traditionally raised a lot of money for the states. I see no reason why the federal government shouldn't leverage this as well. Once the debt has been paid down, then I propose the funds be transferred to the Social Security fund. We could finally fix the solvency issue and protect our seniors for generations to come."

Jeff sat there thinking for a second before responding, "I don't see why we couldn't establish something like this. We can create a subsidiary company under AFC to manage and handle the system. I'll start to discuss it with my team and get back to you during our next meeting on the feasibility of it," he said as he made a few notes on his tablet.

The President smiled, knowing if Jeff thought it was a viable option, he would not exude praise until his team had examined the idea first. "Excellent, Jeff. This next idea is a plan I thought should have been enacted decades ago. It's a radical approach but something that will, in time, help to stabilize global food levels. I'd like to propose the development of a grain consortium."

Stein linked his tablet to the interactive holographic projector on the ceiling of the room. Instantly, a floating image of the world displayed. The President used the program to highlight specific countries, then turned to face his advisors. "The oil producing countries have OPEC. I don't see why the large food-producing countries of the world can't form a grain consortium to both stabilize the price of commodities and ensure enough food is being produced to feed the world. These countries represent our greatest potential for membership in the consortium."

Jeff sat back in his chair and stared at the map as it floated in a circle just above the center of the table. He was thinking about what the President had just said. "I don't see why we couldn't look into this—however, the trick is making it work. That will be the hard part. First, we have to get enough of the large food producing countries to participate in the consortium, and then we need everyone to stick to the prices and food production quotas. It would definitely be hard to enforce."

Grabbing a pen and writing some notes in her notepad, Katelyn Smith, the President's senior trade advisor, asserted, "At a minimum, we need to get Canada, Argentina, Brazil, New Zealand and Australia to be a part of the consortium if it's going to be effective. We'll also need to stop producing corn ethanol entirely and ensure our farmers are running their farms at full production. No more subsidies to farmers who don't grow and sell crops."

Katelyn Smith had been a commodities trader at the Chicago Mercantile Exchange for several decades before she'd started her own financial firm. When it came to international trade, particularly in the area of commodities, she knew her stuff. The President had chosen her to be his senior trade advisor because she was sharp, honest, and direct—qualities he respected. He knew he needed help to turn the economy around.

Jeff interjected, "Another point for consideration is that each country will need to establish a central entity, whether it's a corporation or some other entity, that will coordinate the purchasing and sales of all national food products."

Katelyn nodded towards Jeff, then continued, "Another caveat is that local farmers would need to have a choice in selling their products to local grocery stores and communities or to the government entity. We don't want this to appear like the government taking control of food production, because we're not. As long as we include this qualification, I believe this consortium could work—it will take a lot of coordination and some patience, but I believe we can do it. If you would like, my staff can start to develop the outline for this consortium, and we can start the dialogue with our potential partners."

"All right, then, please have your staffs start work on this immediately, and let's see how fast we can get this moving," the President said, satisfied that this idea had some merit and could potentially work.

Looking at his watch, the President saw they were running behind schedule. "Let's talk about the infrastructure projects, Jeff. Where do we stand with them?"

Jeff tapped away on his tablet, and the holographic map showed new data and information represented on each state. He pulled several states forward to discuss them in more detail. "As you can see, we have 497 bridge projects, 2,667 highway projects and 3,422 high-speed rail projects underway. All of the agreed upon projects in the 2037 Infrastructure Plan are on track."

Switching to a new image on the map, he continued, "The nation's power grid upgrade and security improvement effort are moving forward. The Department of Energy is working with the various utility companies on hardening specific critical power nodes against EMP and cybersecurity threats. DHS and DOE are also stocking up on transformers and other critical components needed to repair and maintain the various critical nodes should something happen to the supply system," Jeff said.

"Good. This will fold in nicely with the 2040 National Defense Authorization and Recovery Act. Our country has been wholly unprepared to deal with any major catastrophes like this for far too long," the President responded.

"This has been a major focus of the National Recovery Working Group, Mr. President. We're scheduled to have a meeting with them next Thursday. I suggest we wait to discuss this further with them," said Monty as he adjusted his reading glasses.

"I agree, Monty. Thank you for keeping us on track. Before we move on—Jeff, I want to make sure that we're diversifying the equipment used in these upgrades. Pay particular concern to products that are built by Chinese firms or subsidiaries. I don't want our power grid exposed because we used the same product in every facet simply because it was cost-effective."

"I agree, Mr. President, and I will personally make sure that's being looked at," said Jeff as he annotated a few items on the map.

Running short on time, the President jumped to the next section of the brief. "How is our manufacturing renaissance going?"

Jeff nodded towards his counterpart. "Katelyn can provide input into the trade aspect, but things are starting to improve a lot. The corporate tax and tariffs have helped with reshoring a lot of manufacturing. With the steady reduction in energy costs and a large supply of labor, it has made America a very attractive place to set up new manufacturing."

Katelyn broke in, "—We have also increased tariffs on competing manufactured products coming from abroad, with special interests towards products from China. We have spent the last two years reviewing the various trade policies and agreements currently in place. A lot of these deals were initially poorly negotiated, which led to our enormous trade deficit. We have since modified these agreements or terminated them. We have effectively evened the playing field for American manufacturers, which has encouraged a lot of them to reshore a majority of their overseas plants." Katelyn used her tablet to display the latest trade levels on the holograph.

"The Chinese, of course, are not happy about the tariffs, but the alternative is that they lose their ability to sell their goods to the American market."

The President smiled at this. *My entire life, the Chinese have taken advantage of my country. Now it's time to take advantage of them*, he thought.

"Good work, Katelyn. I'm all for free trade, but it must be fair trade," said the President. "Let's continue to work on this grain consortium initiative and ensure our trade agreements are strictly fair trade going forward."

"China is in desperate need of both food and oil—the grain consortium would be the perfect tool to leverage those needs to our advantage. We can also add an additional charge to food and oil products being sold to China."

Jeff, sensing that the President wanted to stick it to the Chinese, asked, "Can you explain that a little better, Mr. President? I'm having a hard time following."

"We sell the goods to China for the price we paid through the consortium, and we then add an extra five percent to it. Rather than taking it in the form of cash, we take it in the form of them forgiving that amount of our debt. So, the Chinese would be able to secure a steady supply of food and oil from the US, while we get an even larger portion of our debt paid off. By doing this, the government wouldn't be losing any money on the purchase of the food from our own markets, and at the same time, we would reduce our debt by five percent of each sale made to the Chinese," said the President, clearly excited at the possibility of reducing the debt even further while "getting even."

"I hadn't thought about it like that, Sir. I think it could work, but the Chinese aren't going to like buying the food and fuel from us when they could just buy it directly from the market," said Jeff.

"Normally you'd be right. However, since the Global Depression hit, most of America's food and fuel supply has been reserved for Americans only. Very little has been authorized for overseas sales. We can tighten that restriction even further, forcing the Chinese to have to play by *our* rules."

"All right, Mr. President. I'll start work with the Commerce Secretary, and we'll start putting this into action. I'm also going to meet with our various farmer groups. I want to see what we can do to help encourage our farmers to produce more products and increase the supply going forward. I think food could become the key to our economic success and recovery, at least in the short term, Mr. President," Jeff said.

"Ok, ladies and gentlemen, let's get things moving, and we'll reconvene next week," said President Stein.
****

The Americans quickly implemented the concept of the Grain Consortium, or "the GC" as it was swiftly coined. Through a series of legislation and executive orders, the AFC took the lead in purchasing commodities from American farmers willing to join in the GC. Canada quickly jumped on board, and so did a number of other countries. It would take the rest of the year to fully integrate all the participating members into the Consortium, but the initial concept and American-Canadian partnership had an almost immediate impact. As the first planting season began, farmers in both countries reported a 120% increase in the number of acres planted for the first growing season.
****

02 April 2039
Paris, France

President Stein hated dealing with his European counterparts. Despite having lived in Europe and worked with NATO during the early part of his career, Henry still found that Europe was a continent so fragmented and diverse that it was difficult to get anything of substance done. The US had spent so much blood and treasure on Europe during the twentieth century to ensure they remained a free people. Most Americans no longer believed Europe was worth the sacrificing of additional lives or resources.

The Europeans had so fouled up the Syrian refugee crisis and the Arab Spring in the early 2010s that millions of refugees had poured across their borders and never left. During the following twenty-five years, the demographics of Europe had changed as a result, and despite the central government's having very little in common with the Islamic Republic, a large percentage of their population did. There was a cultural undercurrent of support for the IR and a distrust of the central government by European Muslims.

President Stein had landed in Paris to start a series of important talks and negotiations. As his motorcade made its way through the city to the location of the meeting, he couldn't help but notice how much of the city had changed. There were a lot more minarets dotting the skyline and women wearing headscarves, despite the bans on them. The air hung with a certain darkness that had been not there before. The atmosphere just seemed a bit bleaker, lacking the energy and hopefulness one would expect in Paris.

The motorcade pulled up to the official entrance of the Élysée Palace, and as Henry stepped out, he couldn't help but feel that he was entering a bubble that brought him back to another time in history. As he followed his security agents through the entrance, he was struck by the building's grand décor and ceaseless beauty. Despite all his worldly travels, he was still amazed by his surroundings, like a child who has seen Disneyland for the first time. When he arrived in the Salon Doré, he was jolted back to reality a bit as he realized that he was the last one to arrive for the meeting. This meant that business would begin right away. He took a deep breath and refocused his mind on the task at hand.

Without further hesitation, he extended his hand to greet the man closest to him in the room. "It's good to see you again, Chancellor Lowden. How have you been?"

Lowden took the President's hand and gave him a firm handshake.

"Things are going well. I hear America is experiencing an economic renaissance—you will have to share your secret with us." A wry smile crossed his lips. President Stein tipped his head towards him in acknowledgment and smiled back.

Turning to the next prominent leader in the room, President Stein continued the task of introductions. "Prime Minister Bedford, how are things faring in Great Britain?"

"We're doing great. Things are really starting to turn around. I do want to personally thank you for the generous food prices to England and the EU. This will make a big impact in our continued economic recovery," replied PM Bedford.

In response, President Stein and Bedford shared some polite exchanges that the rest of the room did not hear. The two men were not-so-secret fans of one another and always enjoyed being face-to-face whenever possible. The benefits of teleconferences were a bit overrated in situations like these, especially with the potential security breaches from hackers.

PM Stannis Bedford was a strong leader and worked hard to ensure Britain didn't lose their British identity despite the recent massive influx of foreign immigrants. Unlike his EU counterparts, he wanted to model more of the British economy around what the Canadians and Americans were doing, especially with regards to their trade agreements with Asia.

After shaking each leader's hand, President Stein turned to the group and said, "Our goal in the US is to continue to strengthen our military and economic ties with England, the EU and our NATO partners. To that end, we cannot have our friends starving. The Grain Consortium can be used as both a relief program and as a weapon, if need be. The Consortium is only a month old, and as we get more organized, I can assure you greater quantities of commodities will be made available at reduced prices for those countries in our grand alliance," Stein said with a warm and disarming smile.

The leaders all nodded their approval. They were a very eager audience. President Stein spent some time going over the finer details of the Grain Consortium program. Most of the leaders were taking notes and asking questions during the presentation; they were all very engaged.

As President Stein finished speaking, the group stood for a brief restroom break. As some left the room and others mingled, the Canadian PM, Troy Peck, approached him. "Mr. President, on a different topic, I wanted to thank you on behalf of Canada for the help America continues to provide in putting down the civil unrest in Toronto and Vancouver. These extremist Muslims have been causing all sorts of problems across Canada since the Grain Consortium stopped selling food products to the Islamic Republic."

One of the initial acts of the Consortium had been to stop selling food products to the Islamic Republic. It was a known problem that the IR continued to sponsor terrorist organizations globally and was persistently behind efforts to undermine Western governments. They were also continuing to try and expand their empire into Malaysia, the Philippines, and Sub-Saharan and East Africa. To that end, the Consortium made it known that they would not sell food products to the IR until this behavior stopped.

Canada had experienced a demographic change, as had Europe. Decades of taking in asylum seekers and refugees had changed the religious and social dynamics of the country. The Islamic population made up close to thirty percent of the country. In several cities where the Islamic population was closer to fifty percent, there were movements to insist that these cities be governed by Sharia law. There was also a growing crusade nationwide to move the country to Sharia law and away from the control of the Canadian Constitution.

The government had, of course, balked at this, and civil unrest had followed all across the various Islamic communities in Canada. Tens of thousands of Canadian citizens had immigrated to the IR and were encouraging others to do likewise. Despite the migration of Muslims from Canada to the Islamic Republic, the ones remaining were doing their best to turn Canada into an Islamic country.

The Canadian administration was clearly overwhelmed by the violence, which had spread from Toronto to the rest of the country. Government workers and police officers were routinely being targeted and killed, and several buildings had been bombed. It was during the height of this violence that Troy Peck had called Henry Stein directly to ask if the US government would be able to assist Canada in putting down this uprising by these extremist Muslim communities.

At first, President Stein had been reluctant to get involved. His main focus was on rebuilding America, and thus he wanted to avoid external conflicts. However, once the US intelligence community determined a lot of support for these uprisings was originating from Dearborn, Michigan, and the rest of the Detroit area, the President decided he needed to act in order to keep the same thing from happening within the US.

The President, in agreement with the Canadian government, authorized the use of US military forces in Canada. This included the deployment of 5,600 Military police, 120 judge advocate generals and three brigade combat teams or BCTs. There were also six Special Forces A-Teams assigned to support the BCTs. The results of the military engagement were almost immediately successful. Minor disturbances cropped up here and there, but the large-scale riots were gone and violence was on a definite decline.

It was during this tense period that PM Beck and President Stein secretly began to explore the possibility of the US and Canada holding a national referendum to merge their two countries. It was too early to announce anything publicly yet, but there were a lot of backroom conversations happening behind the scenes.

"Troy, if Canada needs any additional help, please let me know. I'd be more than happy to deploy additional military police to Canada to help augment your government. We've been fortunate in that we have not experienced the same level of violence or uprising by our own Muslim communities. Of course, the problem really isn't with Muslims directly. It has more to do with the one to three percent of radicals within these communities that stir up the problems. As we identify these individuals, we prosecute them under the law or move to deport them," said Stein, trying to reassure PM Peck that things would get better.

The President was eager to get the next part of the meeting started. His arrival had been delayed by nearly thirty minutes, so he felt behind schedule. The leaders filed back in and sat down, and Henry wasted no time.

"Switching gears, I wanted to speak with you all about the growing problems with Russia and with the Islamic Republic." Stein linked his tablet to the holographic device on the table and brought up a floating global map. Next to the map, several intelligence reports, photos and analysis were available for the rest of the group to read through while he spoke. "I feel that at this point, conflict is all but inevitable with the Islamic Republic. It is incumbent upon us to make preparations for this battle and ensure that we win."

As naïve as the leaders of the EU appeared, they also recognized that the massive demographic changes of the last twenty-five years had caused some serious problems between their Muslim immigrants and their European counterparts. The provocative activities of the IR within Western countries and the rest of the world were pushing everyone towards a clash of civilizations.

"Do you really feel that diplomacy will not work?" asked PM Bedford, hoping that his own assessment was wrong.

Stein responded, "At this point, I don't—we've shared our intelligence with you in regard to the Russian build up and the massive troop movement and modernization of the Islamic Republic's military. They're gearing up with assistance from China and Russia. The questions we have to ask are 'How much time do we have?' and 'Who will attack who first?'"

Chancellor Lowden cut in, "—Europe is still recovering from the Depression. We are only now able to adequately provide for our people, and we cannot afford to spend additional resources on a military buildup." He looked concerned while he spoke, genuinely torn.

"Chancellor Lowden, I understand your economic situation. The US has been in the same situation. You and I both know the EU cannot possibly hope to protect itself with a military force of 130,000 soldiers.... The US cannot protect Europe alone. We need Europe to do its part," said Stein, nodding towards the photos and intelligence reports floating on the holographic screen.

"With all due respect, Henry, the US does not need to lecture Europe on protecting itself. With the combined forces of Europe and the US, we can more than hold our own against the Russians. The Russians use quantity over quality, which is our advantage over them. Our weapon systems are more precise, and we can do more with less," Chancellor Lowden shot back.

"That may have been true twenty years ago. However, neither of our countries have invested in new defense technologies, while Russia and China are now leading the world in that arena. A lot has changed. Look at this report here—the Chinese are already integrating robotic exoskeleton suits into some of their combat units. Neither of our countries are even close to incorporating this technology to the same scale they are." The President brought a new set of documents up, showing the initial preparations the US was starting to make.

"Because of these new developments, I have directed our military to begin a slow buildup. We are adding almost 300,000 additional troops to each of our military services. I highly encourage the UK and EU to begin a rapid buildup of forces as well," said Stein.

"Henry, I don't know that I can gain the needed support from Parliament to increase the military. I understand the threat. I'm just not sure I can gain the political support to do what you're asking," said Lowden in a more conciliatory tone.

Bedford concurred. "I fear I will have the same problem. England is struggling, and we still have an unemployment rate of nearly eighteen percent. Paying for an increase in the military budget will be a tough proposition. Our young people are frankly just not interested in being a part of the armed forces, and as you illustrated earlier, our defense technology isn't what it used to be. What you are proposing would take the better part of a decade to achieve, not years like you are implying we need."

The President had known this was going to be a hard sell from the beginning, so he had come to the table with several options. "Gentlemen, I understand the concerns and the problems that you all will face. However, if we do nothing, it may be too late to act. We need to take action now while we still have time, not wait until after we've been attacked.

"To help increase your own economic recovery, I ask that you review and approve the new US/EU/UK free trade zone that you see before you. We will remove any tariffs currently in place and ensure that this trade agreement doesn't outsource jobs away from our respective regions. This will enable goods, services, and materials to be sold between our countries without having to pay an extra duty tax. I have also directed the US Treasury to offer fifty-year, one-percent-interest loans for the sole purpose of rebuilding your militaries," said Stein.

There was a short pause as the leaders in the room looked over the information in front of them. PM Bedford was the first to speak. "This trade deal is excellent news. I'm also glad to see that there will be special provisions in place to ensure this isn't used to outsource either party's jobs, just provide tax-free access to goods and services."

Lowden chimed in. "I agree, Henry. I'll work to have this treaty moved through quickly. As for the military, I'll recommend we increase our reserve forces to 600,000 and then slowly start to convert some of them to active duty. We may need to rely more on *your* defense industry for newer equipment—France and Germany's defense industry is limited in what it can produce right now."

Seeing that he had essentially gotten everything he wanted from the meeting, the President handed his tablet back to Monty and rose from his chair. "Gentlemen, I'm glad we were able to clear a lot of these issues up. I believe we have a dinner to attend in a couple of hours. Let us break for some drinks and a lighter conversation before we eat and share some of this exceptional French wine." The men all smiled. Stein always knew how to keep the mood in the room light.

****

June 20
Washington, D.C.
White House, Oval Office

The Grain Consortium was really starting to take shape as more countries joined and food production continued to increase. Stein wanted to leverage the Consortium to ensure the world had enough food and to lower overall global food prices. During the Great Global Depression of

74

the 2020s and early 2030s, close to one billion people had died from starvation when the global movement of food goods had collapsed. When OPEC and then the Islamic Republic had placed a global squeeze on oil, raising the price of a barrel of oil to over three hundred dollars, things had broken down fast. OPEC and the IR had believed they could exploit their control on oil and gain an incredible amount of wealth from the West. What they had actually done was create a global depression and caused an interruption in the global supply chain—energy and transportation prices had become unsustainable.

However, by June 20, there was plenty to smile about. Jeff Rogers stepped into the room, and Henry stood up to greet him. "Mr. President, I'm proud to report that the Grain Consortium is starting to get up to speed. We have the food agreements in place with the EU and our NATO allies. We have cut off all food shipments to the Islamic Republic, and China has grudgingly agreed to our food proposal."

The President motioned for the attendant in the room to pour everyone a fresh cup of coffee. "Jeff, I'm always amazed at how fast you can make deals happen and get things moving. How do you do it?"

With a smile on his face, Jeff replied, "Well, Mr. President, running P&G has given me a lot of experience in how to establish a truly global supply chain and negotiate deals that are fair to all parties…I've also poached a lot of really good people from a number of Fortune 100 companies," said Jeff with a snicker.

"I anticipate that next year, the Consortium will really start to hit its stride as the group begins to increase food production," Jeff added, taking a sip of coffee. "I'm confident it will, and as the years go by, this Consortium will bring a lot of wealth back to our countries, and more importantly, to our lower- and middle-class workers."

Monty checked his tablet as a new message popped up. The intelligence reports of the Islamic Republics troop movements had finally come in. The President saw Monty had received a message and asked, "So—what news do you have for me?"

Monty looked up and quickly said, "Sorry to interrupt, Jeff. Sir, we've gotten additional intelligence on those troops that were being moved from Southeast Asia to the Middle East. It appears the Islamic Republic has pulled them back to receive additional training. The intel guys believe most of them will return back to Asia, though our sources have said some of them will stay behind," explained Monty.

The President had been concerned about the troop deployments, not knowing if the IR was preparing for a potential conflict with Israel or just moving troops around to consolidate their positions globally. He asked, "Did we ever get a full count on how many troops were arriving from Asia?"

Monty looked down at the tablet for a second before returning the President's gaze. "One hundred and twenty-five thousand troops—our source said about 25,000 will stay behind after their training. It would appear they will be deployed to Iraq to receive additional training."

The President thought for a moment, then asked, "What training bases are in Iraq? What type of training are they receiving?"

Checking his tablet again, Monty replied, "It appears they're receiving additional training in mechanized infantry operations in Anbar Province, and about 15,000 are going to Balad for additional Air Force–related training. That training is most likely being provided by the Russians. Our sources and analysts believe the IR is in the process of reorganizing their military forces and working to unify their training and equipment."

Placing the tablet on the couch seat next to him, Monty continued, "Since we stopped selling them spare parts, they're having to reorganize their military forces with newly purchased Russian- and Chinese-manufactured equipment. Seeing that Saudi Arabia, Iraq, Jordan and Egypt primarily used American equipment, they have to replace virtually everything."

The President snickered at that. "It'll be interesting to see how this plays out over the next couple of years as parts for the F-35, F-18s, F-16s and F-15s start to become scarce. It'll get harder for them to properly field a military until they switch everything over."

Jeff rarely interjected in anything related to the military, but at this point, he added, "They may be using 3-D printing to help with parts. If you have original parts, it's not hard to develop a replica using 3-D printing software, and the printers these days are exceptionally good."

The President thought for a moment. "I hadn't thought of that— you're correct, Jeff. I guess we'll have to factor that in."

Chapter 5
Alliances

June 2039
Riyadh, Islamic Republic
Imperial Palace, The Council Room

"My Caliph, there is a problem that I must discuss with you," said Muhammad bin Nayef, the Deputy Chairman of the Islamic Republic, who often went simply by "Nayef."

"What is so important that you must interrupt my studies, Nayef?" Mohammed Abbas asked as he looked up to see several of the other advisors and ministers entering the chamber.

"Sir, we must find a solution to the food shortages the West has imposed upon us," said Nayef.

Talal bin Abdulaziz, the IR foreign minister, interjected, "I know we have discussed this before, Caliph, but the food situation is starting to become a critical problem. None of the EU countries will sell food products to us either." He was clearly very angry at the situation.

"Haven't our economic ministers worked out a way around this or figured out how we can increase our own food production?" asked the leader of the Islamic Republic.

"Sir, our engineers are working to increase the Nile River Delta area and increase the distribution of water to more lands, but it is a slow process. We have started construction of hundreds of biodomes using the latest in genetically modified seeds to increase production. These solutions will work in the long run, but they are not going to provide us the relief we need now," he replied.

"Then some people will starve while others will not. Until the situation changes, there is not much we can do but pray to Allah for his blessings," Caliph Mohammed said with a bit of heat in his tone.

Nayef knew the Caliph was right. It was just hard to accept that outcome. Knowing he also had to provide some good news if he was going to interrupt the leader's quiet time, he brought up something on his tablet and linked it to the holographic display. Up popped the latest economic and military reports. If there was one thing the Caliph liked to discuss, it was industry and the modernization of the Republic. "Caliph, the food situation is dire, and as everyone has said, we have solutions in development, but they will take time before they come to fruition. However, I'd like to direct your attention towards the progress we have made with regards to the modernization of the military and the Republic."

"Thank you, Nayef. This is an area of great importance to the Republic. We need to build up our own military industrial complexes and secure new sources for weapons and parts. If we can do this and solve our food problem, then the Republic will truly be self-sufficient," Caliph Mohammed said with some return to enthusiasm in his voice.

Nayef continued, "We have been making headway with the Chinese. They are not happy about this new cartel the Americans have formed, but they are in desperate need of food, so they are going along with it for the time being. They have agreed to sell us additional weapons and spare parts if we cut them a deal on oil. I told them we will sell them all the oil they need for thirty percent less than market value, as long as they continue to provide us with weapons and, more importantly, 3-D printing technology.

"The Russians have agreed to sell us their entire line of Armata armored vehicles. We are purchasing three thousand T-14C main battle tanks and 28,000 armored personnel carriers among other assorted vehicles. They also agreed to allow us to manufacture them under license, and we are setting up plants in Riyadh, Baghdad, Cairo and other industrial hubs."

Smiling, Nayef nodded towards Muhammad bin Aziz to continue.

"The Russians have agreed to sell us two thousand MiG 32s and will also let us manufacture a large percentage of them under license. This will greatly bolster our aerospace industry. They have agreed to sell us their newest air-to-air fighter drones as well. These are much cheaper and easier to produce. We have agreed to purchase four thousand immediately, so our pilots can begin to train with them. And once the factories are operational, we will start producing one thousand new drones a year," Muhammad said excitedly.

Nayef happily replied, "Muhammad, I didn't know you were such a shrewd negotiator. This is an excellent deal. I'm very pleased that you were able to secure the manufacturing licenses—it will not only provide highly skilled labor jobs, it will help advance our ability to design and build armored vehicles and combat aircraft…How about food? Are they able to assist us in that area?"

Muhammad relaxed a little as he said, "The Russians can assist us with minimal food this year, but they are in the process of converting large portions of their newly conquered territory into farmland. We will make it through this year's food shortages, but it will be rough."

"How is the training of the army?"

"It is going well. We have instructed the Asian region to build up their regional force to 450,000 troops. The North African region is working to build their forces to 600,000 troops and the central region to 5,500,000 troops. Most of those recruits are coming from the provinces of Iran, Saudi Arabia, and Iraq, and it will take time for this force to become proficient. The Russians and Chinese have both agreed to send us 50,000 military trainers each for the next five years to integrate our forces into the same military doctrine as theirs," said Muhammad.

"Excellent. How has the integration of Iran been going?"

"Rough in some areas and good in others. The military has been a big help in securing the country and ensuring it stays protected. It's some of their former leaders that are causing trouble...not all of them are happy with the assimilation. The drafting of a few million military aged males will certainly help with integrating them into the Republic. If it were not for the military coup, this whole incorporation of Iran would have been a disaster."

"It would have been war. Who would have thought a few billion NAD could have bought an entire country?" replied the Caliph with a snicker.

Before the meeting ended, the Caliph wanted to make sure everyone continued to stay focused on the end goal. "Everyone needs to remember that despite our final integration of Iran into the fold, our ultimate enemy is America and Israel. You need to remember that no matter what your thoughts are on the Americans, they are fierce and ruthless in combat. I've personally fought them, and I know that to be true. Their individual military training is the best in the world—that is why they are such tenacious fighters. We need to train our soldiers to that same standard, so they will not run during a battle but will charge right into it like the Americans. We can beat them, but we need our soldiers to be better trained."

General Rafik Hamza, the Overall Islamic Republic Military Commander, chimed in. "We recently had several thousand Muslim Americans immigrate to the Republic. Some of them, who had previously served in the American military, have agreed to share what they know. We are leveraging their skills and experience, along with our Russian advisors, to help modernize our basic training. The former Quds Force has also been instrumental. Surprisingly, there are some American companies that are also helping us in this area for a price. They are expensive, but they are very good."

"This further reinforces my previous statements that the West only cares about money. They will do anything for money, even train their future enemy."

"Have we moved Allah's Swords to Tanzania yet?"

"Yes, they have been smuggled out of Iran and are now sitting in a shielded warehouse in the Tanzania Coffee House Company. They make regular freighter shipments to America, so when we are ready to move the devices, they should make it through the port security intermixed with the regular cargo shipment. They have a very dense lead shield, so they will not show up on any detention sensors or satellites. I have agents who will load them onto the freighters when you give the order," said General Rafi, IR Special Operations Commander.

"If we could work out a more coordinated first strike with the Russians and Chinese, the Americans would never know what hit them until it was too late," said Muhammad.

"In time, we need to create as much instability inside America and Mexico as possible. The Russians have designs for Europe, and we need to convince them that with America out of the picture they can do whatever they want with Europe. The same argument can be made with the Chinese, but they are going to need to know that we can play our own part," Talal said.
****

June 2039
Beijing, China
Imperial Palace, Central Military Commission Meeting Room

"What are the Americans trying to do with this deal? Starve us to death?" asked Zhang Jinping, the Premier of the People's Republic of China.

"Premier, the American president is working to reduce their debt, a debt of which we hold the majority share. Our country is becoming flush with cash, and the US is starting to buy more of our products again. All of this is good news," said the Premier's Senior Advisor, Jing Xi.

The Premier was clearly angered that the Americans had negotiated China out of ten trillion dollars with the remonetizing of their debt. The US had also imposed severe tariffs on Chinese products coming into America, despite the free trade agreements previous administrations had signed. Now the US had coopted other countries to join their Grain Consortium, further squeezing China. Though outwardly trying to remain calm, the Premier could not hide his ire. The veins on the side of his neck were bulging and pulsating with each breath. The middle of his brow furrowed involuntarily. No amount of "good news" was going to erase the perceived wrongs of the West.

"This food cartel the West has formed is going to force us to play by their rules, or they will simply cut off our food supply," said Jing Xi.

Premier Zhang thought for a moment before responding, "Not only do we have to pay an artificially high value for the food that we buy from them, we have to reduce their debt by five percent of the cost of that food. If our people were not starving right now, I'd have half a mind to tell the Americans to go to hell."

Jing knew the Premier was angry and wanted to assure him that despite these slights by the Americans, all of this was still good for China. "At least they are paying back their debt—there was a time when we thought they were not going to. The value of the NAD is also rising quickly as their economy continues to improve."

"Yes, but all the money we are making from them paying back their debt, we are just paying right back to them to buy food. Not only that— we are reducing their debt by five percent of each purchase. At this rate, they will have the majority of their debt to China paid off in less than half a decade, and our leverage over them will have evaporated."

"True, but the global economy should have improved significantly by then. Our factories are already returning to life," replied Jing.

"I believe that has more to do with the massive weapon and industrial goods sales to the Islamic Republic than anything else. I can't help but wonder if we are supplying a future enemy with weapons that may one day be used against us."

"One can never know these things. Right now, it is a good business opportunity for us to pursue, and the Muslims have not been stirring or causing problems in our country, so we should be thankful," said Jing with a neutral face.

"Mark my words, if the Muslims ever try to rise up in and revolt in China, I'll not hesitate to crush them with the full weight of our military. I will absolutely not tolerate an Islamic uprising in China," said the Premier with a determined look in his eyes.

"The bigger question is, 'What is Russia doing?' They have been building up their military to pre–Cold War levels," said General Fan Changlong, the Vice Chairman of the Central Military Commission.

The Premier looked everyone at the table in the eye as he spoke. "Russia has always had an ax to grind against the Europeans. They have been invaded by Europe multiple times throughout history. Perhaps they feel Europe is in enough of a decline they can enact their revenge or vision of a unified Europe under Russian rule. In either case, it is not our vision or our problem."

Zhang continued, "Our vision is for a unified Asia. Southeast Asia has always been the Rice Bowl of Asia; it has flatter lands and can handle our growing population. It is for this reason that we continue to build and train our forces to become the dominant force in the Pacific and push the Americans out."

He paused, then asked, "What is the state of our military? Are we fully prepared for Operation Red Dragon yet?"

"As you know, the military has suffered like everyone else in China. However, our forces are still strong. The PLA stands at 3.5 million troops, all ready to defend China. We still retain a very limited offensive capability, but we can more than defend our borders. As we continue to expand our light drone tanks and infantry fighting vehicles, we will be ready to secure Southeast Asia. We have three additional supercarriers under construction, and once they are completed, it will bring our carrier force to six supercarriers and three smaller escort carriers," General Fan Changlong said as he highlighted some images of the new supercarriers on the holographic display.

The general went on, "At that point, we will be ready to initiate Operation Red Dragon and destroy the American Pacific Fleet should they try to intervene. We also have another six million troops in the reserves that can be called up if needed. Our current plan calls for us to activate two million of the reserves by the end of the year and begin to train and integrate them into our active army. By the end of 2040, our active duty force will consist of 5.5 million soldiers. A full 300,000 of our infantry will be equipped with the new exoskeleton suits. They will be our shock troops for the operation."

The Director of State Intelligence, Xi Lee, spoke up. "As long as we do not attack Taiwan, I believe we will be left alone if a conflict arises between Russia and the EU or with the Islamic Republic. With India still picking up the pieces from their last war, we do not need to worry about them as a possible threat to us either."

"Our country is safe, Premier, so long as we do not provoke a fight until our carriers are finished," said Jing with confidence.
****

July 2039
Moscow, Russia
Kremlin, Presidential Office

"Mr. President, I'd like to speak with you about the deteriorating situation in the Stans and the Caucasus region," said General Gerasimov, the head of the Russian Military.

"I trust our grip on the region is not slipping?"

"No, Sir. General Kulikov continues to purge the region. However, we are seeing a rise in the number of insurgents and separatist activity, including weapon smuggling, particularly along the border with the Islamic Republic," replied General Gerasimov.

"We have an envoy from the IR this week. I'll speak with them and see what they can do to help shut down these smuggling routes. They want to discuss the issue of a joint military defense agreement," said President Fradkov.

"That could be dangerous," asserted Nikolai Bortnikov, the Director of the Russian version of the CIA, the FSB. Nikolai was another holdover from President Viktor Zubkov's administration. President Fradkov had thought about replacing him but was more scared of what would happen if he tried. Nikolai lived for the FSB, and though he had been part of the Zubkov administration, he was extremely loyal to Russia, if not to President Fradkov. For that reason, the President had left him in power.

"In this we agree, Nikolai. The IR will at some point attempt to destroy Israel and continue the spread of Islam into Europe and America.

They could entangle us into a fight sooner than we want, but they could also be a useful ally. If they do attack the Americans and we provide them with the best weapons possible, then they may be able to bloody the Americans enough that they would not be able to intervene in Europe when the time comes.

"Likewise, we can encourage and aid them in their activities in Europe. If the EU has to put down popular uprisings in their major cities, they will not be able to react fast enough to our invasion," said the President.

General Igor Gerasimov, the Head of the Russian Military, interjected, "Whatever is agreed upon with the Islamic Republic needs to remain in line with our European objective. In all my years in the military, I have never seen the Americans at such a weak moment. President Stein knows this as well and is taking remarkable steps to correct the situation, but he has time working against him. If the IR attacks Israel, the Americans will come to their aid. We need to ensure the IR has the training and equipment needed to deliver several major hits against the Americans. If they can weaken the Americans enough, they will not be able to intervene in Europe and stop us."

Sergei Puchkov, the Minister of Defense, saw the President was weighing General Gerasimov's comment and wanted to reinforce it. "Mr. President, the general is right. I propose that when the IR does attack the Israelis and Americans, we be ready to act. If the Chinese also act when we do, then the chances of success in Europe are incredibly high. They have been building their naval forces for decades in preparation for taking on the American Pacific Fleet. If we could coordinate with the Chinese to initiate their attack shortly after the IR moves, the Americans will be split between Asia and the Middle East. Then we will launch our attack in Europe. We could capture Europe in less than sixty days."

"My intelligence sources suggest the Chinese would be open to organizing an attack with us," Nikolai added.

The President took a puff on his cigar before responding. "Nikolai, continue to work that angle. I'd like to see if the Chinese would be open to coordinating their operation with us. I also want you to look into how we can help the IR in further destabilizing Europe and North America. The more fires we can start before the big one, the better."

"I serve Russia," was Nikolai's response.

Lieutenant General Nikita Sergun, the Director of the GRU, Russia's military intelligence division, was not sure why Nikolai hadn't brought up the information about the East African coffee company his sources had discovered, so he decided to speak up. "There is one other major item I'd like to bring up, Mr. President. As you know, in the past several years, the GRU has been expanding the number of agents we have abroad. Recently, one of my agents discovered something of great value in East Africa," Sergun said, looking to Nikolai to see if he would interject. When he did not, Sergun continued.

"One of our operatives in East Africa has made an alarming discovery. His sources tell him that a freighter arrived from the Islamic Republic last week. His source works at the shipyard as a dockworker. He said one of the containers being offloaded was heavily guarded; it had a biometric lock on the door, and it required a special truck because it was too heavy for a regular truck.

"The dock worker said he believed the shipping container was lead-shielded. When it scraped against another container, it left a mark on the container that appeared to be lead," said General Sergun while displaying several photos on the holograph.

"I had our agent look into this a little further, and he discovered that the container had been delivered to the Tanzania Coffee House Company and placed into a new warehouse on the property. This coffee company also went from having minimal security to suddenly having several dozen armed guards and biometric locks on the doors to its new warehouse."

"So, what are you saying, General Sergun? That the IR shipped a few nuclear bombs or something to this apparent front company?" asked Nikolai with a surprised look on his face.

"Mr. President—Nikolai—that is exactly what I am saying. I have directed our agent there to do whatever he can to infiltrate this company, and we are looking at every angle of this," General Sergun replied.

Nikolai thought for a moment about what General Sergun had just brought up. His agents had known the IR had moved two nuclear devices out of the country—they just hadn't known the location. "Mr. President, if the IR uses these devices against the Americans, and we and the Chinese coordinate this right, we could knock the Americans completely out of the war before it really has a chance to get started," said Nikolai with a bit of excitement in his voice.

"How do you mean, Nikolai?" asked the President.

"If we can convince the IR to use the nuclear devices against key US logistical nodes instead of symbolic targets, they could cripple the Americans' ability to move men and materiel to Europe or the Middle East."

"That is a big 'if'—these Muslims don't always use logic when they fight a war," Minister Puchkov said.

"Nuclear weapons are dangerous to play with, as we saw with India and Pakistan. They nuked the living daylights out of each other, and it's lowered global temperatures by five degrees. Plus, if the Americans get nuked, you can be assured that President Stein will obliterate whoever attacked them," the President said with a bit of concern. "The goal is to conquer Europe, not destroy ourselves in the process."

"That's the beauty of it, Mr. President. The IR would do it for us. If anyone would be attacked with nuclear weapons, it would be the IR," explained Nikolai.

"Continue to monitor the situation, and let's play this one by ear, Nikolai."

****

In the following months, a series of secret meetings between Russia, the Islamic Republic, and China took place as they discussed a strategy for defeating America once and for all. They all had their own reasons for plotting an attack against the US, but for all of these parties, the end would justify the means.

Chapter 6
Saving the Mounties

November 2039
Washington, D.C.
The White House

The last nine months had been terrifying for the people of Canada. The country's Muslim population had risen to over twenty percent following the Global Depression. With the creation of the Islamic Republic and the return to a Caliph, the Muslim minority in Canada wanted to be a part of this historic event. When that didn't happen, they grumbled—loudly, and the more radical groups started to cause some civil unrest. They bombed government buildings and targeted the police and government workers. Once Canada joined the American Grain Consortium and cut off all sales of food products to the IR, the extremist groups erupted.

Extremists within the Muslim communities across the country denounced the Canadian government as anti-Muslim and held massive rallies and protests. Through careful manipulation of the situation by the Islamic Republic, these rallies and protests quickly turned more and more violent, with both sides taking casualties. The IR's public relations machine produced extremely effective propaganda showing images of Muslim children starving and blaming the atrocities on the actions of the Canadian government. They also showed graphic images, telling stories of "peaceful" protesters who were shot or killed by Canadian police. The social media campaign was proving to be incredibly effective in changing the mood within the country.

What resulted was a near-constant conflict—both violent and nonviolent—between the various Muslim communities in Canada and the authorities. In April, a series of bombings targeted police stations and killed 154 police officers. Those in law enforcement were starting to be openly attacked and assassinated, causing further casualties. It was during these trying times that the Canadian government reached out to the US and asked for assistance.
****

"General Branson, the President will be ready to speak with you in a few minutes. He's still speaking with Prime Minister Peck," said Monty.

"Not a problem. I suppose they're talking about the most recent rioting in Montreal. Their police forces were overrun by those Muslim radicals," Branson replied.

"I heard about that this morning. They burned down a police station and killed several police officers, didn't they?" asked Monty.

"Yes, law and order were just restored to the city about four hours ago, after the 5th Battalion, 20th Infantry Regiment arrived and suppressed the uprising."

"The problem in Canada only seems to grow. Their government seems to be paralyzed by this revolt of their Islamic population. They've been hit the hardest in the economic recession with—what—close to thirty percent unemployment?" queried Monty.

"Something like that. I'm a military man, so what I'm most concerned with is threats to our country and what I can do to stop them," replied Branson, always the soldier. He did his best to stay out of politics and wanted nothing to do with the political fighting that often consumed Washington and anyone that dared to get involved in it.

The President's Secretary walked back in the room and with a welcoming smile said, "Gentlemen, the President is ready to see you now."

Walking in to the Oval Office, the two of them saw the President walk towards them with his hand extended. "Mr. President, always good to see you," said Branson as he shook the President's hand.

"Likewise, General. I assume you're here to talk to me about the recent uprising in Canada."

"Yes, among a few other things, Mr. President," he replied.

"General, before we talk about this uprising, I think Monty and I should bring you up to speed on some very secretive talks that PM Peck and I have been having. Monty, if you would explain the situation."

"Yes, Mr. President. General, we all know that Canada has been in some great turmoil for the last five years. Shoot, they've had three different PMs, and their government has all but collapsed several times. This recent uprising by their Muslim populations is the straw that looks to be breaking the Canadians' back," said Monty while taking a sip of coffee.

"We've been in secret talks with PM Peck and Speaker of the House Fultz since our April meeting in Paris. The Canadians are going to hold a national referendum in three months, and the United States is going to hold its own national referendum alongside it. This referendum will allow both countries' people to vote on the unification of Canada with the United States. Their individual provinces would become States in the Union with Senators and Congressmen just like any other state," Monty said as he showed the general the breakdown of the new states that would be formed.

Sitting back on the couch, the general had to catch his breath. "Wow, I must say, I never saw this coming, Mr. President," a flummoxed Branson managed to spit out.

"There has been some talk about this in the press, but nothing serious yet. We've been working to keep it a secret for as long as possible, particularly since we have 26,000 US troops in Canada right now to help provide security," said the President.

"Our intent is to bring this public on Wednesday night during a prime-time speech that both PM Peck and I will be making at the same time. Our hope is that people will welcome this unification. It would certainly help both of our economies and bring additional stability to our borders."

"Well, with Mexico slowly slipping into a failed state, it would be good to know that our northern border is at least secure," said Branson, still in a bit of shock that Canada might become part of the Union.

"Yes, thank you for bringing up Mexico, General. We need to talk about possible scenarios should the Mexican government completely collapse. We cannot have a failed state on our southern border, nor can we allow a drug cartel to take over the country. We may need to intervene militarily."

"Our planners have been thinking about this as well, Mr. President. We've been working on several military contingencies, but things would go a little faster if we had a clear vision of what you'd like to see done in Mexico should things fall apart," Branson said, clearly looking for the President to give more guidance rather than just a broad picture.

"A clear vision, such as us installing a new government?"

"Or taking over Mexico and just annexing it into the Union," said Branson, going out on a limb.

"Annexing Mexico might pay off in the long run, but I fear it would be costly in the short run, General. I think we would need to use the military to eradicate these cartels that currently have almost free rein in the country," said Monty, looking to the President to make sure he had not overstepped his bounds.

"No, I like this idea Monty. If Mexico becomes a failed state and we intervene, we are going to have a military presence there for a long time to put the new state governments and law enforcement in place and ensure it survives. This is going to require a massive commitment on the part of the US," said the President.

"General, inform your planners that if Mexico's government does collapse, we should plan a military operation to eradicate the cartels and to bring Mexico into the fold of the Union. We'll annex them as a US territory until the cartels are wiped out. Then we can hold formal elections to begin building an internal state government and integrate them into the Union like the proposal with Canada. I also think that if we're going to invest resources into Mexico, then America should be the one to reap the benefits from it."

Branson countered, "I was kind of joking about annexing Mexico, Mr. President. The proposal you're asking the Pentagon to put together would be rather difficult to accomplish without a substantial military commitment. I can have my staff work on this plan, but I believe we should also work on a plan to just eradicate the cartels and leave the government intact. We can accomplish both." The last thing Branson wanted the military to do was get bogged down in nation-building—he wanted to keep the force mobile and ready should they need to deploy to Europe or Israel.

Stein rubbed the day-old stubble on his chin as he thought about the general's proposal. "We may ultimately get stuck in Mexico, but if America is going to expend blood and treasure there, then we are going to benefit from it. I'll concede to you that we may need two plans—I'd rather have an alternative to choose from when the time comes. Have your staffs prepare the proposals accordingly then," the President concluded.

Smiling at the concession he just obtained, he replied, "As you wish, Mr. President. I also think we should look at the size of the military again. If we are going to annex Mexico, then we're going to need a solid military presence down there for some years to come."

"How many additional troops do you believe you will need?" Monty asked.

"At least another 120,000 troops," Branson replied. "We'll need that many to clear out the cartels and to establish law and order while we build up the police force and local law enforcement."

"Agreed. We'll speak with Speaker Fultz about pushing that increase through Congress. I believe we should go ahead and increase the size of the military by another 200,000 instead of 120,000, and add an additional 300,000 troops to the National Guard and Reserves. A storm is coming, gentlemen, and we are going to be prepared to meet it head-on."

****

Riyadh, Islamic Republic
Imperial Palace Council Chamber

"Caliph, the Americans and Canadians are going to hold a referendum in three months on a possible unification of North America," said Muhammad.

"A unification of North America? Do you believe this will complicate our plans?"

"No, Caliph, it should not interfere with our plans. However, it does mean that the situation for our Muslim brothers in Canada may get worse if this unification does happen. Currently, Canadian law is a lot more lax than American law, especially as of late.

"This new political party, the Freedom Party, has been pushing through a lot of very tough domestic legislation aimed at giving the government and states a lot more power and policing capabilities. This whole biometric-enabled National Identity Card, or NICs as they call them, is making it so that everyone has to carry and use them to purchase everything. It's making it hard for our sleeper cells to procure items and go unnoticed," said Muhammad.

"As long as nothing interferes with our end goal, then I'm not concerned with what their government does. How many agents have we been able to get into the US?"

"We have a total of two thousand special operations and insurgent specialists in the US so far. They were all hand-selected to ensure they had never been biometrically enrolled in Europe or anywhere else, so when they get their NICs, there will be no record of them being associated with the IR.

"Now that they're in, they have begun to develop their cells and direct-action units. Fortunately for us, the Americans have pretty lax gun laws, so they're acquiring a lot of their weapons, both legally and illegally, with little problem," Muhammad said while sipping his tea.

"We have a little over a year to get things ready. Ensure everyone is in place and ready to execute their missions when the time comes."

The Islamic Republic had been moving select members of their Special Forces and other military and intelligence specialties into the US and Mexico for the past few years. The IR had named the North American operation "Allah's Judgment." Their goal was twofold: to destabilize the government of Mexico and work with the Mexican Army to conduct a coup and then let the cartels run wild, and to cause as much panic and chaos as possible inside the US. This would force the Americans to get involved in Mexico, which would result in a significant portion of the American military becoming committed to that theater of operation. This, in turn, would make them less able to handle any other attacks on their soil.

A large portion of the domestic assaults were slated to be conducted against the American power grid. This would involve attacking transformers, towers, power plants, and dams. Some of the other cells would focus on mass killing events, attacking malls, schools, subway and train terminals, and movie theaters. Then, while the US reeled from these violent acts, the last wave would attack law enforcement and first responders.

With the American Army committed in Mexico and the internal chaos going on inside America, it was believed the US would not have sufficient forces available to prevent the IR from wiping out Israel. This single act would fulfil the great Mahdi prophecy and cement Mohammed Abbas as the lifelong ruler of the Caliphate and usher in a new Islamic renaissance.
****

02 February 2040
Post Referendum Day

"Mr. President, it's official. All votes are in, and the referendum won in the US with 62% of the vote. It also won in Canada with 52%— not as much as we would have liked, but it passed," said Monty with a big grin on his face.

"This is great news. PM Peck is scheduled to call me at 11 a.m. today, and we're going to hold a joint news conference tonight at 7 p.m. here at the White House to make it official. We'll both sign the referendum into law, and that will start the official process of merging our two countries together," the President said happily.

"This is a great day, Mr. President. It is clearly one of the most significant moments in American history, sir. Ten new states will join the Union, and our country will increase in size by over forty percent," said Monty.

"Mr. President, congratulations on the referendum," said Jeff, also smiling from ear to ear.

"Thank you, Jeff. It was a lot of hard work selling this these past three months, and I'm just glad it paid off. I feared it would have been bad politically if it didn't."

"Well, Mr. President, it worked. We have ten new states. I'm going to organize a meeting as soon as possible with their former economics and finance ministers, and we will work to bring the Canadian economy into ours. We will need to work on currency conversions, consolidating their debt into ours and converting their people's money into NADs. It's going to take a bit of time to make all these adjustments, Mr. President, but this is a task I'm really looking forward to," said Jeff said with a serious look of determination.

"I am too. This is a significant point in our country's history, no doubt, and this is also a chance for all of our people to start something new. I firmly believe this will really improve the economy," said the President with confidence in his voice.

"I believe it will certainly help. Their unemployment is still near twenty percent, while ours has finally fallen below six percent for the first time in two decades. There are significant infrastructure projects that will need to be done in Canada, but the sheer volume of natural resources is going to be an amazing boon to our economy. They've been unable to exploit them properly for decades because of a lack of investment and their ridiculous environmental laws," said Monty.

"That is about to change, gentlemen. Monty, we also need to work very vigorously to get the Freedom Party firmly entrenched in the new Canadian states. We need to ensure that they know which party is bringing them this newfound prosperity and security."

"Yes, Mr. President. That will be one of our first tasks. I will meet with Speaker Fultz about this and get the party heads working on getting things set up," said Monty, tapping a quick note to himself on his tablet.

The Speaker of the House, Mike Fultz, was also the Deputy Chairman of the Freedom Party, while the President remained the Chairman. Speaker Fultz's primary responsibility within the party was its expansion and recruitment of candidates. The actual Freedom Party headquarters was located in Tampa, Florida, where Henry Stein had initially founded the group. The party had 7,000 full-time employees spread throughout the country and boasted an incredible candidate research team. Their goal was to find and interview potential candidates for positions in their state that the FP thought they could win.

For the past eight years, the FP had been active in identifying and recruiting candidates to run for every state and federal position across the country. Of course, not every candidate won, but enough candidates were winning at the state level that several states were now FP-governed. As the economy continued to improve, more people left the Democratic and Republican parties to join the one party that truly was doing what they said they would do. Their goal was to bring prosperity back to America and make the nation successful again.

The President, out of necessity, was already starting to turn his attention towards his own reelection. "Remember this is an election year, and the Democrats and Republicans are already going full bore after us. The polls still show us with a very commanding lead, but once the final candidates are determined, it will be a tougher fight."

"I wouldn't be too concerned with it, Mr. President. In the last three years, unemployment has gone down almost six percent, and it's going down one percent to two percent each quarter. We're showing steady economic progress, and more and more people have money in their pockets," said Jeff.

"Thank you for the assurance, Jeff. Let me and the President worry about the political stuff. You worry about integrating the Canadian industry and economy into ours and ensure that the economy continues to improve," said Monty, clearly not wanting another senior advisor in the administration advising the President on the election or political matters within the FP.

"Sure thing, Monty. I didn't mean to intrude into your area. I was just saying, I don't see the elections being a problem for us. I travel the country a lot, and when I'm waiting around in the airports, I often strike up random conversations with people and ask them what they think of the Freedom Party. The vast majority of people love the President's straight talk and his take-charge attitude. I very seldom find someone who has something negative to say," Jeff added.

"That's good to know, Jeff. I do appreciate your thoughts on the matter. What Monty means is that you have a huge job ahead of you, and a lot of our political success will hinge on our success or failure with the economy. Focus on your part of the machine and let us focus on the other parts," the President said with a smile, clearly trying to ensure Jeff didn't feel left out of the inner circle.

****

The spring and summer of 2040 brought dramatic changes to North America as Canada and the United States merged into one country. Ten new stars were added to the flag, bringing the total number of stars to sixty-four (Northern and Southern California, East and West Colorado, East and West Washington State had separated and become their own states during the early 2020s under the Warren administration, and Puerto Rico had also been added as a state during the same timeframe).

The United States continued to see enormous economic growth, especially as employee wages quickly increased. The median household income had risen from $62,400 annually in 2037 to $83,700 by the summer of 2040. Meanwhile, the Republicans had nominated one of their rising stars to challenge Henry Stein and the Freedom Party while the Democrats nominated a familiar name and face, Senator Lowden from Northern California.

England and the EU also continued to grow as the Transatlantic Fair Trade Agreement increased trade and eased movement between the two continents. England and the EU also experienced a sharp increase in emigration as tens of thousands of Muslims were immigrating to the Islamic Republic. The IR was starting to truly turn into the Islamic paradise most Muslims longed for. It was a pure Islamic country, with little in the way of Western influence. The state controlled that, to be sure. Slowly, the IR was starting to solve their food shortage problems through the creation of thousands of biodomes and genetically modified seeds to grow more food per acre than traditional seeds.

The modernization of the IR military continued at a rapid rate. They had increased their military force to nearly three million soldiers, and another two million more were being trained. Russia and China had increased the number of military advisors in the IR to over fifty thousand. China had established a new naval base in Oman, repositioning one of their supercarriers as they continued their expansion into East and South Africa. Russia had expanded their naval base in what used to be Syria. They had also leased an airfield and established a training squadron to assist the IR in training pilots for the new aircraft they were purchasing at a rapid rate.

Russia and China both continued to look for ways to increase their own spheres of influence. China was nearing completion of their additional supercarriers and established a solid footprint in East and South Africa to include the establishment of two joint naval, army and air force bases. The People's Liberation Army or PLA had grown considerably, and so had their provocations towards Taiwan.

Tensions between the two countries continued to build as Taiwan was going to hold a referendum on whether to officially become their own country or continue to hold their claim as the only legitimate government of the Republic of China. President Stein had made it clear that the US was not going to get involved in territorial disputes that did not directly threaten the national security of the US. The US did continue to sell Taiwan as much top-of-the-line military equipment as they wanted. In technical terms, the PLA was now more advanced militarily than Taiwan. The PLA Air Force had thousands of fighter drones and the PLA Navy had six supercarriers. The Chinese Army had also managed to equip and train nearly 300,000 soldiers with the newest exoskeleton combat suits.

The PLA and the Russians' new exoskeleton combat suits integrated both speed and survivability of the individual soldiers. A soldier using the new suit could lift over one thousand pounds, jump nearly forty feet, and run close to thirty-five miles per hour. The helmet worked much like a fighter pilot's helmets did, with a heads-up display that identified targets for the soldier and kept track of how much ammunition the soldier was burning through. It also had a built-in map and mini ground radar, so it could distinguish between friendly and enemy forces in real-time.

The polycarbonate uniform sewn into the mechanical aspects of the suit protected soldiers against flash burns caused by nearby explosions and flying debris, including limited amounts of shrapnel. The suit also monitored the human body and could automatically inject the wearer with additional red blood cells and clotting agents to assist the body in naturally clotting an open wound. Also available were insulin, adrenaline, and stimulants.

The soldiers wearing these suits would be able to operate at such a high level that the Russians and the Chinese would be able to accomplish more tasks with fewer soldiers. The US, UK, and EU forces also had similar exoskeleton suits with similar capabilities but nothing close to these numbers of soldiers equipped with them. This was a very new military technology, and though the US had it, the US had not integrated it into the armed forces to the degree the Chinese and Russians had.
****

With a lot of negative influence and activity by the Islamic Republic, the situation in Mexico continued to worsen despite the improving American economy. Millions of Mexicans were still trying to cross the American border, which had become nearly impossible since the FP had turned the southwest into a militarized border. Aside from the twenty-foot-tall wall separating the two countries, there was also a ten-mile no-man's-land that was heavily patrolled by border patrol agents and drones.

The various cartels and criminal organizations controlled most of the country outside of the major cities, which made life for the average citizen difficult, to say the least. The Mexican government was quickly losing control of the country, which was putting an enormous strain on the situation at the border, as millions of Mexican citizens were desperately trying to escape their crime-ridden country.

Chapter 7
Infiltration

September 2040
Riyadh, Islamic Republic
Imperial Palace, Council Chamber Room

"Muhammad, are we ready for Operation Allah's Fire?"

"Yes, our operatives have infiltrated the Port of Baltimore, the Port of Houston, the Port of LA, and several contracting companies that provide services at two of the major utility companies that provide power to the northeastern US," Muhammad replied, pouring himself another cup of tea.

"Excellent. I am glad that you have included several ports, in case one does not work out."

"As of right now, the primary targets are the Port of Baltimore and the Port of LA. We have people infiltrating the Houston port in case we need a fallback plan. Some of our people believe we should also make use of our liquid natural gas tankers. They would act like mini-nuclear bombs if they were full when they are detonated."

"That is not a bad idea, but the Americans only export LNG, and they only use a couple of companies for security purposes. I am not convinced a shipment from one of our front companies would be able to get through."

Wanting to discuss the main operation and not get dragged down a rabbit hole, Caliph Mohammed said, "Tell me about the plans against the American power companies in the Northeast that you mentioned."

"The primary attack against the northeastern US is going to take place in the dead of winter, when electricity is needed most. The plan for our groups that have infiltrated the power companies is for them to destroy several critical transformer nodes from the inside. One group even plans to destroy one of the power plants directly with explosives.

"When the power goes out, it will cause a number of things to happen. First, people will lose power in the throes of winter, which will prove deadly as it will take more than a couple of weeks to repair. Second, with no power, there will be a lot of looting as people run out of food. Third, we have two hundred fighters broken down into numerous smaller direct-action units that will go on a killing spree all across the major cities. After the first five days, those fighters that are still alive will do their best to fade away into the population and move to their next assignment once they are able to check the draft emails in their accounts."

Huseen ibn Abdullah, the Director of Intelligence, made a point to mention, "We are staggering the attacks to take place over an extended period of time, to cause as much fear and damage to the American psyche as possible. Some of our three- and five-man direct-action units will conduct random and uncoordinated attacks on malls, supermarkets, movie theaters and elementary schools, mostly across small and rural towns, cities and the suburbs outside of the major cities. These attacks will be hard to deter and even harder to predict. We believe this will increase their likelihood of success and cause more casualties."

"How are we going to ensure these attacks coincide with the two nuclear bombs?" asked Caliph Abbas.

"The plan right now is to have the nuclear weapons detonate two days apart from each other. The first one will hit Washington, D.C., during the first day of the new Congress in January of 2041. The vast majority of the government will be in session that week, giving us the highest likelihood of decapitating a large swath of their government. In the evening, the President is supposed to have a dinner with the prime minister of Israel, so it is possible that we may take him out as well," said Zaheer Akhatar, the Caliph's Senior Advisor.

"This is also when we will issue our ultimatum to the US to stop supporting Israel and to leave the Middle East and Europe alone. We know they will not agree to these demands, and that is when we will have the second device detonate two days later. After dealing with two months of terrorist attacks across their country, the blackout on New Year's Day in the Northeast, and then two nuclear bombs, the country will be in a panic, and they will agree to our terms. If they do not, then the attacks will continue, and their economy and country will grind to a halt," said Talal, the foreign minister.

The Caliph smiled a sinister grin. "At long last, we will be able to pay the Americans back for all of the wars they have waged on our lands. We need to remember that when this happens, and the Americans are most panicked, they will lash out and it will not take them long to do so. What contingency plans do we have in place to deal with the Americans once this occurs?"

"We have the most advanced surface-to-air missile defense systems, the same ones both the Russians and Chinese have. Our antimissile laser defense system is now operational and will be able to protect the industrial heartland of our country and the major population centers from any ballistic nuclear missiles or bombers the Americans may try to hit us with," said Muhammad.

"I hope you and our advisors are right. This is going to either devastate the Americans, or it is going to cause them to destroy us. Are the plans for Israel ready?" asked Abbas.

"The operation is ready to start on New Year's Day."

"What are we going to do about the American carrier battlegroup in the Mediterranean?" he inquired.

"Our plan is to saturate their defenses with missiles and then slip in a nuclear missile to finish off the battle group. Once the operation begins, Israel and the Americans will be bombarded with missiles, and while they are raining down, our armored forces will be racing across the border and will drive their army into the sea," said General Rafik Hamza, the commander of the Republic's military, hate and vitriol in his voice.

Clearing his throat, Huseen linked his tablet with the holographic monitor and brought forward several reports. Changing subjects, he said, "Caliph, if you are ready, I have the briefing of our activities in Mexico completed for your viewing." Prior to the formation of the Republic, Huseen had been the head of intelligence in Egypt and had been instrumental in Egypt joining the IR several years earlier. Now, he was the director of the Islamic Republic's intelligence service and had the task of coordinating the myriad of attacks that would take place across North America.

"True to their word, the cartels have held up their end of the bargain. They have thoroughly infiltrated the police and military and are ready to take over as soon as we give them the word. We have also secured the cooperation of numerous senior defense officials."

The Caliph smiled. "This is good news indeed. Have they asked for any additional weapons?"

"They have asked us for two thousand SA-18 man-portable air-defense systems and three thousand additional RPG-7V rockets along with eight hundred additional launchers."

"Why so many MANPADS and the new RPG-7Vs?" asked the Caliph with concern.

I'm not sure how badly that will cut into our own reserves, he thought.

"Their assessment—and I have to concur—is that once the coup takes place, the Americans will most likely intervene. When this happens, they will need to turn to guerrilla tactics. The SA-18s will aid them in shooting down the American drones and pose a huge risk to their attack helicopters. The specific RPG rockets they are asking for are the high-explosive antitank or HEAT rockets, which can destroy or disable just about any armored vehicles the Americans would bring to the fight. They have RPGs, but the rockets are only fragmentation rounds. They needed the newer rockets to take out newer tanks and armored vehicles the Americans are likely to use," he explained.

"I understand now, but do not send them that many. Send them about one third of their request. There is no way they will need more than that. Also, I want you to send a few thousand advisors to assist them in the coming conflict. Our advisors can also help in taking down those American helicopters."

"As you wish. I'll see how many commandos I can get reassigned to Mexico."

"Once the coup takes place, how reliable is their military going to be? Are they going to be effective?" asked Abbas.

"Their military is pretty infiltrated already, and we have several high-level officers on our payroll. The military will be brought in line within the first couple of days. Some units may not respond or go along with the coup, but those units can be dealt with. As for how effective the army will be against the Americans...not very effective. Their plan is to try and hold their own at some strategic locations, and then, between their propaganda and ours, they will try to rally the people against the Americans once they invade. Their plan is to move everything to a sustained guerrilla war, which will drain the Americans of even more troops. With US forces entangled in Mexico, it will limit their options in aiding Israel. Add to that the chaos our sleeper units will be causing, and a large portion of the American military will be unavailable."

"There are a lot of moving parts. How are we going to ensure the American intelligence agencies do not discover this before the operation is able to start?" asked Caliph Mohammed.

"There is no guarantee. We have a lot of activity going on in Africa, and we are starting to stir things up in the EU, mainly in France,

Germany, and England. We just need them to be distracted. This is also why we cannot delay the operation. The longer we postpone, the more likely it is that someone will figure out what we are doing."

"I agree. What other items do we need to discuss?"

"I think we should talk about the nuclear warheads. I still believe that if we use them, the Americans are going to use theirs against us. We can still accomplish our goals without the use of nuclear weapons."

"I know we can make things work without the nukes, but I want to use them. We want to level Washington, D.C., and wipe out as much of the government as possible in the process. They may use nuclear weapons against us, but we are a huge sprawling empire. We can absorb some hits like India did. We also have our laser defense system, and I'm confident we will be able to shoot down their missiles," the Caliph said, rebuffing their concerns.

He continued, "The damage that will be done to America will be devastating. I am just not sure where the second bomb should go off. Part of me wants to have it go off in New York, and then the practical side says we should use it against a target that will cripple their economy."

"I suggest using it against Houston or the Port of Los Angeles. Houston would hurt their energy exports and refinery capacity. Hitting the Port of LA, however, would wipe out their largest and probably most important port, not to mention the damage it will do to the city," Talal said.

"I'll have to take that under advisement, Talal."

"I think it is also time for us to get things going in Mexico. Let's stir that hornet's nest up and get the Americans involved. The sooner they become truly entangled there, the better," said the Caliph, indicating he wanted to end the meeting.

"As you wish," said General Rafik Hamza.

****

Early September 2040
Washington, D.C.
White House

"Monty, we need the President down in the Situation Room," said General Branson with urgency.

"What's going on?" asked Monty with a bit of concern in his voice.

"Monty, this is Jim Wise. We need the President down in the Situation Room ASAP. Please go find him."

"All right, I'll track him down. I believe he was out for a short walk to clear his head," said Monty as he looked for an exit that would lead him towards the Rose Garden.

As Monty was walking towards the Rose Garden, he spotted the President smelling one of the roses still in bloom. "Mr. President, we need you down in the Situation Room—something is going on," Monty said as he moved towards the President.

"Is it really so urgent that it can't wait fifteen minutes? You know I like to take a short walk after breakfast to clear my head before the day's schedule."

"Yes, Mr. President, it's important. Jim Wise, Eric, and General Branson are all down there waiting for you."

"Well, if they're all there, then I suppose it really must be important." Henry sighed deeply, knowing something must have gone wrong that would require him to make a decision he would rather not have to deal with right now.

As the President walked into the Situation Room, he could see by the looks on everyone's faces it was grim news. "Gentlemen, this had better be important."

"Mr. President, it's critical. One of our agents in the Mexican Army told his handler yesterday that the cartels had just received a very large shipment of weapons from the IR—MANPADS and RPG-7V rockets," said the National Security Advisor as he looked up from his tablet.

"We've known for some time that the IR has been shipping weapons to the cartels. We've intercepted some of these weapons shipments in the past—if I'm not mistaken, the Mexican Army has as well. Why is this such bad news, Jim?" asked the President, clearly annoyed at having his morning routine interrupted.

"The cartels are planning a coup, and the Mexican Army is in on it," General Branson blurted out.

"Our source said his unit just received orders directing them to be ready to attack the presidential palace and secure the major government buildings in Mexico City," Jim added.

"What about the rest of their military? Are they in on it as well?" asked the President.

"Not all of the units are in on the coup. Our source said he's going along with the coup plans for the moment, but when it comes time to execute his orders, he's going to move to safeguard the palace and the government buildings, not seize them."

"Have we alerted their President about this impending coup?"

"Not yet. We aren't sure who in the government we can alert without notifying the wrong people. Our source in the military said he believes his commanding general is part of the coup, so informing the military is not going to work, and neither will the police. They've been heavily infiltrated by the cartels, so nothing stays a secret with them."

"So, what's our plan, then? Do we have one?"

"We have the military option we discussed earlier in the year, Mr. President. If the coup does happen, then we can initiate our plan," General Branson said, not knowing if the President would want to act now or play a "wait and see" approach.

"What are your thoughts, Monty?"

"This is a hard one. On the one hand, if we do nothing, then the cartels will more or less take over the country. This will give the IR a willing partner on our southern border, which is something we want to avoid. On the other hand, if we do intervene, it's going to require a lot of troops and resources," said Monty.

"Eric you're the SecDef. What are your thoughts?" asked the President.

"Well, General Branson is right. This gives us the pretext to act on our earlier discussion about this situation. The government is going to fall—we know that. I propose we let this play out and once the dust has settled, then we execute our plan and intervene. This way we can hopefully eliminate the leadership once they have come forward to form their new government."

"You're talking about the plans to annex Mexico?" the Secretary of State asked.

"That's exactly what I'm talking about," replied the SecDef.

"I still think the annexation of Mexico is not a wise move, Mr. President. There are just too many problems in Mexico that we'll be inheriting," asserted the Secretary of State.

"I have to agree with Secretary Wise, Mr. President. We can annex Mexico, but managing it is going to be a difficult problem," Attorney James Roberts said. If the annexation went through, then the Department of Justice would be incredibly busy trying to establish a new legal system with the Mexican provinces.

"What are your thoughts, Jorge?"

The Director of Homeland Security, Jorge Perez, pondered the question for a moment before responding as he steepled his fingers. "America has been dealing with problems from Mexico for nearly a hundred years. The country is rife with crime and totally corrupt. If you're willing to keep Mexico under martial law for a few years and give us time to root out the cartels, I believe we can make it work. I think we should just annex it if we're going to get involved. Putting that much blood, sweat, and tears into nurturing a territory, only to hand them off to revert right back to what they came from would be a supreme waste of time, effort and resources. It reminds me too much of what our country did in Iraq in 2011 that ultimately led to the formation of the Islamic State."

Taking a deep breath in and letting it out slowly, the President thought about what his advisors had said before responding. "I understand the logic and concerns in annexing Mexico. It would solve a lot of problems, but it would also bring a lot of problems that we don't need right now. When I first took office, I told the American people that we would not get involved in foreign wars unless American security was threatened. Because of Mexico's proximity to us and our shared border, I believe this constitutes an immediate threat. With that said, I do not believe America should have to shoulder the burden of nation-building. If America is going to intervene abroad, then we're going to keep what we take, and America will be the one to benefit, not some corrupt government that always seems to come to power once we hand it over," said the President, who had clearly made his mind up now.

"Jim, I want your staff to work up an exercise with the DOJ, DHS and the FBI on how we would begin to implement our law enforcement agencies into Mexico once annexation begins. Let's frame this as an exercise to downplay the possibility of it really happening, but I want a plan ready within the next twenty-one days."

"That's a tight timeline, Mr. President. I'll see what we can do," Jim said as he wrote down some notes in his tablet.

"Well, I guess we wait and see what happens next," said the President as he stood up and left the Situation Room.
****

September 2040
Moscow, Russia
Kremlin, Presidential Office

While situations continued to spiral out of control in Mexico, the Russians continued their covert preparations for their own attack against the European Union. On the opposite side of the world, China and the Islamic Republic continued to plot their own assaults against the Americans and the West. Their ultimate goal was a new world order, where the three nations would rule.
****

"Mr. President, it would appear the Islamic Republic has presented us with a unique opportunity. They are moving forward with their attack on the US," said Nicolai with a mischievous smile.

"Have we learned the full details of the attack yet?"

Nicolai shook his head. "Not yet. We know some of it, and we know they plan on attacking the Israelis," said General Sergun, the director of the GRU, reading the latest intelligence feeds from his tablet.

"Do we know when they plan on attacking the Israelis? What type of assault are they going to launch?" asked Fradkov.

"We believe they are going to launch their attack around the New Year, although we are not sure of the exact date. As of right now, it looks like they plan on launching a massive conventional missile attack on Israel, targeting their military bases and their ability to defend themselves. This raid will be quickly followed up by their military attacking through several predetermined invasion points, so no WMD as of right now," replied General Sergun.

General Sergun loved to use the multidimensional maps and graphs when presenting war plans. They made everything seem more aligned and perfect, or at least they did to him. He cleared his throat and continued. "Their first invasion point is across the Golan Heights. If they can break through, then they will be able to drive deep into Israel quickly. The Israelis know this, so they will send a large part of their forces in that direction. A second front will be initiated from the north along what used to be Lebanon. A third front will then be opened in the south near the American naval base in Eilat on the Red Sea. The fourth front will come from the Sinai, and the fifth attack, which is the main assault, will come through the Jordan Valley towards Jerusalem.

"From what we have gathered, the attack in the Golan along with the assault in the south will happen almost simultaneously, and then twelve hours after the first assaults begin, the other three fronts will begin their invasions," General Sergun said while changing some slides and maps on the holograph.

"It sounds like they might actually have a chance of beating the Israelis if they do not go nuclear, which I highly suspect they will," President Fradkov said, not believing for a minute that the Israelis would not use atomic weapons if they were about to be overrun.

"If the Israelis go nuclear, the IR will as well. I don't believe the Israelis would survive even if they did go nuclear. One point of concern that I'm not sure the IR has fully accounted for is the use of land-based and mobile antimissile laser defenses. These can also be used to target aircraft, and if the Israelis are somehow able to achieve or maintain air superiority, the IR is going to have a much tougher time. Unless Israel receives massive reinforcements from the Americans, they will probably only be able to hold out between five and seven days at best," General Gerasimov said, stealing Sergun's thunder.

"The IR's placement of mobile and fixed antimissile and aircraft laser defense systems guarding Israel will make it hard for them to use their nuclear weapons too," Nicolai interjected.

"What forces do the Americans have in the area that they could use to help Israel?"

"They have a carrier battle group operating in the Eastern Mediterranean and another in the Indian Ocean–Red Sea area along with a Marine Expeditionary Force with about 2,500 Marines. The MEF is about the only unit that could quickly come to their aid. Though there is still an airborne battalion in Italy, that would add another 550 paratroopers to the mix," General Sergun said as he lit another cigarette, ignoring General Gerasimov's request to share one with him.

"It sounds like our hopes and dreams are being answered. The Americans will be bogged down in Mexico and then Israel. They really won't be able to provide any meaningful support to the EU," the President said with a wicked grin on his face.

"That is true. The next test will be Great Britain and the EU," Sergun said.

"Yes, but they do not pose a serious threat to our forces. Our Air Force is on par with theirs these days, and they do not have the ground forces needed to stop us," Gerasimov added as he brushed off Sergun's concerns.

Fradkov thought of an idea that might help further their ruse. "Let's hold a military exercise in mid-January along the NATO lines. We'll make this a joint exercise with our Belarusian and Eastern Ukrainian allies. Let's also include NATO officers to ensure we defuse their apprehension. Once the IR attack is in full motion against the US and Israel, then we can make our move."

"True, Mr. President. We had planned to attack the EU next fall, but the IR is going to make us move our timeline up sooner than we had anticipated. If our winter training exercise coincides with the timing of the IR's attack, we could redirect the training to a full-on invasion of the EU and a combined first strike against the Americans. Our forces will have been dispersed and have crossed into the EU, so neither the EU nor the Americans would launch nuclear weapons at them," General Sergun said devilishly.

"Despite our forces being dispersed, the Americans will respond with nuclear weapons if we use them on their troops. It's part of their standard procedures."

"Mr. President, to launch nuclear weapons, the Americans need their president to authorize it. If he is not available, then it passes down to the Vice President. Next it would go to the Speaker of the House. All of these people will be at the inauguration, and if the IR plan works, they will have decapitated all of the people in the line of succession that could authorize an attack," said General Gerasimov.

"What is the state of our ballistic missile defense system?" inquired Fradkov.

"We have twenty-one pulse beam batteries covering the likely approaches their missiles would take from either submarine launch or their missile silos. In addition, we have recently launched four new weather satellites that are part of our space-based laser missile defense system. Our primary concern would be their stealth bombers; we may be able to identify some of them, but more than a few would slip through our defenses," replied General Sergun.

"The question we have to ask is this—can we inflict enough crippling damage to knock the Americans out of the war at the start and secure the rest of Europe? And can we absorb the damage the Americans are most likely to inflict?" asked President Fradkov. "The other question is—will the Chinese play their part and strike the American West Coast and their Pacific Fleet?"

"During our last talks with the Chinese, they seemed like they would do their part. They want to absorb Southeast Asia and the Rice Bowl it would bring. They may even look to secure Australia, if the Americans are knocked out of the equation. The hardest challenge our forces and the Chinese will have is ensuring we coordinate our attacks to coincide with the Islamic Republic's assault," General Gerasimov replied.

"Yes, it will be a challenge trying to synchronize everything, but I'm not sure we will have an opportunity like this ever again. If we and the Chinese choose not to join in this attack, the Americans will recover quickly and obliterate the Islamic Republic. If we limit our first strike to purely military targets, chances are if the Americans respond, they will likewise limit their strikes to our military facilities as well. The GRU believes our missile defense will help reduce the number of potential strikes we would absorb, so our only real concern is how effective the Americans' missile defense system is," replied General Sergun.

"Let's move forward as if we are going to execute this operation with the IR and the Chinese. If we need to cancel the operation, we can do so right up until the last minute if we believe the Chinese are not going to be able to pull off their end. Perhaps we even let the Chinese launch the first attack, and while the Americans are responding to that threat, we hit them," said the President.

Chapter 8
South of the Border

Mid-September 2040
Mexico City

"Colonel Zedillo, we have received final confirmation. We are to begin the coup at once. Send the word to our people to start arresting the various commanders and military officers we know will not cooperate and replacing them with ones that will. I want this done within the next two hours. We are to commence with the coup by the end of the day," General Galván said with glee in his voice.

"Yes, General. We shall have everyone in position soon," Colonel Zedillo replied. Then he began to type up a coded text message to let everyone know the coup was going to take place that day.

General Guillermo Galván was an egotistical narcissist who had a god complex. He truly believed he could one day become president or take control of the country and lead Mexico to new greatness. His tenacity, skill, and determination had led him to become the second-highest-ranking general in the Mexican Army. For years, he had fought the cartels, until two years ago. One day, he had been approached by a member of the Islamic Republic intelligence service with an offer that had seemed too good to be true—five hundred million NAD to stop attacking the cartels and start cooperating with them.

The Islamic Republic's goal was for Galván to form a partnership with the cartels to take over the country and ensure the Americans would not pose a threat to his government once he completed his overthrow of the current government. If he was able to successfully plan and execute the coup, he would have their full support to become the new president for life.

He would, of course, need to continue to turn a blind eye to the cartels and to change his country's stance towards the US. The IR reasoned with the general that by incorporating the cartels into the government, a prearranged percentage of revenue made by the sale of drugs globally would be given to the government. The Islamic Republic would then ask for permission to base soldiers in Mexico, and he was to accept this offer and extend an opportunity for the IR to establish a military base there.

With the orders sent, Colonel Jose Zedillo felt good as he left the secret meeting with General Galván. He owed his entire military career to the man, and he was confident that when this coup was over and the dust settled, he would obtain a senior position within the government. To help ensure the success of the coup, the general had ensured he would be the commander of the soldiers that protected the presidential palace and the Mexican government. This would help to ensure the general had people loyal to him in key positions near the president, and furthermore, he would be able to control the message the army wanted sent out.

****

When the coup finally happened, it transpired quickly, despite some army units refusing to be a part of it. Their commanding officers were quickly eliminated as well as any other individuals who wanted to resist. During the first hours of the coup, the Islamic Republic's cadre of Special Forces operating in the country assisted the Mexican Army with securing important government institutions and military bases as well as eliminating opposition and potential opposition leaders.

The first two days of the coup were bloody. Thousands of people within the government and media as well as individuals identified by the Islamic Republic's intelligence network were killed, and others with needed skills and political leanings contrary to America were installed. Within two days, the entire country had been secured with help from the military, and the police had no resistance or violence from the cartels.

At first, the US stood on the sidelines to see what would happen. Within five days of General Galván taking over the country, several governors refused to recognize him as the new leader of Mexico. Several military units whose commanders had not been replaced during the coup also revolted when they saw how the cartels and the Islamic Republic advisors appeared to be cooperating with Galván. The situation in Mexico appeared to be quickly dissolving into a civil war as new battle lines were being drawn. Those governors who initially stood up to the military dictatorship being imposed were quickly killed by IR Special Forces units at the request of General Galván. It then became apparent to the US President and his advisors that the level of involvement by the Islamic Republic was much greater than could have been anticipated.

The Islamic Republic quickly recognized the new military dictatorship and even the cartels aligned themselves with the rebels.

After the public recognition, the IR's military advisors and Special Forces in Mexico openly assisted General Galván's forces in "holding the country together." The Islamic Republic had even offered to send an additional ten thousand soldiers to help act as peacekeepers, which General Galván gladly accepted.

For the IR, the situation played out exactly how they had hoped. Mexico was becoming a base of operations that would necessitate an intervention by the American military. The ensuing battle that would rage in Mexico would tie down American forces, keeping them from being mobilized for the coming fight with Israel. Once the Americans did intervene, the IR sleeper agents would then start their part of Operation Allah's Judgment and would rain chaos and terror on the American people for the next three months, until it was time to deliver Allah's Swords.

****

End of September 2040
Mexico

As it became clear that Mexico was going to become a base for Islamic Republic forces in North America and that the Mexican government was going to become a "narco-state"-sponsored military dictatorship, President Stein saw no other option than to intervene in Mexico. The Pentagon had been working on a war plan to capture and then integrate Mexico as a US territory for nearly six months. Units had been identified along with equipment that would be needed. The President only needed to give the order, and within three days, the operation could begin.

On September 26, President Stein gave the order for Operation Brimstone. The President brought in the Congressional leadership of all parties and had the National Security Advisor, Director of the CIA, Director of DHS and the Secretary of Defense brief them on the situation in Mexico and explain the finer points of Operation Brimstone. At the end of the meeting, the President asked for approval for the operation. Support was unanimous from the FP and Republican Party leadership and their representatives. Several Democrats also voted for the campaign, despite most voting against it.

On the morning of September 29, US forces initiated hostilities in Mexico with devastating effectiveness. Before the sun rose, the US launched a series of attacks by land, air, and sea across the US southern border, the Pacific and Gulf of Mexico. Thousands of fighters, drones and cruise missiles hit critical military targets all across Mexico, with hundreds of Special Forces and American paratroopers landing all across the country securing airports, critical bridges and military command and control centers.
****

30 September 2040
Philadelphia, PA

The day after President Stein announced the US was going to intervene in the Mexican Civil War to restore order, the Islamic Republic activated one of their direct-action teams to start their first series of attacks. These outbreaks of violence would continue to escalate in frequency until the final two assaults, when IR agents would direct a full insurrection and rioting of several major cities.

Nagim Abdullah had just finished his coffee and was returning to work when he received a text message. He quickly checked his phone and understood that his group had just been activated. Nagim had succeeded in obtaining a warehouse position shortly after his arrival from Oman a year earlier as a political refugee. He had been recruited by IR intelligence to be a group leader for a direct-action unit in Philadelphia, Pennsylvania, just prior to leaving Oman.

His orders were to obtain a low-level job that would draw little attention and wait to be activated. They had given him three targets to attack. The first was a mall located in the downtown area. If his group survived the first attack, then he would proceed to their next target, which was a movie theater in one of the suburbs.

His orders were simple—spend no more than three minutes in the mall shooting as many people as possible and then quickly get away. Lie low for twelve hours and then conduct the next attack. He would continue to move down his target list until either his team was killed or they completed their mission. Once the assignment was complete, he was to head to Detroit, where the IR had a major operation planned.
****

01 October 2040
Washington, D.C.
White House, Situation Room

Since the authorization of Operation Brimstone, the President had requested an update every twelve hours, until the country had been fully secured.

"Mr. President, the first forty-eight hours of Operation Brimstone have been completed. There were 1,353 bombing sorties since the start of hostilities. We've hit various military and strategic targets all across Mexico, with a special emphasis on hitting the known cartel locations and operations. While this has been taking place, thirty Special Forces A-Teams began hitting every known cartel safe house, drug factory, and leadership residency location. They were either directing the air strikes on the ground or quickly following in afterwards with ground forces to ensure the targets were killed," General Branson said.

Changing presentation slides, he continued. "Delta Force was tasked with attacking the central military command base in Mexico City and quickly apprehended General Galván while they were trying to organize a defense of the city and country. They also captured and secured the presidential palace," General Branson said, giving the President a chance to ask questions before he continued with the brief.

"Please continue, General," instructed the President.

"The 75th Ranger Regiment conducted a combat jump directly onto the Mexico City International Airport and secured it for follow-on forces. The entire XVIII Airborne Corps, all 35,000 of them, completed their combat jumps and hit over a dozen locations across Mexico City. They also landed with their light tactical vehicles and two battalions of the new light tank drones. They are currently securing the remainder of the city and expect to have it fully secured within the next seventy-two hours. One of the first major units we have landing at the airport is a brigade of military police. Once they land, we'll begin to filter them throughout the city to assume the policing duty while we keep our combat forces focused on finishing off the enemy military units.

"Our Navy quickly neutralized the Mexican Navy, capturing what ships they could in port with the SEALs and destroying the ones they couldn't capture. 1st Marines led the charge across Southern California, securing Tijuana and moving through the Baja Peninsula. 2nd and 3rd Marines are making various amphibious landings across the Gulf Coast of Mexico."

Moving to a new slide that showed the US southern border, the general continued with his presentation. "The 1st Armored Division out of Fort Hood is leading the ground invasion from Texas, along with the 1st Cavalry Division out of Fort Bliss. The 4th Army Division has several battalions securing positions across the Arizona and New Mexico borders, with the rest of the division pushing inland through the desert. The commanders on the ground believe the majority of Mexico will be secured within the next ninety-six hours and full occupation of the country will be accomplished within ten days as more follow-on forces arrive and begin to move to every major city in Mexico."

"It still amazes me how fast our forces were able to capture and secure most of the country," said the President, genuinely impressed.

"Mexico isn't that far from most of our military bases, and sharing an almost-2,000-mile border does make it a lot easier to invade. We also had the element of complete surprise, thanks to your speech earlier about the US taking a wait-and-see attitude towards the new government. They were completely lulled into a false sense of security," Eric Clarke said with a smile before turning serious again.

"I want to make sure that once follow-on forces are in Mexico, that we extract our frontline troops, so they are ready for any other surprises. I didn't think the Islamic Republic would have gotten involved so soon, nor that they'd have as many soldiers already on the ground as they did," he added with a bit of concern in his voice.

"They caught a lot of people by surprise with that," said Patrick Rubio, the Director of the CIA. The CIA was starting to catch a lot of flak in the media and from the DoD for not knowing there were already several thousand Islamic Republic troops in Mexico.

"How many casualties have we taken, and has there been much resistance?"

General Branson resumed his brief to answer the President's question. "Resistance was heavy the first day. Special Forces had 60 killed in action, and another 135 wounded in action. The brunt of those casualties came from Delta Force, which was hit particularly hard."

"Why did Delta take so many casualties?"

"They had the toughest, most well-defended target. The military headquarters compound was heavily guarded by Mexican and IR Special Forces. They put up one heck of a fight before they were able to capture General Galván," said Branson.

"Sorry for interrupting—please continue, General."

"During the airborne operation to secure the Mexico City International Airport, the 75th Rangers suffered 19 killed and another 124 wounded. Despite the resistance at the airport, they were able to secure the airport within two hours. They also repelled two separate but uncoordinated attacks by the Mexican Army to prevent us from being able to use the runways to ferry in additional soldiers."

Changing slides, he brought up that showed the casualties for the conventional forces, which were just now starting to get more heavily involved in the fight. "The rest of our ground forces up to this point have sustained 675 killed, and roughly 4,250 injured. A large number of those wounded will be able to return back to their units within a week, so do not let the large number throw you off. The conventional forces are now starting to make contact with the Mexican army units that are fighting for General Galván, which is why the casualty numbers are a bit higher right now. That number should drop as we finish mopping up the enemy units.

"The cartels have also been putting up a good fight, though they are also melting away into the population. We'll need to hunt them down. The MANPADS the IR provided them prior to the conflict have caused us a lot of problems. We've lost thirteen helicopters, 46 drones, and four aircraft that flew a little too low. We're starting to see more use of those new RPG-7Vs rockets as well," Branson concluded.

"Gentlemen, I'm impressed with our success thus far. I want to make sure it continues, so please use whatever resources and troops are needed to pacify the country quickly. I want law and order restored soon, and I want a return to normalcy, or as close to it as possible."

Knowing the domestic aspects of Mexico and America still needed to be discussed, the President changed the direction of the meeting and asked for his domestic advisors to begin their brief. "Moving to domestic matters, Jim, I believe you had some information you wanted to share— but before getting into that, I want to make sure everyone is working towards stabilizing Mexico. I want the FBI to hire an additional 1,500 Special Agents and start to identify Spanish-speaking agents who can start setting up field offices in Mexico. I want the DOJ to start developing their plan for criminal prosecutors and a police force," said the President as he looked over the men and women at the table.

"I have my best people working on this, Mr. President. We have several plans underway right now to accomplish that goal. I will have more details about this in my brief with you tomorrow," said Attorney General James Roberts.

AG Roberts had been a federal prosecutor prior to being named the AG. He was a tenacious prosecutor and had spent his first few years as AG repealing hundreds of presidential memos and directives that previous administrations had issued in direct violation of the Constitution. Churches were no longer required to report their attendance or their membership base. Sharia law was no longer being tolerated in any city in America. The cities and townships that had allowed this now had to abide by the laws of the United States government, not Islamic Sharia law.

The Sharia law challenge had created a lot of problems between those who were Muslim and those who were not. There was a high tolerance for people to practice their own religious beliefs in America, but all religions had to respect and abide by the laws of the United States. Likewise, the sanctuary cities were no longer allowed. City governments that refused to enforce federal law were being denied all federal funding until they became compliant. The city governments that were still in violation after the one-year compliancy period were dissolved, and a state caretaker government was installed until a new election could be held.

AG Roberts had taken a lot of heat for his reforms within the DOJ and the legal system. His primary goal had been to reform the justice department back to its original stated purpose, to return the judiciary back to interpreting the law and constitution, no longer tolerating judges who legislated from the bench. Laws could be struck down or upheld, but no judge could impose a new law or issue an opinion that could be interpreted as a new law. Roberts was a true constitutionalist and loyal party member.

"Excellent, I look forward to learning more about them tomorrow, then. Jorge, can you please go ahead and give us your brief?"

"Yes, Mr. President. The NSA intercepted several communiques between several known IR intelligence individuals and people in the US.

They were not able to glean any usable information from the messages, but they believe they were coded messages, perhaps intended to activate some terrorist cells or just a status report on our operations in Mexico. They still have a few thousand soldiers and operatives operating in Mexico," Jorge said as he clicked through several images of known IR intelligence agents suspected of being in the US and Mexico.

Suddenly, a Secret Service agent walked over to the President and whispered something in his ear. The President's eyes grew a little larger, and his demeanor changed.

"Sorry to interrupt, Jorge—I was just informed that we should turn on Fox News. There's been a terrorist attack in Philadelphia."

An aide quickly changed the 3-D holographic image in the Situation Room to Fox News, where a news update was being aired live from a shopping mall in Philadelphia. A Fox News reporter by the name of Nina Short was in the process of providing an update on the situation at the mall as it developed.

"We are standing outside the Mayfair Mall, where twenty minutes ago, five men were seen running into the food court entrance to the mall, wearing baseball caps and dark sunglasses, each of them carrying an AR-15-style rifle and small backpacks. We were able to interview a survivor, who told us what she saw."

The camera panned to a woman who was clearly shaken and had blood spatters on her blouse. She explained, "Three of the men ran past the food court to the center of the mall and shot at everyone they saw. The two at the food court entrance opened fire, shooting and reloading as they walked through the food court. After what felt like an eternity, they worked their way back to the food court exit. Then I saw a security guard shoot two of the suspects before they killed him. One of the attackers was left behind by his partners while the other was able to retreat out of the mall. I was hiding under one of the tables but managed to catch most of the event on my smartphone."

The camera returned to Nina Short as she continued, "Upon leaving the mall, the individuals sped away in their vehicle. The FBI and police told us they have issued a BOLO for the suspects' vehicle and are asking the public for help or video footage of the event."

"Enough. Turn it off. Do we know how many people were killed, and do we have any idea who the attackers are?"

"I just received an update from the agent in charge at scene right now," said the Director of the FBI as she looked up from her tablet. "She's reporting 87 people killed and 107 people injured. The suspect who was shot by the security guard has been transported to a local hospital for treatment." Audible gasps were followed by an awkward silence.

"She said they plan on questioning him as soon as he's out of surgery. We should have an ID on the suspect shortly as they run his prints and facial image against our databases," Jane Smart said.

"Jane, I want answers soon. Find out who this person is and whether this is a lone wolf attack and if it's related to our operation in Mexico or something else."

"Yes, Mr. President. I believe I should excuse myself and work on this with my people right away, if I may leave?"

"Yes, please get us an update as soon as possible. Keep Jorge and James apprised of any changes. I want the NSA cross-checking this as well."

A chorus of, "Yes, Mr. President," echoed throughout the room.

The President turned towards his National Security Advisor and said, "Mike, can you please give us a shorter version of your brief, so we can be ready to handle this new situation as we receive more information?"

"Yes, Mr. President. The intercepts from the Middle East indicate something is going on. We've seen a lot of military orders and activity within the IR. They appear to be moving a lot of forces to the provinces of Syria, Jordan, and Egypt. Some of these movements appear to coincide with a major military exercise that they're holding towards the end of November; others appear to be new unit assignments to bases in those areas.

"The cause for concern is that most of these units are their Tier 1 frontline units. The best equipped and trained units are all moving to within striking range of Israel, with the majority of these forces and support units being in position around the time of the exercise."

"Why is this important, Mike?" asked the President.

"At first, we didn't think anything of it. However, the Chinese are conducting a massive naval and amphibious exercise throughout December, and the Russians are conducting an exercise of similar size in Eastern Europe in the middle to end of January. This is a lot of military activity by these three nations, all within a very short timeframe, suggesting it might be a coordinated effort and part of a much larger plan," Mike explained.

"Not to discount the information or your group's analysis, but are we sure this isn't a legitimate exercise as opposed to something more sinister?" asked Monty, the President's Chief of Staff.

"Perhaps. Right now, there are several alternatives. I've retasked a lot of our intelligence surveillance and reconnaissance and HUMINT assets to find more information. We'll continue to monitor it and ensure nothing else is going on."

"All right, gentlemen. Let's table this for the moment and focus on the immediate tasks at hand, stabilizing Mexico and reestablishing law and order. And let's identify who these men are that perpetrated this dastardly terrorist attack today."

"Yes, Mr. President," chorused the whole room.
****

02 October 2040
Riyadh, Islamic Republic
Royal Palace, Council Chamber Room

The Islamic Republic had initiated the Mexican coup in mid-September, anticipating that the Americans would intervene in a month or two— not immediately. They hadn't anticipated the swiftness of the American military, or their ability to destroy the Mexican Army and occupy the country so quickly. While it was true that the American Army had been growing in size for the past couple of years, the Republic had still believed the Americans to be years away from being able to deliver such a devastating blow to an enemy. Nearly all past American interventions had been in the Middle East, Asia, and Europe, far from America's home bases. Unlike past interventions, Mexico shared an almost-two-thousand-mile border with the US. Nearly all the military units involved were located within a thousand miles of Mexico City, meaning there was very little in the way of logistical problems or long distances for their forces to travel.

"The Americans have secured Mexico faster than we originally thought they could. Our advisors were unfortunately not able to prevent the Mexican army from collapsing as quickly as it did either," said Huseen, the Director of Intelligence, dejectedly.

"The MANPADS did bring down a number of helicopters, drones, and aircraft, and they should continue to destroy aircraft as the occupation continues. Some of the Mexican military units were smart and faded away quickly as soon as it became clear that the Americans had taken out the military leadership. They are now carrying out guerilla attacks as often as they can," assured General Hamza.

"Our operatives in the country are working to establish a grassroots-level insurgency as we speak. It will take time, but they are confident attacks against the Americans will start to increase in the weeks and months to come," said General Rafi, the IR Special Operations Commander.

"Excellent, General. Please continue the good work and keep us informed. I'm disappointed by how fast Mexico was taken, but I take solace in knowing that our Special Forces and military advisors have inflicted a lot of casualties and will continue to do so. For the rest of our plan to work, we need the level of violence to continue to increase in Mexico in order to tie down the American troops," commanded the Caliph.

"On another note—have the Americans figured out our involvement in the Philadelphia attack?" the Caliph inquired, hoping the answer was no.

"Not yet. They captured one of the attackers, but he didn't know anything that would lead them back to us. I ordered the next group to begin their attack, and they should begin tonight. The first group will begin their second attack in two days—they had to lie low and regroup after the mall attack. I'll initiate the third group right away. By the time we have all eight groups active, the Americans are going to be going crazy," Huseen said with a devilish grin.

Chapter 9
Escalation

October 2040
Beijing, China
The Central Military Commission Briefing

The Chinese had been preparing for a confrontation with the US for nearly fifty years. Decades of cyberattacks and theft of intellectual property had given the Chinese the advantage they needed to not just catch up to the Americans, but advance beyond them in multiple areas. For nearly thirty years, the Chinese had infiltrated various aspects of the American industrial control systems' manufacturing base and embedded viruses and malware that were just waiting to be activated. The Chinese planned on not just dominating the Pacific but replacing the US as the world's leading superpower.

"What is the status of the situation with the Americans? How are things progressing?" asked Zhang.

"Premier, the terrorist attacks in America continue to increase. The assaults against American forces in Mexico are increasing as well. The Islamic Republic was right—as this continues and their attack against Israel starts, it will draw forces away from the Pacific and limit the Americans' options when Operation Red Dragon begins," said Xi Lee, the Director for State Intelligence.

"The Navy is nearly ready as well. We have relocated our fleets to be within striking distance of the exercise location, and I have moved the majority of naval infantry to be ready for the ground invasion as soon as the order is given," said Admiral Wei Shengli, the Commander of the People's Liberation Army Navy or PLAN as he sneered at his Army counterpart.

The rivalry between the PLA, PLA Navy, and PLA Air Force had been going on for decades, with each service commander believing theirs was the most important branch of service to the People's Republic of China. "Premier, we discussed this earlier. It would be the PLA that would lead the invasion of Taiwan, with the PLAN infantry creating a diversion. We do not want to split the PLA Air Force's support between two different amphibious landing forces," said General Fang Wanquan, the Commander of the People's Liberation Army.

The capabilities of the PLA Navy had increased over the last several years with the additional supercarriers. Their ability to go toe-to-toe with the US Navy was unmatched by any other group. It was also the naval infantry that was first to receive the new exoskeleton combat suits, outside of the Special Forces.

"Gentlemen, the attack will continue as planned. Admiral, your forces will destroy the Taiwanese Navy and neutralize the American bases at Guam and Okinawa. I want your naval infantry to capture the airfield at Guam."

"Yes, Premier. I merely offered a second front to split the Taiwanese defenses," said Admiral Shengli.

"I understand perfectly, Admiral. You want to show off your naval infantry and your new toys, and you will...at Guam and then Okinawa. Taiwan is going to be a victory for the PLA. I do not want interservice rivalries to compromise this operation. This is going to be our first engagement against the Americans, and we need to win so we can assert our dominance over the rest of Asia."

"The Air Force is ready to deal with both Taiwan and the Americans on Guam. We are going to time our attack on Guam to coincide with the cruise missile attacks in order to overwhelm their defensive capability. As for Taiwan, we have moved 6,000 cruise missiles, along with 3,000 aircraft and 10,000 drone aircraft, to cover the army's amphibious assault," explained General Xu Qiliang with a smile and a nod towards the PLA commander.

"This had better work, General Qiliang. If the Air Force is not successful, that will make it very hard for the Army and Navy to accomplish their mission. I believe enough has been said about this matter. I want everyone to give me a status update at the next CMC meeting."

****

Late October, 2040
Washington, D.C.
Pentagon

"General Black, what is the status of operations in Mexico? How are things proceeding?"

"We're a month into the operation, and we're starting to see the rise of an insurgency. There've been multiple IED attacks against military patrols, sporadic rocketing of some of our bases, and some small engagements against our troops on patrol—but it's nothing we cannot handle," said General Black, the overall commander in charge of Operation Brimstone in Mexico.

"This isn't going to turn into another Iraq or Afghanistan, is it?" asked General Branson.

"No, Sir, it is not. I still have 70% of the Special Forces community in Mexico, along with additional military police and specialized counterinsurgency teams arriving every day. I have the SF guys busy hunting down any and all insurgent leads as soon as we learn who they are. We also have the entire country covered 24/7 with drones. If we spot a group of armed men moving to engage our patrols, then we engage them. The same happens when someone is spotted putting down an IED. We've also placed bounties on the heads of the insurgent leaders and will pay for any information that leads to their capture or death. We've seen a significant increase in the number of tips, and for the most part, they're starting to pay off."

"How are the work programs coming along there? Are we getting the various projects up and running?" asked General John Branson.

"The Army Corp of Engineers has about 15% of the identified projects underway, and they anticipate having another 20% started in the next couple of months. Even with just 35% of the projects active, it will employ roughly 800,000 people with high-paying jobs, which, when compared to what they previously had—it's almost a miracle. I believe the insurgency will start to die out once more people are employed through the various reconstruction projects."

"Generals, this is a top priority for the President, and not just because of the election in a few weeks. You all are aware of the increase in terrorist attacks here at home. The President wants to get things in Mexico stabilized soon so we can have more of our combat troops ready when and if they're needed," said Eric Clarke, the Secretary of Defense.

"To that effect—General Black, I'm retasking Delta Force back to the US, effective immediately. If these domestic attacks continue, the President may look to task Delta to work with the FBI and DHS in locating and terminating these terrorist cells," the SecDef ordered.

"The loss of Delta Force is going to impact my mission, but I can live with it as long as you leave the rest of my A-Teams and the SEALs, at least for the next couple of months," replied General Black.

"Unless something else comes up, General, I have no intention of taking any forces away from Mexico. We need that mission stabilized and ready to hand over to the provisional governing authority or PGA. The President has also authorized the use of three security firms in Mexico: Ravenwood, DynCorp and Triple Canopy. They'll start to show up once the PGA gets set up, and they'll provide a lot of the security for the DHS, Army Corps of Engineers and DoJ as they begin to setup operations." An audible sigh was heard by the various generals.

"Gentlemen, I know not all of you agree with the President's decision to intervene in Mexico. You may not love the thought of us integrating Mexico into the US, or the use of private military contractors either. The President wants to stabilize the country to a point where a general referendum can be held. The people need to be able to begin national elections for Congressional and Senate seats, along with Governors and State legislature," said the SecDef.

"I'm not against the President's plan—I mean, it will solve fifty years' worth of problems between the US and Mexico. It's just going to be a big adjustment," said one of the divisional commanders.

General Adrian Rice, the Air Force Commander, placed his reading glasses on the conference table. "This is going to be an adjustment for us all. The Freedom Party is not going to be like the political parties of old—we are not going to get involved in conflicts abroad unless either the United States is going to gain from it or there's a direct and immediate threat."

The DIA Director looked tired and complained, "I fully understand the party's stated goals. It just feels like imperial expansionism."

"Gentlemen, we all serve at the pleasure of the President. This is the strategy going forward. I suggest everyone make the best of the situation for the good of the nation or look for positions in the private sector. You are the best officers in the military—that is why you all have been promoted, in some cases far ahead of your peers. The President wants the most qualified people in charge, not the ones who put in their time and believe that 'now it's their turn'" the SecDef reiterated.

The meeting broke up, and each commander went back to their respective offices to brief their own staffs and implement the orders given.

Chapter 10
America Under Attack

End of October
Washington, D.C.
White House, Cabinet Meeting Room

"Gentlemen, last night was the ninth domestic terrorist attack in three weeks. This last attack was at a Republican Party rally, nearly killing the presidential candidate. By the way—do we have a final death toll yet?" asked the President, still in a state of shock.

"Ninety-seven people killed and 232 wounded. On a happier note, none of the attackers survived the attack," said Director Smart of the FBI.

"Senator Landrew is calling for the White House to make peace with the Muslims in order to end these terrorist attacks. She's already using last night's attack in a new campaign ad," said AG James Roberts, shaking his head in disgust.

"I don't want to focus on politics. I want to discuss what we're going to do about this situation and how we're going to make this stop," the President replied, clearly irritated.

"Mr. President, the three terrorists we've managed to capture are starting to provide some good intelligence," said Mike Williams, the National Security Director. "One of the individuals captured was just a foot soldier; he was recruited locally here in the US, so he doesn't know any information about future attacks or other cells. The other terrorist that's talking said he originally worked for the Quds Force as an intelligence agent, and when Iran became part of the Islamic Republic, his mission changed from gathering and reporting intelligence to recruiting and building direct-action units to be used to conduct terrorist attacks."

"Really? I hadn't heard this before," said AG Roberts. "When did the National Security Council learn of this?"

"We opted to use an interrogation team from Joint Special Operations Command or JSOC, and they were very persuasive in getting him to talk. He originally spilled the beans about four days ago, but we didn't want to say anything until his information could be verified. All the information he gave us about his Quds Force contacts, dates, and the Islamic Republic proved to be accurate, so we had no reason to believe he was lying," Mike explained, putting down the dossier of the individual in question.

"I'm always skeptical about information obtained through the use of torture," interjected Director Smart.

"He wasn't tortured; he was just given some pharmaceuticals to help him relax. Eventually, he said that if we were willing to pay him money and place him into our witness protection system, along with his family, he'd tell us about additional future attacks that he knew about."

"I hope you were planning on asking me for permission before you went ahead and agreed to this," replied the President, giving Mike a stern look.

"Of course, Mr. President. As I said, we only just broke him the other day. As a test, we asked him to give us the location and names of one of the cells that was going to conduct another attack. He gave us the names of the individuals who conducted the movie theater massacre, and JSOC should be apprehending them sometime in the next few hours. They've had their safe house under surveillance for the past eight hours. They're just waiting for another member to return back to the house before they execute the raid."

"Mike, if you are going to use your JSOC guys for something like this, then please keep my office and the FBI informed," said AG Roberts, annoyed.

"I agree, Mike. I have no problem with you being proactive, but please stay within the rules we set when I gave you permission to use JSOC on US soil," chided the President. He was clearly irritated that Mike was not keeping the other agencies well-informed.

"Yes, Mr. President. It wasn't my intention to leave anyone out of the loop on this operation. I just wanted to make sure it was real before I got everyone's hopes up," said Mike, who was clearly annoyed at being dressed down by the AG and the President during the meeting.

"All right, everyone, let's get back on track and continue with the rest of the brief. What's done is done. Can you please continue, Mike?" asked the President.

"Yes, Sir. As I was saying, we told the Iranian that if his information about this cell was accurate, then we would agree to his demands and have a letter personally signed by you for his review. If at any time, he provides us with false information or warns the IR, his deal will be voided, and we will deport his family and the rest of his entire extended family. We would also make sure the IR knew he had been a double agent for us."

"Well, this leaves us with some interesting questions and options for what to do next," said Monty.

"Mike, are you one hundred percent confident that these terrorist attacks we've been experiencing have been directed, supported and orchestrated by the Islamic Republic?" asked Jim Wise, the Secretary of State.

"I am, Secretary Wise. What we are trying to ascertain is how many more direct-action units the Islamic Republic has in the US and what their other missions are," Mike replied.

"If that's the case, Mr. President, then this is an open act of war against the United States by the Islamic Republic," said Eric Clarke, the Secretary of Defense, with a bit of heat in his voice.

"The question is—how do we want to respond, and when? Mike, I want full confirmation that this is, in fact, being directed and supported by the Islamic Republic. I want as much factual evidence as possible: money traces, people, signals intelligence…everything. We are going to respond, but I want to make sure we lay out a solid case against the Islamic Republic to both the American people and the world. I also want the other agencies to see if they can confirm or validate your findings. We will not go to war on sole-source reporting," emphasized the President.

"Yes, Mr. President. I'll start working with the AG," said Mike, nodding towards AG Roberts. "We will prepare to present the facts, releasing as much information as possible at the unclassified level."

"Actually, I want to declassify the intelligence in this case. Everyone knows our capabilities and how we gather intelligence. Don't reveal any sources or information that could damage a source or a means of intelligence collection, but make sure the nitty-gritty details and information are there. I want there to be no doubt as to their culpability in this."

Stein turned to his senior military man. "General Branson, you've been awfully quiet. What are your thoughts?"

"I've been kept informed by JSOC on the progress of the interrogations, so most of this information is stuff I've already heard. Right now, I'm trying to look at the bigger picture and figure out what's going on globally."

"Care to elaborate on that, General?" asked the President.

"Let's look back to the beginning of the year. The Islamic Republic started shipping heavy weapons to the cartels in Mexico. The cartels increased their attacks against the government and generally created a lot of internal chaos and instability. Then, the military conducted their coup, and the problems caused by the cartels evaporated. Once the coup happened and we announced our intention to intervene, terrorist attacks start to take place all across the US. We've had nine attacks in the last three weeks, and twenty-three since we started operations in Mexico. The American people are becoming afraid to leave their homes or even go to work."

"That attack against the corporate headquarters at Apple in California and the Amazon warehouse in Tennessee have caused a lot of employees to fear that their office may be next," said Jane Smart, the Director of the FBI.

"Yes, these types of attacks are designed to target and instill fear among the common person. None of their attacks have been against the government, or what we would consider 'hard targets,'" explained Branson.

"But you see a bigger link to this?" Mike asked curiously.

"I do. I believe everything has been orchestrated by the IR to preoccupy us and distract us from their next move so that we won't be in a position to intervene."

"What do you believe this next move will be, General?" asked Monty, leaning forward in anticipation of the response.

"The IR is going to conduct a massive military exercise in December. I believe this exercise is going to be used as a cover for an attack against the Israelis and the US 5th Fleet," said General Branson.

"Hmm, certainly could be. Does the intelligence support your assumption, General?" pondered the President.

Director Rubio suddenly remembered a report he had read two days ago on this topic. "Mr. President, one of our case officers published a report a couple of days ago that mentioned a possible attack against the 5th Fleet and Israel. We had tasked the agent with obtaining more information, and I wanted to vet this information further before we briefed it...I believe General Branson may be onto something. If he has additional information, then it may help us paint a better picture."

"Thank you, Pat, for bringing us up to speed on what your agent found. It has been a well-known fact that the IR wants to destroy Israel, and they believe our continued support and military bases there infringe upon the holiness of the lands of the Prophet. A lot of this does make sense when you picture it all together. I believe you're both right—the IR's next move is probably going to be against our remaining forces in the Middle East and Israel. If that's the case, we should make preparations for it. Any suggestions?" asked the President.

"My advice is that we work on the assumption that this is going to happen and begin to shift specific forces to the area that could quickly be used. We could have a Marine Expeditionary Force conduct a joint military training exercise with the Israel Defense Force at our base in Eilat. It would also reinforce the naval air station and port. This will place 3,500 Marines and their equipment on the ground prior to a potential attack. At the same time, we should have some of our F-35s and F-22s conduct a training exercise, enabling us to pre-position additional combat aircraft in Israel."

"I would also like to add several additional antimissile defense ships to the *George H.W. Bush* carrier battle group. We should also move the 6th Fleet out of Naples to Greece. They can be in position quickly if needed," said Branson as he looked at the faces of everyone in the room, making sure they understood the gravity of what he was saying.

"I'm in agreement, Mr. President," said the National Security Advisor. "It's better to have the forces in place and ready. If nothing comes of it, then at least our forces were able to get some additional training."

"All right, then let's go ahead with the deployments. Perhaps we should also send additional Special Forces teams or some airborne units to Italy."

"We can do that, Mr. President," replied General Branson as he looked at General Black, who nodded, knowing that these forces would be pulled from his resources.
****

31 October 2040
Los Angeles, California

Ibrahim had received a coded message early in the morning, letting him know it was time to activate his direct-action unit. His cell had originally been developed by the Iranian Quds Forces. Now that Iran was part of the Islamic Republic, his unit fell under the IR Special Operations and Intelligence Group. Having seen the numerous attacks happening across America, it was only a matter of time until they would activate his unit. Now it was time to let the others know.

"Najim, the attack is on. Get ready while I make the calls. This is going to be a long day."

Ibrahim had been given some autonomy in determining his unit's targets. The first target was a big one. The unit was going to attack the central police headquarters in downtown Los Angeles, kill as many police officers as possible, and then release any prisoners being held. They had exactly ten minutes to kill as many police officers as they could and destroy as much of the building as possible.

Pending their survival, they were going to break into three groups. One team of two people would take one of the Chevy Tahoes and drive through the varying valleys surrounding LA County, throwing road flares into the dry underbrush to start as many wildfires as they could. The second group would consist of three people, who would also take a Tahoe but would head to Malibu. Their mission would be to go house to house, killing people in their homes until either the police killed them or they successfully attacked ten homes. If they survived, they would fade into the background of the city and await further orders. The third group was to head to Universal Studios and attempt to kill and destroy as much of the compound as possible. This group would be the largest, with the remaining members of the assault team.

Grabbing his cell phone, Ibrahim begin to make the calls to his lieutenants to activate their groups. "Have everyone armed and assembled at our preplanned staging point," he barked.

Walking down to the basement, he removed a couple of boxes that were obscuring a large black trunk. Pulling out his key, Ibrahim unlocked the trunk and did a quick inventory of what he had and what he would need to bring with him. Placing his military-grade body armor on, he quickly loaded six magazines of 5.56mm ammunition for his AR-15. He grabbed another eight magazines and placed them in his backpack. Next, he grabbed his Glock 19 and five eighteen-round magazines. Before he left with his tools for this mission, he placed six radios with throat mics in his backpack, knowing that his lieutenants would need them.

As Ibrahim pulled into the meeting location with his Suburban, he saw most of the group had already arrived. "Ibrahim, everyone is accounted for except Abu Kassim. We are ready," said Mohammed, one of his lieutenants.

Getting out of his vehicle, he told Mohammed, "We need to hit these targets fast and stick to the timeline. If we stay at the objectives too long, additional police will arrive, and we may not get out."

"I understand. We are ready when you give the word. Do you think the twenty of us can really pull this off?" Mohammed asked.

"As long as Saïd doesn't chicken out. When he detonates his van in front of the police station, that should kill a lot of them."

"I don't think he will become a coward at the last minute. He has been preparing himself for this moment for a long time, and I think he is ready," replied Mohammed with confidence.

"We shall see."

Beep, beep. Ibrahim checked his smartphone and saw the go order from his handler. The time had come for him to do his part in this Holy war against America.

"That's it—that's the message. Everyone, get ready. We leave in a minute. Saïd, are you ready for your mission?"

"I am ready. I will not let you or Allah down. I will be a martyr for Islam as we bring Allah's judgment upon America," Saïd said with a wicked grin on his face and a look of burning rage. Saïd's father had been killed by an American drone attack when he was just a child. His mother had brought him up with one purpose in mind: to avenge his father's death.

"You will be greatly rewarded, my brother. May we all die as great a death as you will. Now, start heading towards your target and complete your mission."

As their little convoy drove through downtown LA, they could not help but revel in the chaos they were about to cause. Americans had grown fat and lazy. They were only concerned with their own lives and did not notice anything else around them.

Then they saw it—a big plume of black smoke rising into the sky just a couple of blocks ahead.

Boooom!

A large fireball emanated from directly in front of the LA central police station. The utility truck Saïd was driving had been reinforced with bulletproof glass and armor around the passenger compartment to ensure that he survived long enough to detonate the truck. The truck had been loaded with 5,000 pounds of high explosives and 1,000 pounds of ball bearings to create additional shrapnel. When he reached the front of the police building, it detonated—with an explosion so powerful, it tore the entire face of the building off, along with several buildings across the street. Dozens of people were lying on the pavement and sidewalks, some slowly moving, some discovering the gravity of their wounds. Others lay on the pavement like tossed and torn rag dolls. The screams of pain and cries for help began almost immediately after the shock of the blast wore off.

Speaking through his throat mic, Ibrahim ordered Khalid to have his team drive right towards the hole in the building and start clearing the building. His twelve-man team should be sufficient, considering they were all armed with assault rifles and the police were bound to be shell-shocked from the blast.

"Mohammed, I want you to have your team break into four groups. One group is to walk around and start killing the wounded. I want your other teams to start clearing and killing everyone in the surrounding buildings. We have exactly ten minutes to cause as much chaos and damage as possible, and then we move to the warehouse and regroup for our next mission."

"As you wish. This is a glorious day for us, Ibrahim. I'm honored to be a part of your command," said Mohammed, who quickly turned and ran towards the two vans carrying his team.

As Ibrahim walked towards the heavily damaged Starbucks across the street from the police station, he heard the moan and soft cry for help from a man lying on the sidewalk. His arm had been badly mangled from the blast, and he had a terrible head wound. He reached out his good hand towards Ibrahim, begging him for help. Without thinking, Ibrahim reached down, grabbed his Glock and shot the man in the face, putting him out of his misery.

For some reason, he was amazingly thirsty. As he walked into the Starbucks, he saw what he was looking for—the cooler filled with bottles of water. He grabbed several bottles of water and started walking back towards his command vehicle, a black Chevy Suburban with a reinforced brush guard and bulletproof windows and doors. The sound of automatic fire emanating from the police station was intense—the police were clearly putting up one heck of a fight.

Ten minutes went by quickly. Everyone had returned to the vehicles. Some were bloodied, and others were carrying a wounded comrade. "Ibrahim, we cleared the first two floors of the police station and the holding cells. We released 86 prisoners. We made sure to arm all of them and told them to go cause as much havoc as they could. Khalid lost five of his twelve guys, and two of my guys were killed clearing the buildings around here," Mohammed said as he climbed into his vehicle and took a long drink from a bottle of water Ibrahim had liberated from the Starbucks. Then they all drove away from the carnage they had just inflicted.

Dozens of sirens could be heard as three police cruisers drove past their vehicles, heading towards the police headquarters. "How did you lose two men while clearing that office building?"

"Several employees apparently had concealed weapons. As soon as the shooting started, they quickly shot two of my guys before they were gunned down themselves," explained Mohammed.

"Make sure all of the men are aware that anyone they see could be armed, so we should treat them all as hostiles. Now we will head back to the warehouse to rearm and get ready for our next mission."

Grabbing his cell phone, Ibrahim made a quick call to Sami Abbas. He had recruited Sami two years ago to be the group's primary hacker. His mission today was to disable the traffic cameras in the city and delete the hard drives. "Sami, this is Ibrahim. Have you completed your task?"

"Yes, Ibrahim. It has been done. The cameras are disabled, and the hard drives were deleted. Do you want me to start hacking into the power grid?"

"Yes, do what you can. Any destruction and distraction you can provide will greatly aid the cause."

"I'm on it," replied Sami as he hung up.
****

October was a month of pure terror across most of the US. Since the 2nd of October, sixty-eight terrorist attacks had taken place, striking malls, movie theaters, restaurants, business offices, hospitals and police stations. The entire American way of life and freedom of movement was under attack by Islamic extremists. Forty-two thousand, three hundred and seventy-five Americans had been killed by these horrific attacks, which were now starting to alienate anyone who looked as if they came from the Middle East or practiced Islam.

Mosques were starting to be attacked in retaliation for attacks against churches and synagogues. When a Muslim group in Washington, D.C., held a rally to denounce the attacks against Muslims in America, they themselves were attacked by armed factions within the US population who had had enough of the attacks being carried out by Muslim extremists and looked for a way to vent their anger.

As the presidential election neared, the three political parties made their case to the American people. The Democrats were saying that the US needed to reconcile its past with Islam and the Middle East to achieve true peace. The Republicans were demanding war against the Islamic Republic. The FP continued to stress the economic revival taking place in the US and emphasized the successful capture of hundreds of Islamic extremists before they were able to execute their attacks.
****

07 November 2040
White House

"Mr. President, it would appear that you're going to win by a landslide. Forty states are reporting results in so far, and you've won 38 of them," said Monty as he muted the television in the residence.

"I think you're right, Monty. It looks like this is as good a time as any to declare victory. We've clearly won enough electoral votes to claim it."

"I agree. Four more years, Mr. President—we did it," said Monty. He smiled. *Four more years. Four more years to right this country and the world.*
****

25 November 2040
Washington, D.C.
White House, Situation Room

The President had planned on celebrating Thanksgiving with the troops in Mexico, but due to multiple credible assassination plots, the trip had been cancelled. So, the President enjoyed his Thanksgiving dinner with his family at the White House, and as was customary in the Stein family, they overate and sat around watching football. Unfortunately, things around the world forced the President back to work halfway through the fourth quarter of the afternoon game.

"I hope everyone had a wonderful Thanksgiving. It's unfortunate that we have to shorten our holiday, but the issue with the IR needs to be resolved."

"Mr. President, we have collected enough evidence from the DoJ, FBI, DIA and the CIA to present a clear case to both the American people and Congress to declare war on the Islamic Republic. There is no refuting the evidence. The question now is—when do we start launching cruise missiles?" asked Director Rubio, the head of the CIA.

"General Branson, what is the state of our military forces? How soon can we be in a position to strike at the IR?" inquired the President.

"We have begun a quiet shift in forces from Mexico and other combat divisions from the States to various ports on the East Coast to be moved by transport. We've moved over four hundred Special Forces personnel to Israel, along with a full air wing of F-35s. We also have most of Third Corps arriving over the weekend.

"Fortunately, the IR is also moving a lot of their forces into the local region for their supposed exercise. I suggest we launch our attack soon to preempt them and catch the bulk of their forces by surprise before they can get fully organized," said Branson.

"So, what's the timeline, General? How soon will we have sufficient forces in place to launch an attack?"

"Three more days, Mr. President. In ten days, we'll have Second Corps at the Haifa port, ready to offload and enter the fight as well."

"All right, then. Let's plan to launch our attack on December 1st, five days from now. That gives us a bit more time to get that Corps closer to the action. We also need to start coordinating things with the Israelis."

The Commandant of the Marine Corps spoke up and added, "Sir, the entire 1st Marine Expeditionary Force of 20,000 Marines is also already linking up with the 6th Fleet in the Mediterranean."

"Excellent."

"I would hold off on making any major announcements, Mr. President, until the day before or the day of the attack. If possible, I'd wait until you've given the order. We don't want to lose the element of surprise," said Lieutenant General Rick Scott, the Director of the Defense Intelligence Agency.

"I agree, General Scott. I'll hold off on any announcement until the attack order has been given. Jim, you have a lot of work to do in a short amount of time on the diplomatic front. Eric, I want you to begin a rapid mobilization of National Guard and Reserve units immediately. Activate the units that we know we're going to need, and get the second echelon of forces ready to deploy to Israel as well. I also want more Marines heading that way. Once this kicks off, we're going to need to secure the Suez and a number of other areas that will need their skill set," said the President. He took a deep breath and held it for a moment before letting it out.

"We also need to be ready in case they go nuclear. What are our options, and how do we want to respond? I'd like an answer to that question for tomorrow's meeting, so we can begin to position specific weapons."

"Yes, Mr. President," the men replied in unison. The President got up to leave and return to his family at the residence.

Chapter 11
The Chosen People

29 November 2040
Beijing, China
Central Military Commission

General Changlong Fan, the Vice Chairman of the CMC, had called an emergency meeting to discuss the imminent attack to take place by the Islamic Republic. "General Changlong, the Islamic Republic has been conducting terrorist attacks against the Americans for the past ten weeks. What is new about this situation?" asked Zhang.

"Premier, our intelligence operatives within the US military have confirmed that the Americans are planning to declare war on the Islamic Republic on December first. Their attack will originate from Israel and will include several seaborne invasions as well," replied General Changlong, looking at General Zhang Yang, the Minister of Defense.

"Premier, the information has been confirmed by other sources. Our cybercommand has decoded numerous orders for ships, aircraft, and munitions to be moved to Israel," said the defense minister.

"Hmm…I suppose this could work to our advantage. I had hoped the coming conflict between the US and the IR could have been held off until the start of the New Year."

"The American intelligence agencies have traced all of the terrorist attacks to the Islamic Republic. I suspect they were waiting until they had everything in place and then planned to present the case to their people and to the world," said Xi, the Director of State Intelligence.

"I never understood the Americans' need to justify their actions to the rest of the world. They somehow believe they need the world's permission to act in their own self-defense."

"Premier, this presents us with a unique opportunity. Rather than waiting until the New Year to launch our attack, we could launch our attack on December seventh. The Americans will be heavily engaged in the Middle East by that point, and they will not have the forces available to prevent us from taking Guam and Taiwan," said Admiral Wei Shengli.

"Admiral, you do realize the date you have recommended for the attack is the same day the Japanese bombed Pearl Harbor?" asked the Premier.

"I do. This time, we will finish what the Japanese could not."

"Very well. Proceed with the modified timetable, but make sure we do as little as possible to draw any major attention from the Americans prior to our attack. It has to be a complete surprise if this is going to work to our advantage."

****

29 November 2040
Riyadh, Islamic Republic
Command Bunker

"Caliph Abbas, our intelligence assets are reporting that the American 5th Fleet in Eilat has put to sea and is currently heading on a course towards the Indian Ocean. Our reconnaissance flights out of Egypt have spotted the American 6th Fleet moving towards the Suez," said General Rafik Hamza, the Military Commander of the Islamic Republic.

General Hamza had been the second-in-command of the Saudi Royal Army before the formation of the Republic. He had been trained by the American military and had attended the finest American schools, so he knew the capabilities of the American military and quickly recognized these movements as a precursor to what would most likely be an American attack on the IR.

"What about the Israelis? Has their military posture changed in the last forty-eight hours?" asked Caliph Abbas.

"The Israeli Defense Force has called up their entire reserve force for what they are calling a 'military readiness drill.' Most of the IDF military forces are starting to leave their bases and moving to forward defensive positions. We are also seeing a repositioning of their air defenses and antimissile laser defense systems. Our assumption is that they are moving them around in case we had them pre-positioned by artillery or missiles," explained Huseen ibn Abdullah, the Director of Intelligence, as he laid down a tablet from which he had been reading.

"Caliph, we need to launch the invasion immediately. The Americans and the Israelis have seen through our deception and know we are positioning to launch a first strike against them."

"The Americans have also determined that we are behind the terrorist attacks on their homeland. They have held off on attacking us until their military is in position to strike us," said the Director of Intelligence.

"How soon until the nuclear devices are in American ports?"

"The ships are at sea now. In concert with the Russians and Chinese, I have redirected the ship that was heading to the Port of Los Angeles to move to Baltimore Harbor, and the other ship is heading towards New York Harbor. It will not be in position for another seven days," said Admiral Jaffa Mustafa, Commander of the Islamic Republic's Naval Forces.

"Why the change?" asked Caliph Mohammed.

"The Russians asked that we use the devices to hit two of the larger East Coast ports. This would hinder the Americans' ability to move supplies and reinforcements overseas and would cause considerable infrastructure damage and civilian deaths. The Chinese have also asked that we not attack the Port of LA. They have a surprise for the Americans that requires the port to remain intact," the Intelligence Director said, nodding towards the head of the military.

"Thank you for the clarification, General Muhammed. What is the likelihood of success if you were to launch your attack immediately?"

"Assuming the Navy is able to keep the American carriers occupied and the Air Force is able to overwhelm the American and Israeli Air Forces, my land force should be able to cut Israel in half within seventy-two to ninety-six hours. At that point, we will be able to destroy them piecemeal," said General Abdullah Muhammed. He was the military commander on the ground who would lead the Islamic Republic forces in their invasion of Israel.

Prior to the formation of the Republic, Abdullah had been a general in the Iraqi Army. He too had been trained by the Americans and had initially fought against them during the invasion of Iraq in 2003, when he had been an officer in the Republican Guard.

"General Hamza, how quickly do you believe we will be able to overwhelm the American and Israeli laser defense systems?"

"Nothing is certain or guaranteed when fighting the Israelis and especially the Americans. Our initial assault calls for a massive overwhelming of their systems. We will be using the newest version of the Russian 9A53 Tornado multiple rocket launch vehicles to send an assortment of no fewer than twenty thousand 120/220/330mm rockets at targets all across Israel, with the vast majority being targeted against their airfields and air-defense systems. Ninety percent of these rockets will be launched over a six-hour period. This will provide our aircraft six hours to engage the American and Israeli Air Forces and destroy them.

"Following the first two waves of fighters, our bombers will launch an additional three hundred cruise missiles, specifically targeting the Israeli power generation plants and major transmission nodes. This will disable electricity all across the country, further hindering their ability to coordinate their defenses. The third and fourth waves of aircraft will be our fighter bombers, who are assigned to attacking and destroying the Israeli missile and air-defense capabilities as they are identified. We will have twelve airborne early-warning and control aircraft aloft to assist in directing the air battle.

"The Navy will send all of their missile boats against the American fleet heading towards the Horn of Africa. Between the ten attack submarines and sixty missile boats, they will attack the fleet with over four hundred antiship missiles. We are also launching one hundred ballistic missiles from our OTR-21 Tochka vehicles at the carrier battlegroup. Five of the missiles are armed with a five-kiloton nuclear warhead. It's just enough power to destroy the fleet and minimize fallout to the area. It is possible the Americans will respond with nuclear weapons in retaliation. However, despite this concern, the opportunity to destroy two of their seven operational carriers is worth the risk." General Hamza nodded towards General Muhammed to take over.

"Once the missiles have launched, we have 1,200 various artillery pieces that will begin to fire into the prepared Israeli defensive positions. The artillery will be able to fire a continuous barrage for several hours, providing covering fire for our armored forces as they advance to engage and destroy the IDF and Americans. I assure you, this will not be a repeat of the Six Day War or the War of 1973. This time, Israel will be destroyed." General Hamza spoke with the confidence of a man who had thought about this moment for a long time.

"Then, Generals, let's proceed with the attack. General Hamza, the attack will commence on your order once you have returned to your field headquarters. The rest of us shall remain in the bunkers. We need the leadership to leave for their separate bunkers in case the Israelis or Americans get a lucky shot off and destroy this position."

With that, the military members left to quickly return to their units and begin to issue the orders that would start World War III and the annihilation of the Jewish State.

Chapter 12
Day Zero

29 November 2040
Tel Aviv, Israel
Third Corps HQ

Major General Garry Gardner was promoted to Lieutenant General and given command of Third Corps, which consisted of three divisions. One was armored, one was a mechanized infantry division, and the third division consisted of light infantry modeled around the Brigade Combat Team's concept that the Army was rebuilding.

Lieutenant General Garry Gardner had seen combat in Iraq and Afghanistan during the late 2010s, had participated in peacekeeping operations in the Ukraine, and had recently led the 3rd ID in Mexico. He was a career soldier and had spent his military career in various combat arms units, steadily rising in rank. Once he had been selected for brigadier general, he had been offered the opportunity to obtain a doctorate degree at any university he wanted. Garry had elected to pursue his doctorate from Carnegie Mellon University, where he'd obtained a doctorate in global logistics management and obtained a master's in Russian studies at the same time.

Four weeks ago, Third Corps had been given the order to rapidly deploy to Israel and prepare for combat operations. Most of the soldiers had been arriving by commercial and military aircraft since they were given the order. Their equipment had just arrived eight days earlier and was being moved to numerous marshalling points as the soldiers and vehicles were being fully equipped for the combat operations that were expected to take place within the next thirty-six hours.

The 1st Armored Division, commanded by Major General George Twitty, was at 95% strength and ready for action. The rest of the division was expected to be ready within the next twelve hours.

The 3rd Infantry Division, commanded by Major General Brian Kennedy, was at 97% strength and had deployed to marshalling points near Jerusalem with the IDF. The 1st Infantry Division, led by Major General Paul Brown, had arrived two weeks ago and was at 89% strength. Their equipment had arrived ahead of the battalions as personnel were still in transit to Israel. Most of the division had been in

Mexico when they had been directed to proceed with all speed to Israel and join Third Corps.

Since a portion of the 1st ID was still in transit, the majority of the division was encamped in several locations near Tel Aviv, not far from the airport. It was expected that the remainder of the force would arrive over the next twelve hours. The military had commandeered over four hundred commercial passenger aircraft from United Airlines, Delta, American Airways and Air Canada to move nearly 50,000 soldiers over a four-week period.

One hundred FedEx, DHL and UPS cargo aircraft were also being used to transport enormous amounts of munitions, MREs and other equipment that would be needed to sustain sixty days of continuous combat operations. This would normally be accomplished by the Army Materiel Command. However, with the short notice of this operation, what would normally be moved over a three-month period needed to be moved in thirty days. To ensure US forces were coordinating with the IDF, General Gardner had located his HQ element near the IDF HQ and ensured he had more than enough liaison officers and linguists in both HQ elements.

Major General Lance Peeler was the 2nd Marine Expeditionary Force or MEF commander. His forces were moving with the USS *Gerald Ford* supercarrier and the rest of the US 6th Fleet, which had left Naples five days earlier. Their mission was to get within striking distance of the Egyptian Coast, conduct an amphibious assault to secure the Suez Canal Zone, and destroy the IR forces in the Sinai.

By securing the Suez and the Sinai, the MEF would control the crossing and would reduce the number of borders from which the IR forces could attack Israel. It would also effectively destroy approximately 80,000 IR forces in the Sinai. General Peeler's 20,000 Marines had been part of the initial assault against Mexico and was ready to get back into the fight, especially because of all of the damage and carnage the IR terrorist groups had inflicted across the US. It was time for some payback. They also had the support of 3,500 Marines and a Marine air wing at the Eilat Naval Air Station and Naval Base.

Vice Admiral Lisa Todd was the commander of the US 6th Fleet based in Naples, Italy. She was the first female commander of a US fleet. The 6th Fleet consisted of the supercarriers USS *William Clinton* and the USS *Gerald Ford,* which were to escort the 2nd MEF to the Suez Canal

Zone and assist the Marines in capturing it and destroying the IR forces in the Sinai. The fleet was also tasked with destroying all enemy airfields within a 300-mile radius of the battlegroup.

The battlegroup had just received four additional antiaircraft and missile defense ships prior to departing Naples. Three additional guided-missile cruisers had also joined the battlegroup, bringing the total number of cruise missiles that could be launched from 820 to 1,400. Four munition replenishment ships had also joined the fleet, ensuring there would be more than enough munitions when the order was given to launch the attack.

The 5th Fleet, which revolved around the Supercarrier USS *George H. W. Bush,* had been augmented with a second supercarrier. The USS *Enterprise* had left their home port of Eilat, Israel, to move into position near the Horn of Africa, where they could provide significant air support to operations in Jordan and western Saudi Arabia. Unknown to Vice Admiral Jeremiah Lewis, their fleet was about to be attacked by over five hundred antiship missiles, to include one hundred ballistic missiles, five of which were nuclear armed.

Near Amman, Jordan, General Abdullah Muhammed was receiving the final report on his tablet that all units were in place and ready to commence their attack. The past five years had seen a massive rebuilding of the IR military force. True to their word, the Russians and Chinese had provided the IR with tens of thousands of advanced military vehicles, including the newest main battle tanks, infantry fighting vehicles, self-propelled artillery, multiple-launch rocket system or MLRS vehicles, antiaircraft and antimissile vehicles.

The IR had also received the newest fourth- and fifth-generation stealth and conventional fighters and ground-attack aircraft, including medium range bombers. With nearly 120,000 Russian and Chinese military advisors, the IR was as trained and ready to take on the Israeli and American forces as they were going to get. Knowing that their attack against the Americans would be quickly followed up by the Chinese, and then later the Russians, gave the IR the assurance their war would be successful.

"General Omar, order phase one of the attack to begin. Get our aircraft in the air. Once they are airborne, have the artillery and rocket forces begin their bombardment. Tell the forces in phase two to be prepared to start their attack shortly as well," said General Abdullah Muhammed.

At 2315 hours local time in Israel, 1,600 Islamic Republic aircraft and 4,300 drones took to the skies and headed towards the Holy Land. At the same time, thousands of artillery and MLRS vehicles began their barrage from the borders of former Lebanon, Syria, Jordan and the Sinai, raining tens of thousands of rockets and artillery rounds all across Israel. As the rounds hit their targets, the IR fighters began to engage the Israeli and American aircraft flying over the country. The American and Israeli F-35s and F-22s attacked the IR fighters, scoring six kills for each fighter they lost. At the time of the barrage, there were only 68 Allied aircraft in the sky.

Once Allied radar had detected the IR air armada leaving their air bases, word came down to scramble all available aircraft. Twenty additional aircraft took off just as the rockets hit the runways, preventing additional aircraft from getting airborne. Fortunately, the aircraft not immediately ready for takeoff were well sheltered in their secured enclosures.

The Israeli Iron Dome System immediately engaged the rockets and artillery rounds heading towards the IDF bases, scoring a 91% hit ratio of the targets engaged. Unfortunately, for every rocket or artillery round that was targeted by the Iron Dome, two were still getting through to their targets without any resistance. Once it was determined that the volume of incoming fire was too large for the Iron Dome to protect everything, the Iron Dome switched from protecting civilian targets to shielding critical infrastructure and military bases. While the Iron Dome system was engaging these targets, the fixed and mobile laser and railgun defense systems attacked the IR aircraft and drones that were beginning to swarm over the skies of Israel.

Within the first twenty minutes, several of the fixed land-based laser systems went offline as power transmission nodes and energy generation plants were being destroyed. Power was starting to go out all across Israel. Despite backup generators coming online, their limited generation capability was reducing the number of shots the lasers could fire per minute.

****

Captain Brian Jordan was serving his last tour in the Navy as the captain of the USS *George H. W. Bush* supercarrier. After thirty years in the Navy, it was time to retire to that dream house his wife had insisted they build in Tennessee, near where two of their four children lived. This was his final tour. As Captain Jordan sat in the Combat Information Center or CIC, an alarm went off indicating the E5 advanced surveillance drone had detected a threat to the battlegroup.

The E5 surveillance drone had been in service with the Navy since the late 2020s. The drone used stealth technology and could stay aloft for as long as thirty-six hours. It typically loitered at an altitude of 60,000 feet, providing hundreds of miles of surveillance coverage for the battlegroup. As data from the drone was being received, the threat board suddenly showed hundreds of aircraft and drones heading towards the carrier group. Dozens of smaller missile boats were detected on a course that would bring them into striking distance of the battlegroup as well.

"Sound general quarters, and someone get the admiral in here quickly! Commander, activate the battlegroup's automated defense system. CAG, get your aircraft in the air and engage those fighters and the bomber group."

In walked Vice Admiral Jeremiah Lewis, moving briskly. "Captain Jordan—what are we facing?"

"Sir, we're tracking 62 missile boats, most likely equipped with four Exocet missiles each. There are also 60 medium bombers, 230 Su-43s, and 600 drones heading towards the battlegroup," said Captain Jordan.

"How long until the first missiles come into range?"

"Six minutes," said one of the petty officers.

"How long do we have until those fighters and bombers are in range to launch their missiles?"

"Roughly twelve minutes, if they launch from optimal range. If they launch from maximum range, then it's closer to nine minutes," said a petty officer at one of the radar stations.

"Captain, the fighter CAP from the *Enterprise* and our ship are going supersonic to engage those fighters and bombers. All of our drones are also in the air—ninety fighter drones to their six hundred," said one of the officers manning the battlegroup communication stations.

"The CAG is launching aircraft as fast as he can, about four aircraft a minute right now," said one of the air boss commanders. The admiral issued attack orders to the ships in the battlegroup and ordered the frigates to move further out towards the incoming missile boats to increase the battlegroup's missile defense shield.

The three cruisers in the fleet launched their antiship missiles and engaged the smaller IR missile boats with their railgun turrets. Just as the admiral was thinking this couldn't get any worse, their "eye in the sky" detected multiple ballistic missile launches tracking towards the battlegroup.

Suddenly, one of the destroyers in the battlegroup detected multiple torpedoes in the water. Several torpedoes had locked onto the cruisers protecting the carriers. The ships began evasive maneuvers and increased speed while launching torpedo countermeasures. Four of the eight torpedoes went for the decoys, while the remaining torpedoes zeroed in on two of the cruisers. Both cruisers were hit and quickly began to list heavily to one side, sinking within minutes and depriving the carriers of much-needed antiaircraft and antimissile defenses from their advanced railguns.

The destroyer quickly moved to engage the submarines and fired off two torpedoes of their own. Several of the antisubmarine helicopters reported multiple submarine contacts. They, too, began dropping torpedoes in an attempt to chase them off while the destroyers attacked them. Within minutes, the sounds of several submarine hulls imploding could be heard as the torpedoes made impact.

In the skies over the battlegroup, the Su-43s launched their antiship missiles, adding to the fray of missiles the smaller attack boats had launched. As the missiles fired, it looked like streaks of lightning stabbing in the direction of the American fleet as they began their journey to their targets. Between the IR missile boats and the Su-43s, 480 Exocets were fired at the battlegroup in an attempt to overwhelm their defensive capabilities. Twenty-eight missiles made it through the laser and missile screen and scored hits against the battlegroup. While the Exocets were closing in on the fleet, the bombers launched their two Russian-made P-270s Moskits, also known as SS-N-22D Sunburn antiship missiles. These missiles traveled at three times the speed of sound, carrying 710 pounds of high explosives.

The ocean around the battlegroup was lit up like the Fourth of July as hundreds of missiles, lasers and railguns were fired. Missiles exploded in an almost constant rolling of thunder. Despite the enormous success of the battlegroup's defensive screen, eight frigates, seven destroyers and all three of the remaining guided-missile ships were hit by the remnants of the Exocets' missile barrage. Bright flashes of light could be seen for miles as the missiles hit their targets and the subsequent flames raged out of control on the damaged ships. The sea was starting to look as if it was on fire itself as diesel leaked out from the ships and burned on the surface of the sea.

One Exocet hit the *Enterprise*, causing the ship to shudder slightly despite inflicting minimal damage, while three missiles hit the *Bush*, causing damage to the flight deck. Several aircraft that were still trying to take off were obliterated, and one of the elevators that had been descending in order to move another fighter to the flight deck imploded. Several fires could be seen in the night sky from the *Bush*, while her crew immediately went to work putting them out and trying to repair the flight deck so they could launch more aircraft.

As the Exocets were hitting the fleet, 120 Sunburns began their final approach. Ninety-eight of the missiles were destroyed by the antimissile laser defense system, while twenty-two missiles scored hits all across the fleet. The *Enterprise* took two more hits, one near the waterline causing significant damage to the crew quarters area and the second hitting just below the hangar deck that housed the aircraft munitions. As the missile exploded, it caused several secondary explosions, which tore through the hangar deck and two decks below, killing hundreds of crewmen in a fiery cauldron of death.

Two of the cruisers blew up shortly after being hit with the second round of missiles. The *Bush* was hit by five Sunburn missiles, scoring several hits just above the waterline. One shell hit the hangar deck, killing many members of the aircraft maintenance crew. The remaining missile hit near the engine room, shutting down one of the engines. The *George H. W. Bush* was severely damaged and starting to burn, slowly listing to one side.

As the ballistic missiles began their descent on the remains of the fleet, the last antimissile frigate engaged the missiles with its SM3s and the one pulse laser that was still operational. The captain of the ship was not optimistic about their chances to destroy all of the incoming barrage. They had already expended seventy percent of their own missiles, and the batteries for the pulse laser were low from engaging the last two waves of rockets.

The battle lasted less than twenty-five minutes. Admiral Jeremiah Lewis knew he had lost his fleet as the third wave of missiles, this time the ballistic ones, rained down on the remains of the 5th Fleet. Three of the five nuclear-tipped ballistic missiles detonated at various positions over the fleet. The carrier *George H. W. Bush* took a direct hit and was completely destroyed, disappearing below the waves before the blast evaporated. The *Enterprise* was on the edge of two different blast zones. The carrier was battered on both sides from the blast and badly burnt. Once the fires reached the ship's jet fuel, the carrier sank, taking all hands with her.

Two of the ships in the fleet were outside of the blast zones and survived to report on the engagement. The mood of those who had lived through the attack was grim.
****

Still unaware of the events that were about to take place, 6th Fleet continued moving into position for their part of America's preemptive attack against the Islamic Republic.

Vice Admiral Lisa Todd was being groomed to become a four-star admiral and had just taken command of the fleet in June. As the battlegroup neared Israel, Admiral Todd spent most of her time in the CIC with the ship's captain. She had a gut feeling the IR was going to launch a preemptive attack and was determined not to be caught off guard.

"Captain Carr, we're now less than one hundred miles from our patrol position. Are we detecting any additional increase in activity at the IR air bases or ports?" she asked.

The captain looked to his intelligence officer to provide the answer.

"The E5 has spotted a number of aircraft taking off from various air bases in Egypt—the activity just started less than five minutes ago. The analysts are still trying to determine what they're up to. There are already a number of IR ships on patrols, though we're seeing additional activity in the ports."

"Captain, let's go ahead and move the fleet to general quarters. I have a feeling something is up with the IR, and I do not want to be caught flatfooted. Launch the air wing, but keep them in orbit over the fleet, and be ready for whatever may happen over the next couple of hours," she said as her intuition and training told her an attack was imminent.

"I understand your concern, Admiral. Perhaps we should increase the fleet's speed and get closer to our shore-based air cover," said Captain Carr.

"I agree, let's make haste. Have the MEF ships tighten up their positions and order them to prepare to conduct their amphibious assault of the Islamic Republic if they attack. I want the MEF to head straight for the beaches and secure their targets if the IR decides to start the party early."

****

The quick thinking and gut instincts of Admiral Todd were probably the only thing that saved the 6th Fleet from the fate of the 5th. When the IR missile boats and aircraft headed towards the fleet to fire their Exocets and Sunburn missiles, the fleet was in position to attack them at maximum range and keep them from getting within reach of their missiles.

With the entire carrier air wing already in the sky, they were in quick position to attack the IR fighters and bombers before they were able to get into range. Essentially, the entire IR attacking force had been stopped, with the majority of the assailants destroyed. Only five Exocets and two Sunburns hit the fleet, sinking one destroyer, who took two hits, and a frigate, who took a hit to her missile magazine. The other impacts were absorbed by the rest of the fleet, with no catastrophic damage done.

With the attack blunted, the 6th Fleet launched hundreds of cruise missiles at their assigned targets all across Egypt and the Sinai. The MEF moved into position to assault the Suez Canal Zone, while the Marine air wing began softening up the IR ground forces in the Sinai.

The E5 sentry drone began detecting the sheer volume of missile and artillery fire being directed all across Israel while this was taking place. Admiral Todd directed fifty of the cruise missiles to go after the artillery and MLRS vehicles in the Sinai. Her hope was to reduce the volume of fire being poured across the border and to minimize the possibility of it being redirected at the MEF. She directed half of the air wing to engage the IR fighters that had survived attacks by the Air Force and the IDF and ordered another four hundred cruise missiles to hit Islamic Republic troop, missile and artillery positions all across the Jordan Valley, Lebanon and Syrian border.

What concerned Admiral Todd the most was the fight underway with the 5th Fleet. It looked as if they were being completely overwhelmed by the enemy. Then 100 ballistic missiles showed up on the threat board, adding further concern about their survivability. Within a minute, it was clear that they were targeting the 5th Fleet and not Israel. Her heart sank several minutes later as the screen monitoring the missiles and the fleet whited out and then slowly returned. She instantly realized that one or more nuclear devices had gone off over the 5th Fleet. For all intents and purposes, the 5th Fleet ceased to exist, which was a devastating loss for the US Navy.
****

Lieutenant General Garry Gardner's Third Corps was just about ready for full combat operations. They were still waiting on a few thousand troops to arrive and for additional munitions that were being flown in from the States. He had the 1st Armored Division, also known as "Old Ironside," moving to marshalling position in the northeast of Israel near the Golan Heights, where intelligence reported the largest concentration of IR armored units. Ironside had recently received the new M36 Pershing tanks. This was the newest tank in the Army, replacing the venerable M1A4 Abrams tanks that had been in service for nearly sixty years.

The Pershing was made of a new secret type of alloy that was five times stronger than the armor used in the Abrams. The tank was also the first in the world to field a magnetic railgun, giving it an incredible range and punch. The railgun and fire control system could also switch from ground attack mode to air attack, making the vehicle extremely versatile. When in ground-attack mode, the Pershing could hit targets as far away as fifteen miles and could fire one round every twenty seconds for a sustained ten minutes before it had to drop its rate of fire to one round per minute to recharge its battery bank. The US had roughly four hundred Pershings in service, until the manufacturing sector got up to speed. The DoD had ordered roughly 2,800 units for the Army and Marines.

The 1st Infantry Division, also known as "The Big Red One," was being moved towards the Jordan Valley to reinforce what would certainly be a bloody battle for Jerusalem. The 3rd Infantry Division was marshalling around the Tel Aviv area and was going to be used as a floating reserve to plug any holes in the line or exploit any breakouts.

General Gardner was in a planning meeting with his IDF counterparts, despite it being nearly midnight, discussing the coming operation and what the contingency plans were should the IR launch their attack before the US officially declared war.

Suddenly, the "enemy incoming" rocket/aircraft alarms wailed, and an IDF captain came into the room, announcing that the IR had just launched a massive missile and artillery attack all across Israel. The IDF commanders immediately ordered all aircraft that could get airborne to do so immediately. As the staff was moving to the Joint Command and Control Bunker, where the war was going to be run from, a naval officer approached General Gardner, whispering in his ear that the US 5th and 6th Fleets were both under attack as well.

As General Gardner walked into the Joint Command and Control Bunker, an Air Force colonel said they were scrambling all available aircraft and that the aircraft currently on patrol were engaging IR fighters, though they were outnumbered fifteen to one.

"General Williams, get word back to US Central Command and US European Command that we are under attack by IR forces and we are engaging them. Tell them we will need all the available resources they can provide and get the commanding general on the horn. I need to talk with him. Also, make sure the Pentagon is kept in the loop."

"We are already on it, sir. General Wade said he would like to talk with you as soon as you are available," said Brigadier General Peter Williams, Gardner's Chief of Staff.

"Sir, we're tracking over three hundred missiles heading towards our position, and there are also six hundred rockets heading towards the airport and the 1st ID's marshalling points," said an Air Force major, who was tracking inbound threats with four other NCOs.

"Make sure General Twitty knows he has incoming and to disperse his force. What's the status on our air-defense systems? Are they engaging yet?"

"Yes, Sir. The mobile laser batteries and antiair railgun systems are engaging the incoming artillery, missiles and enemy aircraft penetrating our fighter cover," said an Army lieutenant colonel who, along with six other soldiers, was controlling and coordinating the Army's air-defense efforts. The mixed use of lasers and railguns provided an incredible layered defensive system. The railguns had a range of fifteen to twenty miles and had a quick rate of fire, while the laser systems could hit targets as far away as several thousand miles in the case of a ballistic missile, or several hundred miles in the case of an aircraft. The primary difference, and the reason why they worked as an integrated defensive system, was that the lasers could only fire once every twenty to thirty seconds while the railguns could fire one round every three seconds.

"If our MLRSs have not started counterbattery fire, make sure they are on it. We have to cut the volume of fire down, or they're going to cut us to pieces," directed General Gardner.

****

Sergeant Jordy Nelson and his squad were putting the finishing touches on their machine-gun bunker as part of the Jordan Valley defensive line. The Big Red One was assigned a five-mile area of the valley that, if taken, would give the enemy a clear path to Jerusalem. The Americans were given this patch of ground to defend because this was also the most direct route by which American forces could invade the Islamic Republic and move towards Amman. Hundreds of machine gun and antitank missile and railgun bunkers had been constructed over the past several days as the 1st ID settled into their positions until the invasion order was given. Despite it being nearly midnight, the soldiers were still hard at work.

"Private Miller, how much ammo did you guys bring back with you?" asked Sergeant Nelson as he walked towards several of the younger soldiers.

"We brought ten thousand rounds for the M240 and ten thousand rounds for the M5 AIR."

Nelson nodded. "Excellent work, guys. I want the ammunition and power packs split between the two bunkers so—"

"Everyone, get down! *Incoming!*" someone shouted, interrupting Nelson in midsentence.

The sergeant's team immediately jumped into the trench between the two bunkers and ran for shelter as the artillery rounds landed all across the Jordan Valley and endangered their positions.

What in the name of all things holy is going on? What are we supposed to do now? Sergeant Nelson thought. Looking at the scared soldiers in his team, he collected himself and told everyone in the bunkers, "Be ready for anything, and if you see something, report it to me. If it fires at you, then—light it up!"

155

As the artillery barrage continued, IR infantry fighting vehicles, light drone tanks and the much heavier main battle tanks advanced towards the Israeli and American positions. As they neared, they poured their own direct fire into gun positions and vehicles that the artillery hadn't destroyed.

"Sergeant Nelson, we have enemy tanks and infantry vehicles advancing towards our lines," said one of the privates. Nelson grabbed his night-vision binoculars and scanned the field in front of their position. Just twenty minutes earlier, it had been a lush green valley; now it looked like an alien planet or the moon as artillery and missiles continued to impact all around their positions. Despite the heavy artillery barrage, American soldiers fired their antitank or AT missiles at the light drone tanks and main battle tanks, leaving the heavier railgun positions to attack the infantry fighting vehicles. Thousands of tracers zipped back and forth across the battlefield as both armies were locked in a desperate fight to destroy one another.

The armored vehicles took heavy fire from the railguns, with more than half of them destroyed. The remaining vehicles disgorged their infantry, who attacked the American missile and gun positions. Tanks and armored personnel carriers could provide great direct fire, but they were vulnerable to AT equipped soldiers and the larger-caliber AT railguns, which was why they traveled with their own supporting infantry.

"Everyone—begin firing at those soldiers!" shouted Sergeant Nelson as he raised his own rifle and took aim at the several dozen soldiers about eight hundred meters in front of his position. As Sergeant Nelson engaged one enemy soldier after another, an artillery round landed in the center of a small cluster of enemy soldiers, throwing their torn bodies into the air and across the ground like rag dolls. The smell of smoke, cordite and burnt flesh permeated the entire valley.

After an hour of continuous firing across the American lines, it was becoming apparent that they were going to have to fall back to their secondary positions. The IR was attacking with massive human wave assaults and continuous direct fire from the hundreds of tanks and armored vehicles supporting the infantry. Then, the second and third waves arrived. The casualties and damage caused by the twenty-minute barrage prior to the initial attack had weakened numerous fortifications along the American and Israeli defensive works, creating multiple gaps that the IR were starting to exploit.

Despite the carnage and numerically superior Islamic Army, the training and equipment used by the American and Israeli forces showed why they were the most formidable soldiers in the world.

****

29 November 2040
Washington, D.C.
Presidential Emergency Operation Center

The SecDef and General Branson were still being fed data by their aides about the attack underway in Israel, trying to ascertain the status of US forces. Mike Williams, the National Security Advisor, and his two aides walked into the room. They quickly took their assigned seats and assimilated the same information the SecDef and the general were studying.

The situation was starting to look grim, particularly with the 5th Fleet in the Gulf of Aiden near the Horn of Africa. Jim Wise, the Secretary of State, walked in with Monty. The two appeared to be in a heated discussion. "Those dirty, heartless animals! They really attacked our embassy and executed the entire staff, including the ambassador?" asked Monty in a rather loud voice.

All conversations stopped, and everyone looked at Jim Wise for clarification. Just then, the President walked in. He surveyed the room and walked to his seat at the head of the table. An aide quickly placed a half-frozen twenty-ounce Red Bull on the table for the President. A can that large usually meant the President had a stress-induced headache, which he liked to pacify with excessive amounts of caffeine. Not being a coffee drinker, his choice of poison was Red Bull—always had been throughout his life.

"Jim and Monty, sit down and tell us first what happened to our embassy. Then we'll get right into the rest of the information." The President sighed deeply, thinking to himself, *Perhaps we should have acted sooner and prevented this. We lost the advantage, and now we're paying for it.*

"Mr. President, our embassy in Riyadh has been taken over and burned to the ground. Just as the attacks were getting underway, the embassy said they were coming under heavy attack by several armored vehicles and a tank. The walls were quickly destroyed, and soldiers stormed the building.

"The Marines put up a heck of a fight and managed to destroy all the classified data and the servers before they were killed. One of our diplomats was on his way to the embassy when he saw the attack begin, and he moved away to a point where he could observe the situation and relay it back to us. Shortly after the IR forces had secured the embassy, they walked everyone out of the building that had surrendered," Jim Wise continued.

"The ambassador was among the nineteen people who were captured. News crews filmed as they were all lined up against a wall; an officer walked up to each person, shooting them in the head. They killed everyone at the embassy. Our diplomat filmed it with his video phone and managed to send the video and a short message before he, too, was apprehended. We haven't heard anything from him since," said Secretary Wise, sounding tired but seething with anger.

The President sat back in his chair, looking up at the ceiling for a second before turning back to face everyone at the table. "First things first, I want everyone at the Islamic Republic embassy in D.C. arrested and detained. We'll figure out what we're going to do with them later.

"I know the situation is bad from the looks on your faces, and from what I can see on the screens. Of course, it doesn't help that the media is giving the world a front-row seat as well. General Branson, start from the beginning and bring us up to speed on the situation on the ground and how we're faring."

"Around midnight local time, the Islamic Republic launched an all-out attack against Israeli and American forces, starting with a massive rocket and artillery barrage.

"Intelligence was alerted minutes before the attack, allowing the air and rocket defenses a couple minutes' warning, but not much more. The majority of the IDF air bases have been temporarily taken out of commission until the runways can be fixed. The IR also conducted a massive cyberattack against the Israeli energy grid, causing further problems with our command, control, and communications," explained General Branson.

"Vice Admiral Todd from the 6th Fleet thought something was odd with the behavior of the IR forces in Egypt and brought her fleet to battle stations, ordering her air wings to get airborne. Shortly after that, the IR fleet and land-based systems launched a massive barrage of cruise missiles at the fleet. Over three hundred IR aircraft also vectored in to attack the fleet.

"Because she had brought her fleet to battle stations and had her air wings already above the fleet, they were able to interdict over 95% of the incoming missiles. They destroyed over fifty Islamic Republic ships and shot down 247 of their aircraft. The rest fled the area back to their home bases—"

"—I sure hope she was able to hit them back," interjected the President.

"She was. The fleet attacked every airfield in Egypt and destroyed the naval ports. She also ordered the Marines to secure the Suez Canal Zone and attack the IR forces attacking the Israelis in the Sinai."

"This is great news, General. Tell her to keep beating the tar out of them," said the President, showing a bit of excitement at the thought of really hurting them.

"Mr. President, I need to interject something. Sorry, General Branson, but I need to talk to the President about the 5th Fleet. I just received a FLASH message from Admiral Todd," said Admiral Lewis Juliano with a look of sheer horror on his face.

"What is it, Admiral?" asked the President.

"Sir, the 5th Fleet has been destroyed. They were hit with multiple nuclear-tipped ballistic missiles. We've lost the supercarriers *George H. W. Bush* and the *Enterprise*, along their entire support fleet. Thirteen thousand, three hundred and seventy sailors and Marines are gone," said the Chief of Naval Operations as he sank into his chair.

The room fell silent for a minute as everyone digested what they had just been told. The loss of two supercarriers and more than 13,000 Sailors and Marines was a lot to take in.

"Admiral, before we discuss how we're going to respond to that particular attack, we need to assess the rest of the situation. General Branson, tell us about the situation on the ground."

The general nodded. "The 1st ID has taken the brunt of the IR attack in the Jordan Valley. The barrage did a considerable amount of damage to their vehicles, and they've been getting hit with multiple wave attacks of both infantry and light drone tanks. They're putting up a brave fight, but they're starting to fall back to their secondary positions.

"Two brigade combat teams from the 3rd ID are moving up to reinforce them as we speak in order to plug up the holes in the lines. The Israelis were hit hard on their southern border, and just as it looked like they were going to have to fall back, the 6th Fleet hammered the IR with their cruise missiles. When the Marines landed along the Gaza strip and the Suez Canal, the IR force withdrew towards the southern section of the Sinai to block the Marines from cornering them. Admiral Todd's air wing and the Marine air wing should finish them off soon.

"The Israelis are holding the line along the Lebanon border, and the 1st Armored Division completely blunted the IR armored assault. Those new Pershing tanks are performing far better than anyone expected. They absolutely pulverized those frontline Chinese and Russian tanks the IR is using," said General Branson with a hint of a smile.

"General Gardner is requesting the XVIII Airborne Corps to reinforce him immediately. Third Corps and the IDF have taken a beating. General Gardner says they have already sustained 5,340 KIAs and about the same number of WIAs."

"Mr. President, these are some heavy losses. This is close to 20,000 men and women killed and at least another 10,000 wounded in the first hour of the war. I recommend we surge troops to Israel and hit the IR with some tactical nuclear weapons of our own," Eric said. He looked at Admiral Juliano, who nodded in agreement.

"I agree, Mr. President. The IR just hit us with nuclear weapons— we need to respond in kind, or they're going to use them again," said Admiral Julian as he highlighted a submarine that could be used on the holographic display. "We have a sub in the Arabian Gulf and another one not far from where the 5th Fleet was located."

"General Scott, Director Rubio, what are your thoughts on a proportional response to the IR's use of tactical nuclear weapons?" asked the President, searching for more consensus on the use of nukes.

"The US has had a long-standing policy of proportional retaliation. The IR detonated three tactical nuclear weapons over the 5th Fleet, and these weapons were in the one-to-five-kiloton range. If we were to respond with tactical weapons in the ten-kiloton range, I believe that would be a proportional response. The next question is—what type of targets do we want to hit?" asked General Scott as he nodded towards Director Rubio.

"Not only has the IR conducted a nuclear attack against our forces, they have carried out sustained terrorist attacks against our country for the last two and a half months. More than 20,000 civilians have died from these attacks, and they have also conducted continuous cyberattacks against every facet of our economy. They have attacked our very way of life, and they aren't done attacking us at home. Now that they have taken the gloves off, it's time we do the same and hit them with that proverbial big stick we still have," Rubio said, anger burning in his eyes.

"The IR laser missile defense system is going to be challenging to get through, but not impossible. The key to any laser defense system is power. I recommend that we conduct a series of strategic attacks against their critical infrastructure. It's still experimental, but we can use our new hypersonic ramjet cruise missile, the X59. It travels at Mach 10, making it nearly impossible to acquire and target by laser. In addition, a laser needs to hit the missile for at least three seconds for it to cause enough heat to cause an explosion. The X59 travels too fast for that. It can carry -pound high-explosive warhead, or it can transport a variable nuclear warhead. We only have fifteen of them, but we could begin full production at once," said General Adrian Rice, the Air Force Chief of Staff.

"Mr. President, the public is going to demand we hit the IR with nukes. They will want their pound of flesh after the last three months of terrorist attacks. We need the IR to understand that these types of attacks are not going to be tolerated and we will respond with overwhelming force."

"I understand the frustration, Monty. I want to make sure we hit them hard, but I also want to make sure this doesn't spiral out of control either. With the 5th Fleet gone, what does our antiballistic missile defense capability look like in the Middle East now?"

"Sir, the 6th Fleet packs more than enough punch to deal with any ballistic missile attacks by the IR on either Israel or US forces. Unless the IR starts to use nuclear-tipped artillery rounds, we can take them down," said Admiral Juliano.

"All right, gentlemen, let's hit the IR with a taste of their own medicine. Take out their power grid. Hit them with the thirty-kiloton warheads. Also, ensure that at least two of the missiles devastate their ability to export oil by destroying their two largest terminals. I want the

161

Straits of Hormuz heavily mined and some subs sitting out there to pick off any shipping, either entering or leaving. The minute their power is down and their laser defense system goes offline, I want those sites destroyed," the President said.

"We need to disable their laser defense system quickly, and then we'll systematically destroy their ability to continue this war."

"Yes, Mr. President," rang the chorus of voices.

With the plans in place to strike back at the IR, the President left with Monty to prepare his address to the American people.

It was dinnertime in America, and as families sat down to eat while glued to the news of the war, the President went on national TV and radio to explain the situation in the Middle East and the nuclear strike that the IR had conducted against the US 5th Fleet. The President assured the American people that the US was responding in kind and soon the IR would feel the wrath of American nuclear weapons as well.

The following morning, the President gave a second national address, laying out the facts of the terrorist attacks against the US and the links between those attacks and the Islamic Republic. The sheer number of casualties coming in from the Middle East was also staggering. The President asked Congress to issue a formal declaration of war against the Islamic Republic and declared a state of emergency and martial law.

All governors were asked to activate any of their National Guard units that had not been activated yet and to begin to use those forces to protect the critical infrastructure buildings and nodes in their states. Within an hour of war being formally declared, the President asked for all able-bodied men and women to join the armed forces to assist in the protection of their families, homeland, and way of life.

The Islamic Republic responded to the President's declaration of war and the nuclear attack on their own country by issuing one of their own. They vowed they would not stop until Israel was destroyed and the Americans were removed from the Middle East. Within hours, five additional terrorist attacks were carried out against civilian targets in the US, attacking several power plants and transmission nodes.

As police and first responders arrived, they were attacked by several terrorists who had chosen to stay behind and kill as many police as they could before detonating the remaining IEDs and vehicle-borne IEDs they had lined along the roads. These attacks only furthered the hatred brewing between the Muslims and non-Muslims living in America, particularly when a small country church was attacked and all 103 parishioners were crucified on crosses on the county road leading to the church. There were nineteen children among them. Muslims all across America were starting to be attacked in retaliation. The police did their best to protect both groups of people, but it was becoming harder and harder to keep the two sides apart.

****

29 November 2040
Israel
Third Corps Headquarters

The US struck the Islamic Republic's power generation plant at Ras Tanura on the Arabian Gulf, the Abqaiq plant in the same area, and also the Ar Riyad plant, destroying 13,391 Megawatts of power production and effectively disrupting sixty percent of the power generation capability in the heart of the IR. The city of Buqayq was completely destroyed in the nuclear attack, along with the oil terminals and ports of the cities of Ras Tanura and Al Khobar and its oil terminals and port.

Several power generation plants in Iran, Iraq, and Egypt were also destroyed, along with the cities they were near. The IR government denounced these attacks, citing the hundreds of thousands of civilians killed, and demanded the US be sanctioned by the United Nations. The Russian government immediately denounced this blatant attack against civilian targets by the US, as did China.

The European Union asked that all parties refrain from further use of nuclear weapons and asked for a pledge to keep the war conventional. The President of the United States announced that any further Islamic Republic use of nuclear weapons against US forces or Israel would result in a substantial nuclear response by the US.

Meanwhile, General Gardner had been awake for nearly thirty hours as reports from the frontlines continued to pour in. The 1st Armored Division had gone from being on the defensive to taking the fight to the enemy. They had broken out of the Golan Heights and were pushing the IR forces back to Damascus. Because of the success of 1st Armored Division, the IDF had been able to root out the IR forces in Lebanon and shifted forces from that front towards Jerusalem.

163

****

Undisclosed Site in Israel
Allied Underground Command Bunker

One of the colonels running the J3 or Joint Operations group for Third Corps gave an update on the situation on the ground. "The 1st ID has been in constant contact with IR armor and infantry fighting vehicles for nearly twenty-four hours. They had to fall back past Jericho and found themselves less than four miles from Jerusalem. The IDF moved two additional battalions of light infantry just before dawn to reinforce American-Israeli forces and took up positions throughout the hills approaching Jerusalem."

"Tell General Twitty I need him to commit the rest of his division to the defense of Jerusalem. Unless the Israelis tell us otherwise, we are going to turn Jerusalem into a meat grinder," said Gardner. He was reading from one tablet and then another, each with up-to-date aerial reconnaissance and reports from the front.

"General Twitty is already on it. He moved his HQ to the west side of Jerusalem so he could be closer to the battle. I also have that report you asked for and photos of that platoon from 1st ID that had been captured yesterday. It would appear the rumors are true. The IR crucified all of the prisoners to motivate their own forces, showing that even the Americans can be beat," said Brigadier General Peter Williams with a look of anger and disgust on his face.

"This is getting out of control. They're not only killing those who are wounded or captured—they're now crucifying them? How many prisoners of theirs do we have?"

"A few thousand. Most of them are from 1st Armor's area of operations," said General Williams.

"Hmm…I'm not going to kill their prisoners, at least not yet, but since they're making this a religious war, then let's hit them where it hurts. Tell General Twitty he's to destroy the Al Aqsa Mosque near the Temple Mount. I want it flattened as soon as possible."

"I'm not sure the Israelis will let us blow it up, Sir. They're currently protecting it," said Williams in protest.

"I will take full responsibility for this, and if the President or the SecDef wants to relieve me of command, then so be it. I will not let our soldiers be crucified by these jihadists without retaliating."

"I believe we should coordinate this with the IDF. Perhaps we can arrange to have a film crew on scene to video its destruction."

"Make it happen."

****

The Israeli cities were being devastated by the almost constant missile and artillery barrages. While, the Iron Dome was extremely effective, even it could be overwhelmed. Multiple power plants had been taken offline by cyberattacks or damage sustained from the barrages, and this was starting to have an impact on the Israelis' ability to sustain its rocket and missile defense systems. The Iron Dome system was running out of missiles, and the railgun and laser systems were running out of power. Their own self-sustaining power generation could provide enough power for air defense, but with a continuous barrage all across the country for more than eighteen hours, they needed additional power to sustain their defensive effort.

Word spread quickly through the American and Israeli ranks about the crucifixions, which only spurred them to fight harder. As the fighting continued, the 1st ID stopped taking prisoners and started to kill any wounded or surrendering IR soldiers they saw. Without informing the Israeli prime minister or his own higher command, the Israeli major who was in charge of the soldiers guarding the Al Aqsa mosque, let soldiers from the 3rd ID place explosives throughout the mosque and stood by as they detonated them.

Within seconds, the entire building collapsed and was nothing more than a smoking ruin. The people that hadn't fled Jerusalem couldn't believe the mosque had just been destroyed. No one knew if it was an errant missile that had destroyed it, or if it had been intentional. It didn't take long for pictures and video of its destruction to spread across social media.

A BBC news crew who had been filming the fighting from a vantage point near the mosque was reporting on the battle that was taking place a few miles from Jerusalem when they saw a number of soldiers entering the mosque, then leaving just as quickly. A couple of minutes later, the famed mosque was completely destroyed. Every Muslim around the world saw the destruction of this holy site, and many took to the streets, shouting, "Death to Israel and America!"

The Israeli prime minister was quick to denounce the destruction, saying the IDF had no part in its demolition and quickly blaming the Americans. General Gardner provided a short statement to the media saying that he had authorized the destruction of the Al Aqsa mosque of his own volition in retaliation for IR units crucifying captured American soldiers, of which there was plenty of video evidence. Had the situation on the ground not been so precarious, the Israeli prime minister would have insisted on General Gardner being replaced. As it was, Jerusalem would have fallen within a day if the 3rd ID hadn't been able to stop the IR.

****

Near Amman, Jordan
Islamic Republic Military Headquarters

General Abdullah Muhammed could not believe the success his army was having against the Americans and Israelis. Admiral Jaffa Mustafa had come through and destroyed the entire 5th Fleet! Two aircraft carriers and all of their support ships—if only he had been able to destroy the carriers in the Mediterranean, his victory could almost be assured. Those two carriers had destroyed his Sinai force, which would have placed additional pressure on the IDF.

The campaign in the Jordan Valley was going exceptionally well. The American 1st ID had put up a fight, but ultimately, they had to fall back. Even with the American 3rd Infantry Division coming to their rescue, it was only a matter of time before Jerusalem would fall. He had 200,000 light infantry moving into the valley to begin the final assault to take Jerusalem.

"General Muhammed, General Hamza wants to know what we are doing to stop the Americans from advancing and capturing Damascus. They are at the outskirts of the city already," said General Ishmael Omar, General Muhammed's Chief of Staff.

"Tell General Hamza I have ordered three divisions of armor to reinforce Damascus. I'm also diverting additional attack aircraft and helicopters as well. That should satisfy him...doesn't he realize the goal is to cut Israel in half? Damascus is not important. Capturing Jerusalem is."

"I will inform him right away, Sir. Before I leave, we received word that our forces have captured Eilat and the American-Israeli naval base there.

"The IDF retreated to the Ovda Israeli air base just north of there. General Ibrahim also reported that he had finally secured Ir Ovot all the way to Dinoma on the eastern side of the Sea of Galilee. He has asked for permission to use his reserves as he makes a push to capture Be'er Sheva."

"Tell him he has permission to use his reserves and prepare to fight the American Marines. Once he secures his objectives, he needs to be ready to move towards the Sinai and push those Americans into the sea."

IR forces were starting to break through the Jordan Valley defenses. They had poured over 600,000 soldiers into the valley to fight 12,500 American soldiers and roughly 60,000 Israelis. After twenty-four hours of hard fighting, they were now less than four miles from capturing Jerusalem. Then the news that the Americans had destroyed the Al Aqsa mosque sent every soldier into a religious frenzy against the Americans. Hundreds of thousands of Muslims protested in virtually every major city in the world. Close to two million people from Iran, Iraq and Saudi Arabia were moving towards Mecca to pray and to volunteer to fight against the Americans and destroy the spawn of Satan, the Jews.

Caliph Mohammed played this up in numerous broadcasts he televised from a hidden underground bunker. The IR Public Relations Ministry was broadcasting news reels of the destruction of the US 5th Fleet and the nuclear detonations destroying the Americans. Videos of the massive missile and artillery barrages pouring into Israel, videos from the frontlines showing destroyed Israeli and American armored vehicles, and the most startling images for the West, Israeli and American soldiers hanging from crosses with the city of Jerusalem in the distance—all of these played on near-constant loops on any television station that the IR could control.

Shortly after those videos were shown, the pope came out with a statement. He was less ornately dressed than on some other occasions, but the gravity of the situation called for quick action and less ceremony. "This treatment of Christians and Jews is intolerable. If the Islamic Republic succeeds in capturing Jerusalem, they could destroy everything sacred to the Christian and Jewish religions. I declare that this wanton destruction and desecration of life by the Islamic Republic is a crime—not just against humanity, but against the Christian and Jewish religions. I call on my brothers and sisters in faith to stand together against these horrible atrocities. We must take up the call to action."

Within days, tens of thousands of Catholics and Protestants from across Europe were either joining the military or looking for ways to join the Israeli Defense Force militia units that were originally established by the Vatican but quickly sprang up in Italy, Germany, Poland, the United Kingdom, and Ireland. This movement quickly spread to South America, where the word of the pope carried a lot of weight.

The Vatican had all but called this a holy war against Islam. Tens of thousands of Muslims in Italy converged on the Vatican in protest. Very quickly, many Muslim communities across Europe began to riot and take to the streets, attacking Christians and Jews in response to the pope's message.
****

29 November 2040
United States, Undisclosed Location
Mt. Weather Station, Presidential Command and Control Bunker

Within hours of the Pope's message, tens of thousands of Muslims converged on Washington, D.C., in protest. Several hundred young men used the protest as a cover to get close to the Capitol building before launching their attack. They broke from the protest march and ran for the various Capitol building exits, shooting police and security guards as they encountered them. Several dozen attackers were engaging the Capital Police near the main entrance while a group of seven individuals managed to break into one of the emergency exits. Within seconds, they were running through the hallways of the Capitol, throwing grenades into offices and shooting everyone they encountered. Two other groups of attackers were able to enter through other emergency exits and began their assault.

As additional police officers and SWAT team members engaged the attackers, they were able to block them from the House Chamber, where a number of the senior Congressional leadership had evacuated. A similar attack was also underway at the Senate building and two other government agencies within D.C. The protest rally quickly spiraled out of control as police shot the protesters and several gunmen hidden amongst the crowd continued to shoot at the police.

Thirty minutes after the start of the attacks against the Capitol building and the Senate, the President activated the continuity of government plan, which began the dispersal of all elected officials to various command bunkers as the US government went underground. The President also moved the American military to DEFCON One, bringing all US forces to the highest level of readiness. This placed all US overseas military bases on a war footing in anticipation of combat operations.

Rioting and protests were starting to spring up all across the US as the various Muslim communities reacted to the destruction of the Al Aqsa mosque and the Pope's message. Other Muslim groups began denouncing the barbaric acts the IR was perpetrating on the US and Israeli soldiers with the crucifixions, pleading for all sides to remain calm.

****

"Mr. President, the rioting is starting to get out of control in some cities. Just as we believe things are starting to calm down, some nutjob starts shooting Muslims or Christians or Jews, and once again the situation is a boiling cauldron of fury and rage. The National Guard is still mobilizing and getting into position in the major cities, but something has to give," said FBI Director Jane Smart.

"We need to give it some time, Director. Order is not going to be restored immediately—the National Guard needs time to get in place, DHS is still getting the detention processing camps established and so on. I just authorized curfews, as well as the use of deadly force against the rioters. If things don't calm down over the next forty-eight hours, we'll look at the situation again."

"I understand, Mr. President. We have more than just a detention problem. There are literally hundreds of cities experiencing this problem, and the gangs in some of the major cities are also taking advantage of the situation. On top of it all, I have the ACLU breathing down my neck crying foul everywhere," complained the Director of DHS.

"This war is almost forty-eight hours old. I don't give a crap what the ACLU says right now. We are under martial law, and under the 2015 and 2039 Defense Authorization Act, I'm operating within the legal bounds of the law. Let's move on to a status update on the war—where do we stand, General Branson?" asked the President, clearly frustrated.

"Mr. President, everyone is aware of the atrocities the IR has been committing against our forces. I'd fire and replace General Gardner for destroying the Al Aqsa mosque, but right now he's in the thick of it, and I think pulling him out would cause more problems than it would solve," replied Branson.

"I agree. As you said, it would cause more issues at this moment, so we're stuck having to turn a blind eye to it at the moment. Please continue."

"The 1st ID is less than two miles from Jerusalem. In some locations, the IR forces are even closer to the city. Our forces have been getting mauled, and they have been in almost continuous combat for nearly forty-eight hours. General Gardner has ordered the rest of the 3rd ID in to reinforce them. The 1st Armored Division broke through the IR lines and quickly advanced to the outskirts of Damascus. Gardner has ordered them to swing south and try to put more pressure on the IR forces in the Jordan Valley.

"The 2nd MEF has secured the Sinai and the Suez. The 6th Fleet is reporting a massive troop movement from Cairo heading toward the Suez. The Marine air wing is engaging them along with the 6th Fleet. I've directed Admiral Todd to do what she can to assist our troops in the valley. We still don't have air supremacy, but the more pressure we can put on the IR air forces, the better," said Branson.

"Where's the rest of the Air Force in all of this? When will we have control of the skies and start to pound these guys into the dirt?" demanded the President.

"Soon, Mr. President. We are moving the USS *Intrepid* to the Mediterranean. Their battlegroup should be on station in four days—they are sailing at flank speed," said Admiral Juliano.

General Adrian Rice, the Air Force Chief of Staff, interjected. "The 81st Fighter Drone Wing has arrived in Sigonella Naval Air Base, Italy. The Wing consists of one thousand F-38 air superiority drones and six hundred FA-38 ground attack drones. The 80th Fighter Drone Wing has arrived at Aviano Air Base, Italy, and they consist of the same number and type of aircraft. The 80th is engaging the IR Air Force in Turkey and their naval assets left in the area. The 81st is going to focus solely on providing support to our forces in Israel once our forward air bases in Crete are back to being operational. As soon as air superiority has been achieved over Israel to the best of our capability, the ground attack drones will move to their forward bases so they can provide quicker ground support.

"The 80th ground attack aircraft will also move to Israel as soon as possible. I've ordered two additional F-35 squadrons to the region, and our cyber guys are constantly sending new viruses and worms to any of the old US aircraft that the IR still has in their possession. So far, we've managed to keep them grounded, so I'd call that a win."

"How soon until additional reinforcements arrive?" asked the President nervously.

"We lost two transports carrying reinforcements a few hours ago. We have another 3,000 troops waiting in Italy once we can secure the skies a bit more. Most of the XVIII Airborne Corps is still in Mexico, so they aren't going to be available for at least another week. The issue we face is getting enough troops mobilized and deployed to Israel to make a difference.

"The troops we would traditionally have available are either tied down in Mexico, already deployed in Israel, or conducting antiterrorism activities here in the US. We have one brigade from the 82nd that is en route to Italy and will be ready to jump into Israel as soon as there is an opportunity," said General Jeremiah Smith, the Army Chief of Staff. A worried look covered his face. "With your permission, I'd like to prepare Fifth Corps to head to Israel as quickly as possible."

"How soon could they get there?" asked the President.

"I have the orders drafted, and the Corps has been placed on ready alert for deployment We can start to have them move to Norfolk for embarkation immediately. They should arrive in nine days with their full equipment load," replied General Smith.

"Before we deploy more troops to Israel, we need to secure the Straits of Gibraltar. The British are holding their end—the issue is the IR side. At first, they posed no significant problem once our aircraft from Britain paid them a visit, but I'm concerned that this may change now that we are going to need to move a lot more ships through there," explained General Tyler Black, the Commandant of the Marine Corps. General Black looked like your typical Marine. He had a bulldog's face and could stare down just about anyone. His first concern was his Marines, then his country.

"I suppose you have a plan, General?" inquired the President, raising an eyebrow at the general.

"I do, Mr. President. I have the 4th MEF about a day away from the Straits as they move to reinforce the 2nd MEF in the Sinai and the Suez. I'd like to drop a battalion and their equipment to secure the area. The British forces on Gibraltar have said they would provide air support for the battalion and, if needed, medical support."

Stein thought about that for a moment before responding. "All right, General. Secure the area, and then get the rest of those Marines to the 2nd MEF. General Gardner has ordered one of your brigades there to retake our base at Eilat. The situation around Jerusalem is only getting worse, so the more Marines we can get in country, the better." The President rubbed his temples as his migraine continued to get worse. He looked exhausted, practically haggard from the lack of sleep and immense pressure.

"Mr. President, we need to make a decision about Jerusalem and whether we want General Gardner to hold it or withdraw to a more defensible position," interjected General Branson, pouring himself a refill of his coffee.

"I'm afraid the IR has already made that decision for us, General. If we surrender the city, they're going to kill everyone in it and destroy any Jewish and Christian historical sites. We need General Gardner to hold the city at all cost, even if it means house-to-house fighting. The civilians need more time to evacuate. I spoke with the Israeli prime minister, and he said they're evacuating as many civilians as possible out of Israel to Italy." The President let out a heavy sigh. "Generals, you all have your orders. Continue to manage the war as we've discussed and have your updates ready for our next meeting in…four hours."

As the President got up to leave, his Chief of Staff was hot on his heels. "Henry, you need to make another address to the nation soon. The people need to be reassured that things are OK, and we are in control. The COG has really spooked a lot of people. There are lines of people fleeing the major cities, heading to the countryside. People aren't showing up for work, and basic services are starting to break down," explained Monty.

"You are right as usual. Please schedule a broadcast for 5 p.m. today. When's our domestic briefing?"

"In a couple of hours. You have some time to catch a short nap, if that's what you were thinking."

"Thank you, Monty. You know, aside from my wife, you probably know me better than anyone else."

****

The President gave his third address to the nation in a few hours, this time to reassure the American people that things were fine and they should return to their homes and jobs. The President informed the public that the National Guard would remain on the streets with the police to help maintain law and order. The best thing people could do for the war effort was to return to their homes and their businesses, as the country and the soldiers in the Middle East needed their support.

In this same period, the FBI and DHS had apprehended 74 individuals before they could carry out further attacks. This brought the total number of captured terrorists to three hundred and twenty-nine. Four hundred and sixty-two thousand people had applied to join the military in the first forty-eight hours of the war. People were angry, and they wanted payback.

Despite large numbers of people wanting to leave the big cities after the initial use of nuclear weapons by the IR and the terrorist attacks on the Senate and Capitol buildings, American nationalism was at an all-time high. Riots and demonstrations both for and against the war, along with pro-Muslim and anti-Muslim rallies continued. Some turned violent, and there was a lot of vigilante justice going on. Local and federal law enforcement was doing their best to maintain law and order, though they often fell short.

****

02 December 2040
Islamic Republic Underground Command Center

"Caliph Mohammed, I bring good news. General Muhammed has finally captured Jerusalem. The American and Israeli forces have fallen back to less than ten miles from Tel Aviv. General Hamza believes his forces will be able to secure Tel Aviv within the next three days."

"Our Air Force has taken a terrible beating, Caliph. We have lost nearly 1,200 aircraft since the start of operations, and 4,000 fighter drones were destroyed. We still have 2,300 fighter drones, but these constitute the last of our operational air force," said General Ishmael Malik, the Commanding General of the IR Air Forces.

"General Hamza, I'm pleased that we have finally secured Jerusalem. General Malik, you bring up a major concern. Have we been able to get our laser defense systems operational yet?"

"Yes, we have about forty percent of them back online. The Americans were able to destroy ten of our sixteen ground-based sites with cruise missiles. The majority of our mobile defense systems are at the front line, leaving us vulnerable. We have started to pull some of them to help protect our critical infrastructure. The Russians are helping by connecting their power transmission nodes into ours. As they are able to provide more electricity, we should have the rest of our laser batteries operational," explained General Malik with an optimistic look on his face.

"It was a smart move on the Americans' part to destroy our power plants. Aside from shutting down our laser defense systems, it has plunged most of the Republic into the dark."

"Fortunately, we also have a lot of industrial grade generators and two Russian nuclear-powered ships in port—they are providing a substantial amount of power," said Admiral Mustafa.

"Their attempt to take out the reactors at Fordo failed, though we are letting them believe they destroyed them. We have that weak idiot President Obama to thank for giving us the time to reinforce it beyond their capability to destroy it a few decades ago," said General Malik.

"The American cruise missiles are really starting to cause some problems. Aside from electricity shortages, they are attempting to destroy our infrastructure, making movement across the Republic incredibly difficult. It is making it hard to move additional reinforcements and supplies to the front lines.

"We have over two million volunteers in Mecca and Medina right now that need to be transported to the front. A lot of them are being moved by commercial busses, which is helping. Once they arrive, we are providing them with basic small-arms rifles and a minimal amount of ammunition. General Muhammed is having them formed into shock brigades—he plans on using them in human wave attacks and then his professional units will follow in behind them," said Malik.

"Let us hope that with these numbers, we will be able to overwhelm their defenses and finally crush the Jews."

"Caliph Mohammed, if I may—I'd like to discuss our operatives in the US. The Americans have captured ninety percent of our remaining operatives, so it is going to be difficult for us to carry out the final attack once the nuclear packages have been delivered," said Huseen ibn Abdullah, the Director of IR Intelligence.

"Abdullah, your agents have exceeded our wildest dreams in attacking the Americans. Over 20,000 of them have been killed, and you have struck fear in their hearts. I would like all operations there to stop until we are ready for the final attack. Let's conserve the few remaining agents we have for our final acts of destruction," replied Caliph Mohammed, smiling broadly at the thought of detonating two nuclear bombs inside the US.

Chapter 13
The Dragon Awakens

02 December 2040
Beijing, China

Premier Zhang was on his way to a meeting with the Central Military Commission to discuss the plans to finally reacquire their lost province, Taiwan, and become the supreme power in Asia. The war in the Middle East was becoming a bloodbath; the Islamic Republic had hurt the Americans badly when they'd destroyed the American 5th Fleet. The destruction of the 5th Fleet had given China a few new options that they had not previously believed possible. With the Americans sending the USS *Intrepid* battlegroup to the Mediterranean, the US 7th Fleet would only have the USS *John F. Kennedy* to rely on, which was located in the Pacific Northwest. With only one US aircraft carrier down near the Indonesian Islands, hammering the Islamic Republic, they would not be able to intervene with Taiwan or Guam.

The only real concern is the American submarines, thought the Premier.

As the Premier walked into the room to meet with the CMC, he noticed several of the generals in various heated discussions. If there was one major weakness within the Chinese military, it was the various rivalries and the desire for each branch of the PLA to be the dominant branch.

"General Wanquan, are we ready to secure the rest of Asia?" asked the Premier. He took his seat at the head of the table while the rest of the CMC members took their own seats.

"The Army is ready to cross the border and secure Southeast Asia. When the attack begins against Taiwan, our forces will cross into Vietnam, Laos, Cambodia, and Myanmar. Once these countries have been overrun, our forces will continue south and west until we have Thailand and Singapore. We are ready," replied General Wanquan, the Commander of the PLA.

"My naval infantry are ready to secure Guam as soon as you give the order. Our sources have reported that the Americans have not reinforced Guam and appear to be fully occupied with the Islamic Republic. Two battalions of Marines left the island yesterday to join the battlegroup near Indonesia," said Admiral Wei Shengli, the Commander of the People's Liberation Army Navy.

"Premier, our original timetable was to attack Taiwan and Guam around the New Year. With the Americans involved in Mexico and now the Middle East, they are stretched thin. My advice is that we move our timeline forward by at least three weeks. With the Americans sending more troops to Israel, they will not have the option of also intervening in Asia, or have the ability to challenge us with the loss of their two supercarriers," said General Zhang Yang, the Minister of Defense.

"You bring up a good point, General Zhang. Upon further consideration, I will agree to move the timeline forward by two weeks. We should capitalize on their precarious situation before it changes. In the meantime, I want our cyber forces to begin their attacks against the American military and economy. The more problems the Americans are forced to deal with now, the fewer resources they will have later."
****

03 December 2040
Be'er Sheva, Israel

Sergeant Joe Thornton had joined the Marines four years earlier, looking for adventure and a chance to serve his country like his father, grandfather and great-grandfather had done before. They had been jarheads, so it was a family tradition for the Thornton men to join the Marines out of high school or college. Joe had done well and had been promoted to sergeant just prior to the deployment to the Middle East.

Now he had a squad of leathernecks he was responsible for, and within five days, half of his platoon was already dead or wounded. His squad had been flown into the Sinai on one of the Marine Corps' new Razorback assault helicopters to secure Ismailia, which was a critical city on the Suez. His company met minimal resistance upon landing, and with support from the Razorbacks, they had quickly secured the city and their portion of the Suez. Securing the Suez was critical to the defense of Israel as it blocked any possible reinforcements from Egypt and North Africa. It also provided the Navy with several port facilities which could be used to offload more equipment for the Marines.

The newest aerial addition to the Marines was the Razorback assault helicopters. They were a cross between the V-22 Osprey and a

Cobra attack helicopter. They sported the same tilt-rotary system the Osprey had, except there were two smaller rotors per side, one behind the other, and they were enclosed in an armored ring protecting them from ground fire. They were also considerably smaller and very quiet in comparison to a traditional helicopter.

The Razorbacks' armament included eight antitank Hellfire III missiles and forty-six 2.6-inch antipersonnel rockets on each side, and a front mounted 30mm railgun that delivered an incredible punch and fire support. It had a crew of two pilots and two crew chiefs and could carry twelve soldiers into combat. The Razorback was the first fully armored assault helicopter, and it replaced not only the venerable Cobra gunships but also the Ospreys as the primary assault helicopter for the Army and Marines. The V22 was a beast of an aircraft. It was 57 feet in length with a wingspan of 45 feet, and the Razorback was 68 feet in length and had a 40-foot wingspan. Both had been in service for barely a year, so there was a limited number of them available for the Army and Marines, and they were in high demand.

After the initial success in securing the Suez, Sergeant Thornton's company was ordered to assault the IR forces near the strategic city of Be'er Sheva. This city was a crossroad junction leading to many different cities within Israel as well as several highways. The IDF was making a last-ditch stand to block the IR advance, and it desperately needed reinforcements.

The 2nd Marines were going to assault and secure the cities of Nevatim on Highway 25 and the city of Hura along Highway 31. This would place most of the Marines behind the main IR forces and would compel them to halt their advance on Be'er Sheva. With Marine Aviation support and assurances from Admiral Todd with the 6th Fleet, Major General Lance Peeler, the Commander of 2nd Marines, was determined to make the IR pay for crucifying captured American forces. His Marines would disrupt the IR supply lines and force them to have to fight his Marines. The Marine armored units had secured the cities of Eilat and Aqaba, blocking the IR advance into southern Israel. Now it was time to go on the offensive and take the fight to the enemy.

Sergeant Thornton's company had assaulted the Islamic Republic lines at Nevatim, and with support from three dozen Razorbacks, they had quickly destroyed the IR's armor, infantry fighting vehicles, and light drone tanks in the area. They secured the critical highway network supplying the IR's main force near Be'er Sheva. The company had been in near-constant contact with the enemy for seventy-two hours, and it was starting to show; his men were exhausted, and so was he. In addition to limited air support and their Razorbacks, there was a self-propelled 155mm Army artillery battalion assigned to support their position, which was facing continuous contact with the enemy. The IR was now starting to use massive human wave attacks.

"Sergeant Thornton, I'm pulling your squad off the line to get some rest. I can't give your men a long break, but I need to start rotating the squads in the company before everyone drops dead from exhaustion," said First Lieutenant Jack Lee. Jack had taken over command of the company two days ago, when the captain had been killed during one of the IR's suicidal human wave attacks.

"The men will appreciate it—not sure how much longer we can function in our current state. Some of the guys are starting to fall asleep during lulls in the battle, and my fear is they won't wake up fast enough to respond to a new assault," Sergeant Thornton replied, leaning against the wall of his foxhole.

"It's a problem the entire battalion is facing. That's why I need to get your squad some rest while we can. We're pulling one squad from each platoon and giving them an hour and a half to sleep before rotating the next group in. We will continue this rotation for as long as possible," the lieutenant said, sounding optimistic about the sleeping plan.

Sergeant Thornton was glad his squad was the first to get some rest. Before the lieutenant left to go inform the next squad, Thornton asked, "Sir, do you know when we are going to get some replacements? Nearly half our platoon is gone."

"There are two thousand Marine reservists that just landed in Siganella yesterday. Word has it they're supposed to start filtering in within the next forty-eight hours. Of course, that assumes we'll still be alive in the next forty-eight hours."

"If they keep sending these human wave attacks and that constant rocket barrage, you may be right," said Sergeant Thornton dryly.

****

The 1st Infantry Division lost Jerusalem after two days of house-to-house fighting through the suburbs. General Gardner had ordered them to fall back to the surrounding hills and suburbs on the west side of

Jerusalem. Sergeant Jordy Nelson's platoon was exhausted and running on fumes. Nearly five days of constant combat was grinding them into the dirt. His company had lost nearly sixty percent of their original force by the end of the first day. After unrelenting rocket and artillery barrages, they were quickly faced with nearly 300,000 IR troops fighting to capture Jerusalem. When the 3rd Infantry Division had reinforced them four days ago, the 1st ID had lost nearly 4,200 soldiers of their original 12,300. With the loss of Jerusalem, General Gardner had folded the two infantry divisions together since Major General Paul Brown and his staff had been killed in Jerusalem during one of the many IR bombing runs. Both divisions were down to less than forty percent strength, and until reinforcements showed up with additional senior officers, having them operate under a joint command only made sense.

When the US's 80th and 81st Fighter Drone Wings arrived from Italy and Cypress, they immediately made an impact. The drones were slowly beginning to retake the skies over Israel. The ground attack drones had moved to forward air bases in Israel, and despite the air bases coming under rocket and artillery attack, the drones were starting to take a bite out of the IR artillery and rocket forces. The greatest contribution the drones had made thus far was whittling down the IR's artillery, which had been devastating the Allied defensive positions.

The key advantages the American soldiers had over their IR counterparts were their superior training, infantry weapons, and body armor. With some air support, they were finally starting to halt the massive uncoordinated IR human wave attacks. Word had spread through the Allies that these human wave assaults were waged by civilian volunteers with little in the way of training. They might have had numbers, but they lacked courage and conviction in their cause once the artillery and rifle fire started to cut through their ranks.

Chapter 14
European Craziness

03 December 2040
Brussels, European Union

The EU was experiencing a rash of violence against Jews, Christians, and Muslims all across the Union. After the destruction of the Al Aqsa mosque and then the condemnation from the Pope, the Muslims living in Europe had exploded. There had already been strong support in the Muslim communities for the Islamic Republic, and once hostilities broke out against Israel and the United States, hundreds of thousands of Muslim men began traveling to Turkey to join the Islamic Army. Turkey had left the NATO alliance to join the IR, which created a lot of friction between the EU and Turkey. The border between Greece and Turkey, which was already a source of friction, quickly became a fully militarized border.

To complicate things further, the American embassies in Paris, Rome, Norway, Sweden, Finland, Spain, and Germany were brutally attacked on the third day of the war. The embassies were pummeled with multiple vehicle-borne IEDs and RPGs, and then they were directly assaulted by hundreds of "protesters," as the European media was calling them.

The Germans had caught wind of the threat and had prepared accordingly. When the attack there was about to get underway, hundreds of German police and counterterrorism units intercepted the attackers. The outcome was a massive shoot-out in central Berlin that resulted in two vehicle-borne IEDs going off, causing considerable damage to the neighboring buildings.

In Great Britain, the British arrested most of the attackers in the middle of the night and prevented the others from getting close to the embassy.

The Paris attack was perhaps the most disturbing. The French had been dealing with hundreds of attacks between Jews, Christians, Muslims, and rioting across the country. Despite intelligence sharing between countries within the EU, they were caught unprepared for the attack against the embassy. Ten individuals attacked the French police guarding the embassy with machine guns, killing them quickly. One individual unslung an RPG-7VR and blew apart the Marine guard station next to the gate, killing the two Marines and security contractors.

Within seconds, a cargo van drove directly into the front gate and exploded a 1,000-pound bomb, destroying the primary and secondary gates. A second van drove through the newly created hole in the embassy security and drove straight for the front entrance. Three security guards opened fire on the van, killing the driver. As the van slowed down, someone detonated the bomb, exploding three thousand pounds of Semtex high explosives. The vehicle-borne IED blew the entire face of the embassy right off, creating multiple new entries into the building.

Five additional vans arrived and disgorged thirty heavily armed men, who quickly stormed the embassy. In less than five minutes, they had captured the ambassador, the deputy ambassador, and twenty-three employees. They were quickly moved to the vans and driven away while the remaining armed men began killing everyone in the building and waited for the police to arrive. By the end of the day, 136 US and French nationals were killed during the attack, and an additional 61 police officers were killed as well. The next day, a video was posted showing the ambassador and the twenty-four other individuals crucified and their bodies set on fire; their screams were horrific. This same type of attack occurred at the other embassies, with the ambassadors and their staffs also being crucified the following day. The brutal manner in which the diplomats were murdered further infuriated the President and the American people, and President Stein was furious with the EU for not providing better security for the embassies.
****

"Chancellor Lowden, we have started the call-up of the reserves. Our active duty forces are now on high alert and ready to deploy to the cities when you are ready," Minister of Defense André Gouin said as he looked at the faces around the table.

"I do not like the idea of deploying the military into the cities, but we have to do something. The rioting and the attacks on the American embassies are too much. President Stein was enraged when he called me this morning."

"Perhaps if President Stein had kept his generals under control and not destroyed the Al Aqsa mosque, we wouldn't be having this conversation," replied Minister of Foreign Affairs Paolo Prodi.

"I might have done the same thing if I had been in General Gardner's position, after seeing video of our soldiers being crucified. That is beyond barbaric," said General Volker Naumann, the EU Military Chief of Staff, shooting a stern look at Minister Prodi.

"Gentlemen, arguing is not going to change the situation. We have to deal with it and move forward. I want solutions, not arguments."

"If you want to solve the problem, then we need to encourage the Muslim populations in our countries to leave and join the Islamic Republic. As long as they are here, they are going to cause problems. They refuse to assimilate and learn our languages, and they demand that our women dress more conservatively and wear a headdress. French women are scared to go out in public in certain areas of Paris for fear of being attacked," said General Naumann, looking each person in the eye.

"Chancellor, I do not believe it is possible for us to evict them from our country, at least not peacefully. What we can do is deploy the military into the cities to return law and order. As Muslims are apprehended for violations of our laws, they can be moved to a detention facility we intend to set up in Marseille. From there, we will load them on freighters and send them to Algeria or Tunisia, both IR members. If the IR will not accept them, then sink the ship in the harbor," said André Gouin as he took a sip of espresso.

"I cannot even believe you would suggest such a thing," said Paolo as he pointed angrily at Gouin.

"Enough!" shouted Chancellor Lowden. "We, as the government, need to have a unified plan and deal with this problem immediately. Paulo, I understand your concerns, and I share them as well. However, the state of the world has changed so much in such a short time. While the majority of the Muslim populations in our countries used to be peaceful, we can no longer say that is true. The last five days have resulted in over nine thousand people being killed, and four times that many injured. We cannot continue to debate this. I do not like this plan at all, but I can see that it is the only plan right now that will work. Minister Gouin, order the military into the cities. General Naumann, crush this uprising."
****

05 December 2040
Washington, D.C.

White House, Situation Room

After spending several days in the underground bunker, the President returned back to the White House, albeit with a significant military presence protecting the residence, in addition to the regular detail of Secret Service. Despite his advisors saying he should continue to stay underground with the rest of the government, the President was adamant that he needed to be in the White House and project to the American people a sense of calm. It was imperative that people stop panicking and do their best to return to their daily lives.

The President met with the CEOs and head producers of each of the major news networks and insisted that their coverage start to focus on the positive aspects of the war—victories, defeats of the enemy, winning—the economy, and other stories rather than coverage aimed at scaring the public and further inciting rioting and violence between American Muslims and non-Muslims. The news agencies agreed to refocus a majority of their coverage to topics that would hopefully help to defuse the growing violence and panic that was starting to run amok. Even the journalists, usually keen to find the most salacious stories possible in order to rack up their ratings, realized society would not function if everything imploded. They knew they could do something to help bring some calm to the situation and moved to do so.

While the group waited in the Situation Room for President Stein to arrive, General Gardner gruffly addressed the group through the secured video phone. "Does the President understand how many casualties we're sustaining? We need more reinforcements now, or we may lose the rest of Israel," he asserted.

"General, we know how many soldiers you're losing, and so does the President," said General Aaron Wade, the Central Command Commander.

"Sorry I'm late, gentlemen. Monty and I were held up in the economic meeting. Please, let's start the briefing," the President said as he sat down at the head of the table. "Before we move to Israel, update me on the situation in the EU and our forces there."

"Our forces in the EU remain in a state of high alert. The bases are also receiving additional security from the EU, so we're confident they're as secured as they can be," said replied General Branson.

"Well, I'm glad the EU is finally doing something to protect our people and buildings from their unruly mob," said the President.

"We have moved close to 300,000 troops to Italy and Germany. Our biggest challenge is getting those troops into Israel. We do not have full air supremacy over Israel. We've had to focus on using only military cargo aircraft to bring in reinforcements, which has slowed down the number of reinforcements we can send each day. Nine civilian aircraft were shot down over the past four days, trying to break through. No civilian pilot is willing to take the chance now," said General Rice, the Air Force Chief of Staff.

"General Rice, how many troops a day are we sending into Israel right now?" inquired the President.

"We are flying in thirteen thousand reinforcements a day. I would also like to add that we have lost sixteen C-17s and four C-5s—roughly four thousand troops were killed. We just aren't able to get enough reinforcements to the front," said Rice.

"Fifth Corps just arrived at the port of Ashdod. They're offloading their equipment as we speak. They've been under a lot of artillery and rocket fire, slowing the offloading of their vehicles. The equipment and troops that are offloaded are immediately being moved to General Gardner's Command," explained Admiral Juliano, reading from his tablet.

General Gardner broke in to add, "As these troops are becoming available, I'm filtering them into the front line where they're needed. It will still take several days to unload their equipment. I'm feeding most of the Corps into the front line as infantry for the time being."

"Mr. President, I know you're aware of how dire the situation is here in Israel. If we are not able to get more reinforcements to Israel within the next twenty-four to thirty-six hours, I'm not confident we're going to be able to hold on to northern Israel and Tel Aviv. If we lose Tel Aviv, the Army will have to pull back to Be'er Sheva and Gaza," asserted General Gardner with a worried yet determined look on his face.

"General Wade, what's your opinion on the situation?" asked the President.

"I have to agree with General Gardner, Mr. President. If we continue to try and hold northern Israel and Tel Aviv without reinforcements, General Gardner's force may be cut off from the rest of

Israel and surrounded. Then it would only be a matter of time until they're wiped out," replied General Wade with a solemn expression.

"General Rice, what else can the Air Force do to improve the situation?" asked Stein.

"Mr. President, we're in a tough position. The IR continues to move hundreds of thousands of troops to Israel. They have already lost over 300,000 troops, and more keep coming. Presently, there are 540,000 IR troops fighting in Israel. The IDF has taken some horrific casualties too. The Israelis have lost 154,000 troops. On our side, 31,235 soldiers and 18,432 sailors have given their lives in sacrifice to our country."

"I know the losses are terrible, General Wade. What is the solution? How are you going to get more troops into Israel and stop the continued IR reinforcements?"

"The USS *Intrepid* battle group has arrived on station, and we've moved another six hundred fighter drones to Europe, most of which are currently in Cypress. We're going to make a massive air assault that we believe will finally give us air superiority. I've ordered our strategic bombers to Europe as well. Once we have air superiority, our bombers will begin attacking their reinforcements and supply lines. Of note is our cruise missile stockpile—it's down to thirty-seven percent. I've ordered 12,000 additional cruise missiles to Europe, but it will drop our strategic reserves down to twenty-eight percent," said General Rice.

"I've been in discussion with our cruise missile suppliers, and they're now working 24/7 on producing more cruise missiles. They're even adding several new production lines to increase their production capacity," said the SecDef, trying to ease concerns over the possibility of a munitions shortage.

"That's a whole other issue, getting the economy on a war footing. We knew a war was coming, but I don't believe we thought we would lose this many troops and this much equipment this fast. We're only eight days into the war, and we're already running low on munitions, infantry vehicles, tanks, aircraft and naval ships," the President said with a bit of concern.

"Mr. President, there's another issue we still need to discuss. As you know, the country has been experiencing an incredible amount of cyberattacks against the DoD and private industry. Some of the attacks have been going after the critical infrastructure, which is concerning," said Mike Williams, the National Security Advisor.

"This is becoming an issue for the DoD as well. We're starting to see bogus equipment requests and orders for personnel. We have to divert manpower to address the issues created by the cyberattacks, which is hurting us in other areas," the Secretary of Defense said.

"Where are these attacks originating?" asked Stein.

"We've tracked them to various organizations and groups within China. Most of them have some connection with the PLA," said Lieutenant General Rick Scott, the Director of the DIA.

"Is this a potential precursor to something, or are they trying to just take advantage of the situation?" asked the President with trepidation in his voice.

General Rick Scott's parents had lived in China while working for an American company. General Scott had become fluent in the language and studied at the University of Beijing before obtaining his master's degree from Yale through the Army ROTC program. General Scott believed the true threat to the US was Russia and the Islamic Republic, not China. His strong belief that China's interests lay not in attacking the US but in stealing technology was blinding his perspective.

"From the DIA's perspective, it does appear they may be up to something. The challenge with the Chinese is that over the past two years, they've been conducting land and naval exercises in and around Taiwan and the South China Sea. These exercises have always been preceded by an increase in cyberattacks, making it difficult for us to determine if this time, there may be something more to the equation. The first few times, we certainly thought something was amiss, but after four more exercises, we assumed it was part of their training drill," General Scott said with an air of confidence.

"Mr. President, the problem I have with this assessment is that this time around, they've more than doubled their number of ships and troops as part of this exercise. The more alarming part is that a PLA Naval Task Force is conducting their exercise between Taiwan and Guam. My concern is that if this isn't an exercise but a pre-positioning of forces, we could be hit pretty hard. We're in a weak position in the Pacific right now. If there were ever a time to invade Taiwan and assert dominion over the Pacific, this would be it," asserted Admiral Juliano.

"The DIA has evaluated that as well, and we believe they are posturing. The Chinese economy has been growing immensely the last three years. Our repayment of our debt has left them flush with cash, and our economic recovery has increased demand for their products. Our analysts don't believe the Chinese would be willing to throw away the American market by attacking our base on Guam or anywhere else.

"They may take a risk and go for Taiwan, and if they do, there is little we can do to stop them. However, we believe that would be the extent of it," General Scott insisted.

"Admiral, if we wanted to shift additional assets to the Pacific, what do we have available?" the President inquired.

"Sir, we just pulled our third aircraft carrier from the Pacific, and most of our naval assets are engaged in Indonesia. The most we could bring to bear would be eight additional submarines and two fighter drone squadrons. We have, at most, two battalions of Marines at Camp Pendleton we could move to Guam, but that's it," explained Admiral Juliano.

"Look, I don't want to be caught off guard by the Chinese. We already got sucker-punched by the IR with those nukes. I don't want to get hit by the Chinese like that as well. General Black, I want you to send every additional Marine you can to Guam. Tell the base commander to be ready to repel a potential Chinese invasion, should it come to that. I also want to start evacuating all military dependents from Guam," directed the President.

"Admiral Juliano, I want you to deploy that additional fighter drone squadron. Also, move additional hunter-killer submarines into the waters around Guam. If the Chinese surface fleet does make a move towards Guam, then our subs are to target the Chinese capital ships. This is important, Admiral Juliano. I'm authorizing the use of nuclear torpedoes, but only if the sub commander believes it's necessary and would significantly damage the PLA Navy fleet, understood?"

"Yes, Mr. President. I hope it doesn't come to that, but I will relay those specific instructions."

"General Lewis, is the Air Force able to maintain air superiority over Guam with assistance from the Navy and Marines?"

"Yes, Mr. President. We have two squadrons of F-22s, two squadrons of F-38 fighter drones, and three medium-range drone bomber squadrons, which are currently being used in support of our operations in Indonesia. They could easily be retasked to protect Guam. We still have plenty of antiship ordnance on Guam to supply our air wings, should it be necessary," General Lewis said with a devilish grin.

"Excellent, General. I was hoping you were going to say that. Now, moving to the cyberattacks—since the Chinese have engaged in a full-scale cyberattack against the country, I want our entire cyberwarfare capability launched against China. Target their banking, energy, and transportation sectors. If we can turn the lights off in the country, then do so. It's time we start to show the Chinese what it's like to be hit with cyberattacks at the same level, and perhaps a bit worse. Oh, and General Black and Admiral Juliano, if hostilities were to erupt between China and the US, then I want those specific locations where the cyberattacks are originating from to be immediately eliminated—is that clear?" asked the President with a sternness not often heard in his voice.

"Yes, Sir," came the synchronized response.

****

10 December 2040
The Middle East

Between the seventh and twelfth day of the war, the US Navy and Air Force had moved 185,000 US soldiers and Marines into Israel and the Egyptian Suez Canal Zone via military and commercial aircraft, military, naval transports and civilian cruise ships. This massive influx of US forces into Israel was the deciding factor in being able to repel the near-constant human wave attacks from the IR forces. Hundreds of thousands of soldiers and civilians had been killed in less than two weeks, mirroring the destruction of most of Israel and the entire Palestinian area in the West Bank and Gaza. The IR had lost their ability to threaten coalition air forces by the end of the eighth day of the war when the US Air Force conducted a massive air raid comprising of nearly two thousand fighter and fighter bomber drones and nine hundred cruise missiles. They destroyed every IR air base within three hundred miles of Israel.

Once the Allies had regained air superiority, the tide of the war quickly shifted as the IR supply lines and reinforcements came under tremendous pressure. The IDF and US forces were able to stabilize the frontlines and slowly pushed the IR forces back, reclaiming territory and Israeli cities. As the IR forces withdrew, they ensured no civilians survived and did their best to level every building, increasing the number of defensible positions.

Every yard of land was being heavily contested as casualties on both sides continued to mount. The IR had lost 400,000 soldiers, and another 170,000 were listed as missing. The IDF were reporting nearly 197,000 killed and missing soldiers. From the US, 72,340 had perished or were missing, and nearly twice that number were injured.

With large portions of the Islamic Republic operating on limited power and subject to rolling blackouts, it was becoming nearly impossible for them to move additional soldiers and equipment to the frontlines. However, the Russian Federation succeeded in integrating the IR power grid into their own along their shared border in the Caucasus region around the eleventh day of the war. Russia began to provide the IR with nearly 65% of their power, restoring most of the country back too normal while emergency repair crews began to fix what power plants could be mended after the American nuclear and conventional attacks on the first day of the war.

Russia also moved the Second Shock Army into Turkey and insisted on a dialogue with the Israelis and Americans to put an end to hostilities. While the Second Shock Army was being assembled in Turkey, the First and Third Shock Armies were being positioned along the EU border to begin their winter training exercise.

Caliph Mohammed was adamant with the Russian foreign minister that the IR would continue to fight and did not want to pursue talks with Israel and the Americans. They believed if they could continue to send reinforcements and received enough replacement equipment from Russia and China, they could continue to grind the IDF and American forces into submission.

The Russian foreign minister had to remind the Caliph that neither Russia nor China could supply the IR with essentially a new military overnight. It would take years to replace the equipment that had been lost, not to mention the training of military members to operate it. The best course of action was to negotiate a ceasefire and insist upon retaining the conquered land. The foreign minister assured Caliph Mohammed that once Russia declared war on the EU and US, hostilities with Israel could be restarted almost immediately. With great reluctance, the IR asked for a ceasefire with the Allies. Whether President Stein would listen was another question entirely.

Chapter 15
Operation Red Dragon

10 December 2040
China

"We need to get the Premier to start the war. The Americans have already reinforced Guam, and these cyberattacks against our transportation infrastructure and other aspects of the economy are starting to get worse," said Director Xi Lee. He was starting to become concerned that the Premier might be getting cold feet.

"I agree with you, Director. We will pressure the Premier to make the decision today at the CMC meeting. Admiral Shengli and General Wanquan will also insist that the war start today," General Yang said with a bit of urgency in his voice.

"For the sake of China, we must start the war today...the Americans have had too long to prepare, and I fear this preparation is going to cost our forces," insisted Xi, not trying too hard to hide his trace of anger at the indecisiveness of the Premier.

China was supposed to have attacked the Americans yesterday but had held off once the cyberattacks against the Chinese economy had begun to have some serious effects.

Premier Zhang walked into the secured bunker under his official residence for the final CMC briefing before the government moved to the war-time bunkers burrowed deep in the Da'Anshanxiang Mountains just west of Beijing. As Zhang walked to the head of the table, he could sense the tension in the room.

The generals were angry with him for not starting the war according to the original plan, but he had his reasons. He wanted to ensure his generals were loyal to him and to China. Inspector Ma Keshi, the head of the secret police, had suggested holding off on initiating the war as a means of testing his generals to determine if they would listen to him or find a way to disobey him. If one or more of them had found a way to start the war without his direction, then Zhang and Inspector Keshi would know who was loyal and who could not be trusted. Inspector Keshi had wanted to hold off for three days. However, Zhang realized that holding off for even a day might have provided the Americans with more time to prepare, leading them to lose the element of surprise. No, today was the day that China would rise and secure her destiny as the dominant power in Asia.

"Generals, Admiral, please take your seats," said Zhang.

"Premier, we must start the war today!" said Admiral Shengli angrily.

"My task forces are ready, and any further delay is going to raise too much suspicion."

"Admiral, please keep calm and sit down. I held off on starting the war yesterday as a test. I wanted to assess each of you to see if you would obey my orders or if you would find a way to start the war on your own. You all have passed my test, and I am now confident in your loyalties. We begin the war today. This is the day of the Red Dragon. I want all command-and-control functions moved to their secured bunkers and the military brought to full readiness," said Zhang. "Please issue your orders, and let's move as a group to the CMC bunker at Da'Anshanxiang."
****

Operation Red Dragon had been in development for nearly forty years. It encompassed a wide variety of tactics, including corporate espionage, industrial sabotage, and placement of thousands of sleeper agents throughout Asia and the US. Once activated, the PLA would begin to turn off critical industrial control switches and routers in virtually every satellite in space with the exception of Russia, China, and the IR. All other nations' satellites would simply turn off and become space junk.

The loss of critical communications satellites, GPS and military surveillance satellites would blind the Allies and give the PLA a short window of opportunity to move forces and conduct attacks without anyone seeing what was going on. With satellite communications down, it would be difficult to coordinate a response or even call for help. The disruption in satellite communications would quickly be followed by tens of millions of internet routers and various industrial control systems burning out in America, Japan, Korea, the European Union and India.

Great Britain and Australia would be minimally affected since most of their internet switches and routers had been converted over to a product solely built in the UK. That company was one of the few targets that the Chinese had not fully infiltrated prior to Red Dragon. The breakdown in global communications would be nothing short of catastrophic and, in the eyes of China, would lead to a quick victory.

The PLA Navy had been maneuvering as if they were going to attack the US air and naval base at Guam. Once the global communications systems went down, the task force that was headed to Guam would quickly change direction and hit the American facilities at Okinawa, Japan. Then they would turn back to Guam, knowing that the Guamanians would receive no assistance or help from their bases in Japan. With the American naval and air forces in the Pacific destroyed, there would be little to stop China in their conquest of Asia.
****

10 December 2040
1943 hours
The Hive, Northern Virginia

During the early years of the de Blasio administration, the government had begun building a series of regionally based deep underground bunker complexes for the government and scientists to retreat to in case of an apocalyptic event, such as catastrophic climate change, a solar flare, or an unchecked Ebola outbreak. President de Blasio was, if nothing else, paranoid about climate change, and he had spent billions of dollars building these networks that he believed could one day save America should it come to that.

When President Stein had been sworn into office, rather than abandoning the bunkers, Stein had them expanded to include a multitude of civilian functions. Each hive network consisted of fifty underground levels that started with two ground levels and then three basement levels. From there, the hive began a series of fifty underground floors that started at four hundred feet below the surface. Each floor was separated by fifty feet of earth, reducing the likelihood of one floor collapsing into another—each floor was essentially a self-sustaining little city. At a half mile wide and three miles long, each floor had immense space that could be divided and partitioned off as needed. Every fifth floor could be converted into a self-enclosed farm that was able to raise chickens, fish and grow produce via hydroponics. The bunkers had all been equipped with sustainable energy generation from geothermal sources below, allowing each bunker to have sunlike UV lighting 365 days a year. Once operational, each farm floor could grow enough food to sustain five thousand people indefinitely.

The design of the floors resembled the design of the human DNA code as it descended into the earth. Only a small portion of each floor was parallel to the one above and below, reducing the likelihood of one floor collapsing onto another. President Stein, along with a select number of senior level individuals, determined that these new bunker series would replace all the older government bunkers and could be used for more than just housing the government. As they were completed, the government would move most of its research activities to the hives and lease some of the floors to select American firms for their own R&D. These facilities could truly be secured from the public and prying eyes…and hopefully acts of sabotage or espionage.

When the nation's satellites and communication systems went down, the Secret Service believed Washington, D.C. or the President might be the target. "Mr. President, we need to move you and your staff to the hive now," announced the senior Secret Service agent as he entered the Situation Room.

"What is going on, George? Should we go down to the Presidential Emergency Operation Center?" asked the President.

"No, Mr. President. We believe everyone should be moved to a more secured location."

"All right, everyone, let's move with the Secret Service. I assume we're heading to the hive in Virginia?" asked the President.

"Yes, Mr. President. The Secret Service signed off on its operational use two days ago, relegating Mount Weather and other locations to be mothballed."

"Mr. President, I just received word from the Pentagon that our satellites have gone offline," the SecDef said with a look of concern.

"What do you mean, our satellites have gone dark?" asked the President as the group began walking through the White House on their way to the West Lawn.

The federal government had switched phone providers to Verizon and broadband to Google Net two years earlier as part of a diversification of the government's critical infrastructure protection program. This change was probably the only reason the government had been able to hold together in the wake of this recent attack.

"We're not sure yet," replied Eric, who was talking to someone on his cell phone. "It appears to also be affecting GPS and the Internet."

General Branson was on the phone, yelling at someone to figure out what was going on, when he turned to the President and said, "One of our subs in the Pacific just sent a message saying the Chinese are attacking Taiwan. The skipper also reports that he has lost communications with our forces in Japan and Hawaii."

This is the last thing we needed...the Chinese to join the war, thought the President.

As the fully armed Razorback assault helicopter took off from the West Lawn and raced away from the city, the President emerged from thought and announced, "We need to find out if the loss of our satellites is a result of a direct attack by the Chinese. I also want to know what else the Chinese are up to in Asia."

The helicopter dropped down to near treetop level as it accelerated to over 200 miles an hour, speeding its passengers away from the danger of being in Washington. "Admiral Juliano is in the other Razorback with the rest of the team right behind us. I'm sure when we land, he'll have more information for us," Monty said while talking to someone on his smartphone.

****

Lieutenant General Rick Scott, the Director of the DIA, had arrived at the hive thirty minutes before the President and the national security staff. His first priority was to find out how bad the cyberattack was and figure out what still worked. He had been on the phone with the DoD and DIA CIOs, and so far, the most they could tell him was that the Uninet routers and switches had been infected with some sort of malware that caused them to overheat and essentially burn out.

For the last fifteen years, the DoD had been upgrading its IT infrastructure with Uninet hardware, meaning most of the DoD's IT infrastructure had been effectively destroyed. The CIOs explained that the problem was much worse than just the DoD systems. They had been in touch with their DHS and DOJ counterparts, and they were also facing the same problems. Director Scott hit the speed dial on his phone to the Director of Homeland Security.

Within the first couple of minutes of his conversation with Director Perez at DHS, Lieutenant General Scott learned that AT&T was down and so was Sprint, along with nearly half of the country's internet providers. Apparently, Verizon was one of the few internet and phone providers who had not used Uninet's hardware and had not been affected by the malware attack.

"General Scott, the President and the rest of the National Security Council will be arriving in ten minutes. We assured the President that the Chinese wouldn't launch an attack against us…what are we going to do now?" asked Colonel Bauser, General Scott's Chief of Staff.

"We were wrong. I was wrong to doubt General Wright's warning. I suspect the President will probably fire me once he knows we made the wrong call."

Brigadier General Joshua Wright was the Director for Intelligence or J2 at the DIA. Several of his analysts had determined that there was a high likelihood that the Chinese and Russians were going to attack the US and Europe within the week. Their assessment had been dismissed by Lieutenant General Scott due to lack of intelligence supporting the assessment and countering information from the economic and geopolitical analysts. All of this had become a moot point once the satellites had started to go down.

The President's helicopter arrived at the hive entrance, and he and his staff were immediately led to waiting elevators that would take them to the fiftieth floor. The fiftieth floor of the hive had been designated as the presidential level. It had a residency for the first family along with the national security staff. There were also numerous offices and secured conference rooms to conduct the government's business. The next five floors above them were dedicated to various essential departments of the government and their staff.

Once the President and the National Security Council arrived, the hive went into complete lockdown. Thirteen hundred Marines moved into the facility and took over internal security in coordination with the Secret Service. Five hundred Army Rangers, fifty Special Forces, and three thousand Army infantry soldiers would provide external security, scattered across every approachable position to the site. The US government had gone to ground and was hunkering in for the long haul until the situation with the nationwide communications blackout could be sorted out.

As the President got off the elevator and walked to the National Security Council briefing room, he saw that General Scott had already

196

arrived and was clearly getting the room set up and gathering information for a quick briefing.

"General Scott, we've been in transit for the last hour. I need an update on what we're facing," said the President with urgency in his voice.

"Mr. President, I spoke with Director Perez, who's also en route to our position. He told me his department also lost communications. They believe it had something to do with Uninet routers and switches within the government IT infrastructure. I've talked with the CIOs at the DIA, DoD, DoJ, DHS, DoS, NSA and CIA. They've *all* experienced the same problems. All Uninet routers and switches suddenly overheated and burned out at the exact same time. Our assessment is that they had been compromised prior to installation with some sort of sleeper malware waiting to be activated," said General Scott with a worried look.

"Good God, this is worse than we could possibly have thought," said Mike Williams.

"They've also destroyed our communications and GPS satellites," Admiral Lewis said.

"So essentially, we're blind and unable to communicate with our forces abroad or here in the US?" asked the President.

"Sir, it's a bit more than that. AT&T, Sprint, GoogleNet, Comcast, Cox Cable, and Time Warner are all down. Cell phones, internet, just about everything. We're not entirely in the dark. The government's cell and phone carrier is Verizon—so far, they're the only phone and internet provider that's not down. They didn't use the Uninet hardware. Right now, we don't even know if this has hit the Europeans or how this is affecting our forces in the Middle East," General Scott replied.

The President immediately took charge of the situation and rapidly fired off orders to his staff. "First things first. We need to get communications back up ASAP. General Rice, see how many communication drones we have in the US and get them deployed immediately. We need to get military data communications back up at once. Also, someone get on the horn with the CEO of Verizon. Let him know that for the time being, the federal government is going to nationalize their company and infrastructure until the other companies can repair or replace all of the Uninet routers and the switches and are back operational. We need the government functional, and if Verizon is the only content and data provider operational, then they just became our number one priority to secure and use. Work out a generous compensation package for them and ensure that they begin to assist the other providers in order to get services back up and running," directed the President.

The attack against the American critical infrastructure grid caught most Americans by surprise—though some companies were better prepared than others to deal with a situation like this. Thousands of private companies began to assist the government in restoring the communication grid in the US. Google and Facebook had wireless internet drones and blimps they used in remote locations around the world. They immediately deployed that capability in the US, which greatly helped to restore communications within America.
****

10 December 2040
1543 hours
Pacific Ocean, near Pearl Harbor

Three *Shang*-class Type 96 nuclear-powered submarines entered their optimal strike range of the US Naval Facilities at Pearl Harbor, Hawaii. As part of the first strike of Operation Red Dragon, their mission was to destroy the 7th Fleet Headquarters and any ships within the harbor. Upon receiving a message stating the that American satellites and communications were down, two of the three submarines fired four cruise missiles towards predetermined land targets, while the third submarine fired three cruise missiles at the Honolulu International Airport. One nuclear torpedo was launched towards Ford Island, which would effectively destroy the deepwater facilities upon which the US Navy relied.

The cruise missiles quickly found their marks and met no resistance since the communications and electronic grids within the naval facility were still offline. They quickly decimated the 7th Fleet Headquarters and numerous other strategic facilities at Hickam Air Force Base, Camp Smith, and the Honolulu International Airport. The final and most devastating element of the attack was the nuclear torpedo. When it exploded, it destroyed dozens of naval ships in port, along with the equipment needed to service the surface fleet. The damage caused by the mini-nuclear explosion was immense and destroyed the use of Pearl

Harbor for years to come, essentially neutralizing the military there for the duration of the war.
****

11 December 2040
0120 hours
Okinawa, Japan
Kadena Air Force Base

During the communications and satellite blackout, the PLA Navy had maneuvered two of their carriers and the rest of the battlegroup to within ninety miles of Okinawa. While it was still early in the first hour of confusion among the American forces, forty-six J36 attack aircraft began their bombing of Kadena AFB, destroying the runways and numerous aircraft. The battlegroup had launched 190 cruise missiles at the air base and Marines stationed throughout the island. The Japanese Defense Force was able to destroy several of the J36 aircraft while their naval forces moved to engage the Chinese battlegroup. With the bulk of the American naval forces fighting in Indonesia, Japan was on their own. Since the American bases on Okinawa were neutralized, the PLAN carrier battlegroup changed course towards Guam to finish destroying the bases' capability and remove them as a threat.
****

11 December 2040
0120 hours
Straits of Taiwan

With the start of Operation Red Dragon, the PLA Navy and PLA Air Force launched a massive barrage on the Penghu Islands in the Taiwan Straits and began their amphibious landings to secure the islands. The PLA bombarded the main island with thousands of cruise missiles and several hundred short-range ballistic missiles carrying 20,000-pound warheads. They devastated the Taiwanese airports and major command-and-control centers, flattening them like bugs under a fly swatter. The missile and air bombardment of the main island lasted for nearly twenty-four hours before the PLA landed troops on the main island.

Dozens of PLA and PLAN ships were destroyed in the straits by Taiwanese missiles and artillery, slowing the PLA advance but not stopping it. The Americans had sold the Taiwanese their advanced mobile antiaircraft and antimissile railgun systems over the summer. The Taiwanese leveled these weapons to face the ocean and began to add their own devastating fire into the invasion force. These systems were also having a destructive effect on the PLAAF. Within minutes of taking off from their bases on the mainland, they were already within range of the railguns. If it hadn't been for the swarms of thousands of PLAAF drones involved in the attack, the PLAAF might have suffered even worse losses. The railgun defensive systems were beginning to limit the level and frequency of air support that could be provided to the ground forces.
****

11 December 2040
0220 hours
The Border of China, Vietnam, Laos, and Myanmar

At the start of Operation Red Dragon, 1.1 million PLA soldiers advanced across the Chinese southern border into Vietnam, Laos, and Myanmar. Vietnam had been the Rice Bowl of Asia for over a century, so the capture of Vietnam by the Chinese was paramount to stabilizing their nation's food supply. Myanmar would give China deepwater ports on the East Indian Ocean, along with vast amounts of arable farmland.

Thailand, Cambodia, Malaysia, and Singapore were next on the PLA's list. With control of Malaysia and Singapore, the Chinese would control the straits of Malacca and with it the shipping lane of nearly sixty percent of the world's exportable goods.
****

11 December 2040
0542 hours
Riyadh, Islamic Republic
Command Bunker

"Caliph Mohammed, the American satellites and communications systems are down. We have received word from the Chinese that they have commenced their attack on the Americans," Zaheer Akhatar, Mohammed's senior advisor said with glee.

"Excellent. How soon until our packages arrive in America, Huseen?" asked the Caliph, eager to knock the Americans out of the war in the Middle East.

"The liquid natural gas tanker is at the Panama Canal now, and it should enter the lock shortly. Once it does, our people will detonate it as it reaches the optimal spot. With the destruction of the canal, the Americans' ability to move between the Atlantic and Pacific will be crippled. Since the Chinese have plans for the American West Coast, we have moved the Swords of Allah to the East Coast. The first ship has arrived in New York Harbor. Once the captain receives the order, he will move his ship towards the Hudson River until he is adjacent to the New Port Center in New Jersey. Inshallah, he will deliver the first of Allah's Swords," explained Huseen, the IR Intelligence Director.

"Is that the best location to deliver Allah's Sword?" asked Mohammed.

"That location will ensure the vast majority of the buildings in lower and mid-Manhattan will be destroyed. It is also one of the heaviest populated areas in Manhattan and next to the Greenwich and SOHO districts. This is where the wealthiest people in the city live."

"How many casualties do we anticipate?"

"At least one hundred thousand dead from the initial blast, then close to five or six times that number over the next several days as people start to die from radiation poisoning and the general chaos this is going to cause," explained Huseen with an evil sneer.

"The second Sword is still on track to hit Washington, D.C.?" asked Mohammed.

"The ship docked in Baltimore two days ago. Allah's Sword has been offloaded to a lead-shielded delivery vehicle. When you give the order, our operative will drive the vehicle to Washington and deliver Allah's Sword near the Capitol Building. It will destroy everything within a half-mile radius of the event, with severe damage extending as far as two to three miles away. We anticipate fifty thousand casualties initially, and that toll will rise to nearly three to four hundred thousand over the next several days."

"Huseen, I thought the casualties were supposed to be significantly higher than that. What changed?" asked Mohammed.

"The American government has gone to ground. They instituted their Continuity of Government plan. The vast majority of administration functions are no longer being conducted in Washington, D.C., and have moved to their various underground complexes. Before you ask if we know where these locations are—we do not. The ones we knew of have recently been decommissioned, which means they have newer ones that we have not found yet," replied Huseen.

"Perhaps we should move the last Sword to a better target, then?" inquired the Caliph.

"Sir, the goal was to destroy the symbol of American power, Washington, D.C. Even if the government is no longer operating out of Washington, we can still destroy the city," said General Rafik Hamza.

"Destroying the city has been one of our major goals. However, we only have one of Allah's Swords left to use. I want to make sure it is used where it can cause the most damage and hurt and kill the most Americans possible. We can have several of our direct-action units in the area start fires all across Washington and attempt to burn it, but Allah's Sword is special. What other targets should we consider?"

"If this is your final decision, then I propose we use Allah's Sword on Baltimore. It is already in place. All that needs to be done is to move it to the downtown area and then deliver it. We would destroy one of their largest seaports on the East Coast and cripple a key aspect of their rail and road infrastructure. The casualties from this should be several hundred thousand people initially, and eclipse a million within a month," said General Rafik Hamza.

"There are better targets than Baltimore, General Hamza. Demolishing Philadelphia would destroy a naval yard, along with one of their oldest and most notable cities," Zaheer Akhatar said.

"Zaheer, the drive to Philadelphia is further than the drive to Washington, so the chances of the device being detected are much higher. Philadelphia does have the naval yard, but Baltimore has one of the largest deepwater ports on the East Coast. With New York Harbor reeling from the destruction of the first device, destroying the Port of Baltimore will hurt the American military far more than the demolition of one of their naval yards," General Hamza said with a bit of annoyance at being challenged by Zaheer. Although Zaheer was the senior advisor to Caliph Mohammed, Rafik did not like or trust him.

"Enough. You both bring up good points…I believe General Hamza is right. Destroying a second East Coast deepwater port is going to cause more problems for the Americans. Our Russian brothers have not attacked yet, but the destruction of a critical deepwater port will not only aid our war in Israel, it will aid the Russians' attack against the EU. Huseen, issue the order for the LNG ship to destroy the Panama Canal immediately. Twelve hours after the canal has been destroyed, issue the order to deliver Allah's Sword to Manhattan. Then, I will issue the Americans their warning to surrender and withdraw from Israel, or we will deliver a second Sword of Allah."

"Caliph, once we do this, we have to expect the Americans to respond with their own nuclear weapons. We saw what they did to us when we used tactical nuclear weapons on the 5th Fleet. They hit us pretty hard, with over a dozen nukes. We are only just now beginning to restore power to the country, and we lost nearly sixty percent of our laser missile defense systems. I fear the use of a nuclear bomb in New York City is going to destroy us," said Talal bin Abdulaziz, the IR foreign minister.

"I understand your concern, Talal, and the Americans *will* most likely respond with more nuclear weapons. But this is our chance to hurt the Americans at home. For nearly a century and a half, the Americans have waged war in our lands and killed our people by the millions. This may be the Muslim world's last chance to really hurt the Americans, and I intend to take it."

"Caliph, we are grinding the American military down in Israel. The Chinese have just entered the war and are hitting the Americans hard. The Russians will launch their attack soon. We need only to stay the course, and we will achieve our victory without nuclear weapons."

"You speak wise words, Talal. However, we already have Allah's Swords in place—"

"—If we do this, we will lose the Republic. The Americans will destroy everything in retaliation, and even if we do win with Russian and Chinese help, we will not have a functioning country for our people to enjoy our hard-won victory," said Talal, almost pleading with Mohammed.

"If I may, Caliph—as the senior military commander for the Republic, I have to agree with Talal. I want to nuke New York City just as badly as you, but I also want to live to enjoy our victory, and my soldiers will want a country to return home to. With the Chinese and soon the Russians entering the war, it will not be long until we have destroyed Israel and permanently removed the Americans from the lands of Allah. Then we should let the Russians and Chinese destroy America for us," said General Hamza with a somber look.

Caliph Mohammed sighed deeply. "You both have given me pause. Huseen, continue with the attack on the canal. Have our operatives continue to hold on to Allah's Swords. We will wait and leave them in place for the time being."
****

14 December 2040
Kremlin, Moscow

"Generals, the Islamic Republic has been battling the American and Israeli forces for sixteen days. How can they possibly have lost 13,000 fighter drones and over sixty percent of the aircraft that we sold them and the pilots that we trained?" asked President Mikhail Fradkov, still in shock.

"The American antiaircraft and antimissile railgun systems have proven to be far more effective than we believed possible. Their new Pershing main battle tank also has this technology and completely destroyed our frontline battle tanks we sold to the IR. They were able to engage the IR tanks at maximum range, never allowing the tanks to get close enough to fire a shot. When a few of the tanks were able to get a shot or two off, the rounds just bounced off their new armor," said General Gerasimov with an anxious look.

"General Sergun, the GRU assured us that the Americans had not been able to produce these new railgun weapon systems in sufficient numbers to be a problem, yet, they are completely destroying entire drone armadas, and our state-of-the-art tanks cannot get close enough to fire a shot at their tanks. What do you have to say for yourself?" asked the President, clearly irritated.

"Mr. President, the Americans only have one division of Pershing tanks with the new railgun systems. That group is currently bogged down in Israel. They do not have another division of these tanks that can be deployed to Europe. Their mobile and fixed antimissile/antiaircraft railgun systems are also limited in number. They have deployed the bulk of these units to their military forces in Israel and now in Asia to fight the Chinese—"

"—Yes, but they are mass-producing these weapons, are they not?"

"Yes, Mr. President. They are, but it will take time before they have sufficient numbers."

"This still creates a problem for us. Have they shared this technology and the plans with the EU? Are they now producing these weapons as well?"

"Our sources have confirmed the Americans have provided this information to their European partners, and yes, the EU is now starting to produce these weapons. Again, this is a very advanced technology. It's not something that can be mass-produced and deployed quickly. It took the Americans nearly three years to produce enough tanks to field one division. We have time on our side, but only if we act soon," said General Sergun with a look of confidence.

"If we were facing the Americans and the EU at full strength, then these new weapons would pose a significant problem for us. As it stands, the Americans are heavily engaged in Israel and Mexico, and now they have to deal with China. They are not going to be a factor in Europe," said General Dmitri Kulikov, who had recently returned from Central Asia.

"General Kulikov, how soon could the First and Third Shock Armies invade the EU?" asked the President.

"I need three days for both army groups to be ready once you give the order. The Third Shock Army will cross into Western Ukraine and then travel to Romania and Hungary. The First Shock Army will cross into Poland and drive towards Germany. The EU army is not large enough or prepared enough to stand against two experienced combat army groups."

"Do you agree with General Kulikov's assessment, General Gerasimov?"

"I do, but we should wait until Christmas Eve. Let's see what the Chinese do these next two weeks."

"The destruction of the Panama Canal sure caught the Chinese by surprise. They had originally wanted to capture it."

"They should have worked that out with the IR," said General Kulikov with a smirk on his face.

"Prepare your forces, General Kulikov. The attack will commence on December twenty-fourth. It will make for a warm present to the EU and America from Russia."

"Mr. President, I have one last question before I leave to prepare my forces. Will the MiG 40 be ready?" asked General Kulikov, determined to get a truthful answer.

"Sergei, what is the status of the new MiG?" asked the President, knowing that Kulikov would put the screws to him if he believed he was being misled.

"I had lunch with the CEO of Mikoyan, Artem Gurevich, and he assures me that the MiG 40 will be ready at the end of this week. They have completed the software patch and testing of the system as of today. With the modified timeline, there will be 120 aircraft available with thirty additional aircraft being completed each month," responded Sergei Puchkov, the Minister of Defense.

"I do not mean to dismiss the MiG, but how will 120 aircraft be a deciding factor?" asked Kulikov.

"The MiG 40 is a unique aircraft. Aside from its ability to fly at Mach 3 and a range of nearly nine hundred miles, it is the only aircraft that not only uses stealth technology but also incorporates a translucent fiber-optic exterior camouflage that mimics its surroundings. This means that the aircraft is invisible to the naked eye. It has virtually no radar signature and can only be tracked by the heat it emits, making it nearly impossible to detect until it is too late. It can carry a total of eight missiles or six guided munitions," replied Sergei.

"It will be impressive if it finally works," said Alexander Manturov, the Minister of Industry and Trade. He did not believe the aircraft warranted the immense amount of money and resources it was consuming.

"This aircraft has cost a fortune," asserted Anton Shoygu, the Minister of Finance. "This is like the American JF-35 program—a trillion-dollar program for one aircraft line."

"Gentlemen, this aircraft will be effective, even if a few more bugs have to be worked out, and when it is utilized, it will be the most advanced aircraft in the world. The Americans have nothing like it—this aircraft will dominate the skies long enough for us to win the war," replied President Fradkov with confidence.

"I look forward to using it to secure the skies over Europe for my ground forces. It had better work," General Kulikov said with a hint of skepticism in his voice.

Chapter 16
Unholy War

15 December 2040
Tel Aviv, Israel
General Gardner's Headquarters

With nearly 290,000 US forces in Israel, President Stein reluctantly gave General Gardner his fourth star and overall command of US forces in Israel. The President was still mad at General Gardner for the destruction of the Al Aqsa mosque. However, despite his displeasure with his actions, Gardner was becoming a brilliant military tactician and had grabbed victory from the jaws of defeat.

General Wade, the CENTCOM Commander, and his planners were developing a plan to invade Turkey via Greece once the situation in Israel had been stabilized. In the meantime, they were still working on how to move 140,000 soldiers in Germany and 110,000 troops in Italy to Israel. There were still another 350,000 troops on the East Coast waiting for transport to Europe, which had become more complicated with the loss of US satellite communications and GPS.

General Gardner walked into an underground command bunker that had been commandeered from the IDF, ready to address his senior officers and NCOs. "Everyone, listen up. We're going to have to deal with the fact that we don't have satellite communications or surveillance and, yes, there is a serious disruption to our supply lines. We train for this junk, so just get over the loss—we have a war to win," barked General Gardner. "The Air Force is providing continuous drone surveillance and communication flights across the battlefield, the Navy is continuing to ferry reinforcements from Italy, and the 80th and 81st Drone Attack Wings have been tearing into the IR supply lines and frontline troops. They have also lost nearly 460 ground attack drones, so we won't have as many available for close air support—keep that in mind as well.

"For the last eighteen days, we've been getting our butts handed to us on a platter, and now it's time for us to go on the offensive. We're going to encircle the IR forces in the Jordan Valley and cut them off from the rest of their army. Once we have them encircled, the 307th Bomber Wing is going to conduct a massive carpet bombing of the entire valley.

Their attack will quickly be followed up with the 80th and 81st Drone Attack Wings, and a massive napalm attack will finish them off." Audible whistles could be heard throughout the room.

"Major General Kennedy, the 3rd ID has been doubled in strength, re-equipped and supplied. Tonight, your forces are going on the offense. The Marines have been slugging it out with the IR forces in Be'er Sheva for over a week. The 80th Air Wing has been pounding the crap out of the IR forces in that sector for the last eighteen hours to soften them up. I want the 3rd ID to pass through the Marine positions and hit the IR hard, then drive your division to Arad and onward to the Masada Forest Preserve near the Dead Sea. Be prepared to hold that territory."

General Gardner turned to the next divisional commander. "Major General Peeler, the 4th Marines are going to move through your lines and support the 3rd ID by holding the line from Beit Kama, Lahav and Meitar, where they'll form the left flank of General Kennedy's defensive line. The 80th Air Wing will provide continuous air support to your division's forces, so use them as needed. Moving to the north, Major General Preston, your 4th ID is fresh and about to get bloodied. The IR forces have been making a push again at Umm al-Fahm. Your division will need to push the IR forces back and then secure Ein Harod-Ihud down to Beit She'an. It is imperative that your division hold this line. The IR is going to press your troops hard in an effort to cut our forces in half. You absolutely cannot let this happen, no matter the cost to your division. Your position is perhaps the most important in this whole attack scheme." General Preston nodded in acknowledgment of the significance of his mission.

"Major General Twitty, I need the 1st Armored Division to bring the hammer down and close the back door. Your division is to push through the 4th ID at Beit She'an and drive hard to Zubaydat, As Salt, Jericho and Almog along the Dead Sea. This area is good tank country, but you'll need to watch your six with Amman to your back. It's imperative that the 1st Armored and 3rd ID hold your positions at the Dead Sea. This will leave the IR forces nowhere to go."

"The IDF, along with the 101st Airborne, will hold the line in front of Lod, Rehovot and Kiryat Gat. Once the bombing runs are completed, all divisions will move forward and shrink the perimeter until we secure the entire valley," General Gardner ordered.

General Kennedy raised his hand. "Once we've destroyed these pigs, are we going to get our payback for their crucifixions?" he asked.

The Marine commanders, who were beyond enraged, jumped in. "We found 153 Marines crucified when we resecured the Ben-Gurion University campus near Negev the other day," blurted General Peeler, eyes burning with rage.

"I know everyone wants payback for the crucifixions, and I assure you we will have it. Once the battlefields have been secured and the grave registration units move in, they're going to bury the IR forces in mass graves. They'll do their best to identify the IR soldiers so that they can be properly marked. Prior to the graves being filled in, they have been instructed to cover all the bodies in pig's blood, which the Germans and Brits have supplied. We have documented over 5,000 crucifixions of US forces, so we will bury their dead in pig's blood in retaliation. They believe that this will prevent them from entering paradise, so we will test that theory."

A few laughs, snickers and whoops could be heard, mostly from the NCOs.

This was a tactic used by General "Black Jack" Pershing in the Philippines prior to World War I. The US had taken possession of the Philippines during the Spanish American War of 1898. In 1911, a Muslim uprising had taken place in Mindanao, and General Pershing had had the insurgents shot with bullets dipped in pig's blood, and then their bodies had been buried with the guts of the pig. This had discouraged future jihadi attacks. General Gardner's staff wanted to take a page from history and see if it would make a difference in this war—any small advantage that could be gained was something worth pursuing, no matter how strange or unconventional it might be.

"If anyone has further questions, please stay behind and direct them to Brigadier General Williams. I want everyone ready to move within the next twelve hours."
****

15 December 2040
The Hive, Presidential Briefing

"Eric, are the other hive locations operational yet?" asked Monty.

"All thirty sites are operational. We've located and moved every member of Congress and senior government official along with their families to the secured locations. There should be no more high-level assassinations," said Eric Clarke in a serious tone.

"I still cannot believe the Chinese would openly assassinate our elected officials," said Jorge Perez in disbelief.

"The world powers seem to be trying pretty hard to put us down for the count," said Monty angrily.

"Is the President going to sign the executive orders for the Trinity Project today?" inquired Director Perez.

"We are still going forward with the program? I thought we had agreed to table that," said Jane Smart, the Director of the FBI.

"We had tabled it, until the Chinese killed all but three of the Supreme Court justices and Senator Landrew. Between the Muslim extremists in our country and the Chinese sleeper agents, the President made the decision to move forward with it last night," explained Monty.

"I understand your concern with it, Jane. If it doesn't work, then we'll shut it down," said Director Perez.

"Call me old-fashioned, but once this program goes live, I highly doubt it will ever be turned off. It'll become too powerful a tool to simply cancel it."

"Right now, we need to stop these terrorist attacks and bring some sense of security to the American people. The war in Israel is finally starting to turn in our favor, but the Chinese have really hit us hard," explained Monty with a bit of concern in his voice.

The Trinity Program was the culmination of decades of identity intelligence collection, social media monitoring, big data and predictive behavioral analysis, all rolled into one program. Essentially, the program would scan people's social media pages, blogs, and other easily obtainable information and analyze the behavioral characteristics of every single person in the US and around the rest of the globe to provide a predictive analysis as to whether or not that individual posed a security threat. Because of the use of biometrically enabled national identity cards, the purchases people made could also be included in the profiles being generated.

Once the parameters for the search were entered into the program, the system could immediately go to work providing real-time data of threats, including their locations, who they were connected to, and a detailed dossier of the activity of the individuals who met the program's requirements, justifying them as a valid threat. Once a link to a known threatening individual had been made, a warrant for further investigation would be acquired from the Foreign Intelligence Surveillance Court. Then the program would begin to go through the individual's emails, phone calls, text messages, banking records, etcetera, until it had built a complete dossier of the individual for analysts and senior leadership to determine their next steps. Once activated, the Trinity Program would become the most complex and detailed profiling and surveillance program in the world.

By 2039, biometrics had become a major part of the American economy and a major component in reducing crime throughout the country. Through federal grants, the Department of Homeland Security had assisted cities and communities throughout the country in installing traffic and surveillance cameras in public places and buildings, similar to what London and other British cities had done. The network of cameras covered the vast majority of public spaces, making it easier to track the movement of suspicious individuals.

Of course, the Trinity Program was highly classified, with less than twenty total people in the government knowing about its existence, including the two programmers who had built it. There were also several checks and balances built into the program to ensure it wouldn't be used for a political or discriminatory role outside of its stated mission to protect the homeland. All four agency directors, in addition to the President, Speaker of the House and Senate Majority Leader, had to agree on the search parameters and any modifications before it could be used or changed.

As Jane and Monty were engaged in their intense discussion about the Trinity Program, the President walked into the War Room. He could tell by the awkward silence that followed his entrance to the room that he was interrupting something. "Sorry for the intrusion. I know I'm a few minutes late, but let's go ahead and get this meeting started."

"Mr. President, we've broken the briefing down by theaters of operation as requested. The first theater we're going to discuss is Asia," said Colonel Alisa James, a sharp Air Force officer who had been the Defense Attaché to China just four months prior. Her unique knowledge of Chinese military capabilities had attracted the President's attention during a briefing at the start of the war with the IR, and she had been his preferred briefer ever since.

"In Taiwan, the PLA has landed nearly 215,000 troops and effectively split the country in half. The Taiwanese Defense Forces believe they should be able to hold their current positions for at least another month and will continue to do so for as long as they can. The TDF destroyed nearly twenty percent of the invasion force's ships and shot down over 1,300 Chinese fighter drones. Ultimately, the TDF will have to surrender if they're not reinforced, but at present, they're tying the PLA down and costing them thousands of casualties a day.

"We have three attack submarines in the area that have been hitting the Chinese surface fleet on and off for the last three days with some success. They were able to destroy a PLAN heavy missile cruiser along with two roll-on, roll-off heavy transport ships, which will probably hurt the PLA and PLAN logistically more than any of the other ships sunk thus far."

"In Okinawa, the PLAN and PLAAF have destroyed our Naval, Marine and Air Force bases on the island. Most of our aircraft that hadn't deployed prior to the surprise attack by the Chinese were destroyed on the ground. The 12,200 Marines, sailors, and airmen are working with 15,000 Japanese Defense Forces or JDF to prepare the island for a potential invasion. Unfortunately, we do not have any capabilities within the region to evacuate our military members from the island. Should the Chinese land ground forces on the island, *our* forces are on their own.

"The North Koreans and Chinese haven't made a move towards South Korea yet. We aren't sure how long this will last. Admiral Libby, the PACOM commanding general, has ordered all American forces in Korea to withdraw to Japan. The South Koreans have activated their entire reserve forces and are moving to fill in our positions as we withdraw.

"The Japanese have provided over a dozen heavy lift transports to assist in moving the heavy equipment to include tanks from Korea to Japan. The JDF has also moved three of their five carriers into Korean waters to protect the transports. Admiral Libby has stated that all American forces should be out of Korea within the next seven days, bringing the US forces in Japan to around 42,000.

"Aside from the attack against our bases on Okinawa, the Chinese have not attacked the Japanese Defense Forces. Intelligence does not believe there's a separate deal being worked between the Chinese and Japanese, but the Chinese don't appear to be concerned by the JDF at present."

The President interjected, "Colonel James, before you go any further—can you please tell me if the JDF plans on assisting the US in fighting the Chinese?"

"I believe that is a question Secretary Clarke or Secretary Wise could better answer," said Colonel James, turning to them both.

"Mr. President, I have spoken with the prime minister of Japan, and he has told me that Japan is going to try and remain neutral as they continue to mobilize their reserves," replied Secretary Wise.

"Jim, kindly remind the prime minister of our mutual defense agreements, and that America is depending on Japan to honor those agreements. If they're holding out for a few more days or weeks so they can mobilize their reserves, I understand. However, we need their help in challenging the PLAN in the Pacific until our other carriers are operational," said the President, clearly annoyed that yet another ally had not come to the aid of the US.

"Yes, Mr. President."

"Colonel, please continue."

"Yes, Mr. President. Our forces on Guam are surrounded. The PLAAF and PLAN have been hitting them round the clock. It would appear they are going to invade the island sometime within the next twelve to twenty-four hours. The Navy lost four attack submarines in the last twelve hours in the waters around Guam, and the Air Force has expended nearly all of their remaining fighter drones attacking the PLAN armada—"

"How many PLAN ships are in this armada?" asked the President.

"According to our last surveillance drone, there are three Chinese supercarriers, along with their supporting ships, and what appears to be roughly 90,000 naval infantry forces," said Colonel James. "These naval infantry forces are equipped with their newest exoskeleton combat suits. These are the best trained and equipped troops that the Marines and Air Force will be facing."

"Between the Air Force and Marines, we have 21,200 personnel on the island. Most of the family members have been evacuated, but some are still on the island. As of five hours ago, the base had suffered the loss of 2,312 servicemen and women killed, with nearly twice that many wounded. There have also been 964 civilian casualties."

"General Black, can the Marines repulse their invasion?" asked the President, knowing the chances might be small.

"It will be tough, Mr. President. I'd like to say they can, but with no air support, reinforcements or assistance, they will ultimately fail. I do believe they could defend the base and island for a few weeks, maybe a month. Do you want my Marines to try and hold out?" asked General Black, knowing where the President was going with his question.

The President didn't want to make General Black responsible for issuing the command to hold the island and essentially commit to losing over 15,000 Marines. He needed to be the one to give that order.

"I do, General Black. The longer they can tie down the PLAN, the more time it gives the Navy to attack and sink their ships while they're in a contained area. I hate the idea of losing more service members, but surrendering without a fight is just going to give the Chinese an operational air base in a key position in the Pacific, and our forces will be moved to God only knows what kind of POW camp the Chinese are running."

"I'll inform the commander on the ground that he's to prepare to hold the island for as long as possible, destroy the remnants of the runways and then heavily mine them. It will slow the Chinese down, and hopefully the Japanese Defense Force will get involved soon. They could potentially relieve, or at least resupply our forces there," said the general with a solemn shadow cast over him.

"Thank you, General Black. We will do everything in our power to make sure that those Marines do not make a sacrifice in vain," replied the President.

"Thank you, Sir."

Colonel James paused a moment and then broke the awkward silence that hung in the air. "Moving on to Southeast Asia, Mr. President. The Chinese 7th and 8th Army Groups have rolled across Vietnam, Laos, Cambodia, Myanmar and most of Thailand. Intelligence suggests that they'll move on Malaysia and the Philippines next."

"What are the Australians doing in response?" asked the President.

"The Royal Australian Navy is conducting hit-and-run attacks on the PLAN in the area, but in general, they're pulling their forces back from Indonesia to northern Australia. I recommend we withdraw our forces from Indonesia as quickly as possible, along with the rest of our naval assets, and move them to northern Australia and prepare a new defensive line," General Branson said while pulling up a holographic map of Australia.

"We are in no position to stop the PLAN right now; they have three supercarriers heading towards Malaysia. Our best option is to withdraw as quickly as we can and prepare a defensive line in Australia. Until we can regain control of the seas, we need to be cautious with our remaining carrier group."

"I concur, Mr. President. For the time being, we need to play defense with the Chinese until we can retool and get our shipyards going," Admiral Juliano said while opening a file on his tablet.

"We have ordered the construction of eight new supercarriers, and we're pulling another eight out of mothballs to get them in the fight. It's going to be three to six months to get our mothballed carriers into the fleet, and close to three to four years for the new ones to be completed."

"I assume we are activating most of the Ghost Fleet, correct?"

"Yes, Mr. President. The Navy just issued a contract for 200,000 workers to retrofit the Ghost Fleet and get it operational. We've also activated the entire naval reserve force, and they're going to start reporting for Fleet duty within the week," said Secretary Clarke, nodding to Admiral Juliano.

"Sorry for getting us sidetracked, Colonel. Is there anything else with regard to Asia that we should know?" asked the President.

"There is one other item. We know the Chinese have several military installations in Africa and the IR. One of our subs in the Indian Ocean spotted two Chinese convoys. They followed them until the convoys split, so they followed the one heading towards their naval and land base in former Yemen. The other convoy appeared to be heading towards their base in either Madagascar or Tanzania."

"Hmm….so our forces may start to see Chinese ground forces in Israel soon. General Gardner, did you catch that part?"

"Yes, Mr. President. I'll see if the Air Force can task some of their drones to that location and see if we can spot the convoy as it comes into port," said General Gardner via the 3-D holographic image.

"Colonel, thank you for bringing us up to speed in Asia. Let's transition to Mexico and the Panama Canal before we discuss Europe and the Middle East."

"Mr. President, I've authorized four private military contractors to provide security for the DOJ, DHS, and reconstruction efforts in Mexico. This will allow us to withdraw an additional 60,000 troops from Mexico and bring our total troop count to around 45,000 from the 105,000 currently there. I'll leave the reconstruction status for the DHS brief later today. Moving to the Panama Canal...well, it's a mess. The Corps of Engineers believe they can have the locks repaired within the next thirty to forty-five days. We are also sending 9,300 troops to provide additional security for the canal; it's become too important of an asset for us," Secretary Clarke said.

"I'm amazed the canal can be repaired in that amount of time, Eric. I thought we might have lost use of it for much longer," said the President with a hint of optimism.

"We thought it was going to be out of commission longer as well. Thankfully, the blast wasn't a nuclear or a dirty bomb, so it's just a matter of repairing the infrastructure, as opposed to decontaminating everything prior to working on it."

"I know I'm changing subjects, but how is the recruiting going?" asked Secretary Perez from DHS.

"Surprisingly well. The first week of the war, we had 2,300,000 volunteers. The issue we face right now is processing them all and getting them into training. It's taking nearly three weeks to get a new recruit to basic training. We have twelve new basic training locations being opened, and we've tripled the size of the existing sites. Last week we had another 1,700,000 people join," Eric said.

"Do we still need to look at a draft with these numbers?" asked the President, hoping to keep the armed forces an all-volunteer force.

"Yes, Mr. President."

"Even with nearly four million people joining the military in the last seventeen days?" asked the DHS Director, a bit surprised.

"Four million men and women is a lot, but this war is going to need a lot more. We're facing a Chinese military that's close to forty million strong with their active and reserve force. The Russians have activated their entire reserve, bringing their total force to over six million, and the Islamic Republic still has over six million troops, despite the losses they're incurring in Israel.

"We also need a lot of tech-savvy recruits for our drone and other technical programs. A lot of these training programs are in excess of six to eighteen months. Even with accelerating the training, it's going to take time to field these new soldiers. In the meantime, we've lost 71,242 service members in Israel, 32,435 service members in Asia and 2,352 in Mexico. These are just our KIAs. Our wounded are nearly triple that," Eric said with a deep sigh. He rubbed his temples, unable to hide the stress.

"We're going to need an army closer to ten to twelve million strong and a complete retooling of our entire economy to accommodate war production in order to win this war, and it will take years, not months."

Monty broke in and quickly asked, "Things aren't *that* bad, are they? We're about to crush an entire IR army in the Jordan Valley."

"It's not that they're dire right now…it's the combined weight of Russia, China and the IR that will eventually crush us. We have no blocking force in the Pacific right now, leaving Hawaii, Alaska and the West Coast exposed. The Russians are about to enter the war, and they'll most likely roll over the EU within six months. With the Russian and Chinese navies and most of our carriers and naval forces destroyed, there's little we can do to stop the Chinese or Russians from taking Hawaii or Alaska, or making a move into our Canadian states," explained CIA Director Rubio.

The President saw the realization of what Director Rubio had just said, and he knew he had to regain control of the mood and thoughts of his advisors before they began to think the situation was hopeless.

"Gentlemen, America has been in tough positions in the past, and in each case, we have risen above them to new greatness. This will be no exception. Our soldiers are using the most advanced infantry rifle in the world; we have already seen it make a difference in Israel. Our new Pershing tanks are unrivaled on the battlefield. They defeated the best Russian and Chinese made tanks near Damascus, and it's that same railgun technology that cut down over five thousand IR fighter drones that swarmed over Israel.

"The American soldier is the toughest killing machine in the world, and we will win this war! It may not be in six months, or even a year, but mark my words—as long as I'm President, we will fight this war through to victory. We are Americans. We are not just the greatest country on earth, we are the most innovative and craftiest devils in history. If any of you doubt that fact, then I ask you to resign immediately, and we will replace you with someone who will work tirelessly for complete and total victory," said the President, eying all of his directors, generals, and advisors.

The room became silent. The few who had doubts about America's ability to win this war quickly lost them with the President's fiery pep talk. Monty broke the silence. "So that everyone is aware—the CEOs of General Motors, Ford and Chrysler have assured us that their entire manufacturing capability is in the process of switching over to manufacturing armored vehicles, tanks, drones, missiles and anything else we need. They will no longer produce any new American vehicles for the duration of the war and will focus solely on building military equipment. Wal-Mart and Amazon are assisting with the logistics and movement of material across the US and to the operational theaters. Lockheed, Boeing and General Dynamics have ramped up production to 24/7 operations producing cruise missiles, fighter and bomber aircraft, along with our entire suite of fighter drone aircraft."

Secretary Gibbs also added, "The Treasury Department has also begun to seize all IR and Chinese assets in the US, including businesses, buildings and other assets that the Chinese and IR subsidiary firms have in the US. We have also frozen the bank accounts of all government and private individuals from those countries, and we are in the process of seizing those financial assets as well."

"The rest of the banking community has been made aware that the US will not do business with any financial institution or corporation that has a joint venture with these countries or that has financial dealings with them. The seizing of assets alone has netted the federal government 1.8 trillion NAD in cash and $5.6 trillion in physical assets, such as buildings and businesses," said Joyce.

"What are we going to do with the money and assets from these seizures?" asked Secretary of State Wise.

"The cash is going into the regular federal budget. I assume it will be used to help fund the war. The physical assets will be sold on the open market for any US persons or corporations to purchase. The proceeds from these sales will also go into the government coffers—"

The President interrupted to add his thoughts. "—We did not start this war, nor are we going to allow these countries and their people to benefit financially from the conflict or sabotage our war efforts. The money being seized will be used to directly fund the war. Director Perez, can you tell us about your meeting with the various heads from the Silicon Valley?"

"Yes, Mr. President. Yesterday I had a meeting with the heads of Google, Apple and some other IT corporations in Silicon Valley. They have agreed to shut off internet access to China, in addition to the entire IR. We'll be instructing them to move ahead with cutting off the Russians as well. Cutting them out of the internet, or at least the seventy percent of it that Silicon Valley controls, is going to have a devastating effect on them," said Director Perez with a smile.

Secretary Wise looked puzzled. "How did you manage to get them to go along with this? I would've thought they would've balked at losing money from those markets."

"They initially did balk at it; they even said they would ignore our directive. Then Secretary Gibbs joined our meeting and said their assets would be frozen for aiding and abetting the enemy during a time of war if they didn't go along with the program," Director Perez said with a smirk.

"That's actually a good point. By continuing to provide them services, they are essentially giving them aid by greatly enhancing their ability to communicate and continue cyberattacks against us. I guess I hadn't thought of it in that way," responded Secretary Jim Wise. He flashed a look of admiration at Gibbs and Perez for pulling this deal off.

"Since Russia has already been brought up, let's discuss them briefly before we break. There are a lot of orders that need to get issued and a lot of coordination that needs to be done," said the President. He was starting to feel almost overwhelmed by the enormity of the decisions he was having to make.

An Army brigadier general began briefing his portion of the meeting. "General Dimitri Kulikov, their Central Asian military commander and the general who led their Red October War, has been transferred to Europe. He has brought the Third Shock Army, which has been battle-hardened for the better part of the last two years in Central Asia. The First Shock Army has moved to the western Ukrainian border while the Third Shock Army is in Belarus, not far from the Polish border. Both Army groups have doubled in strength in the last six months, bringing their total number to 1.7 million soldiers each. They've also moved four million second-tier troops that will be used for replacements and occupation duty when the time comes."

"They also have the Second Shock Army assembling in Turkey, which could threaten our forces in Israel or the EU via Greece," General Branson added.

"Will the EU be able to hold them?" asked the President, knowing the chances were slim.

"Not a chance, Sir. The EU has activated their entire reserve force of 1.2 million soldiers, but they're not ready for combat. The EU's active force is around 660,000, and most of those soldiers are underequipped and undertrained to face the Russians. The Russian Army isn't like the old Soviet Army. This new army is well equipped and well trained. At this point, the EU will be more of a speed bump unless they are seriously reinforced," replied the general.

"Do we have a timeline for when they may attack?" the President asked.

"Our agents were able to identify the launch date for their attack. It'll take place on December twenty-fourth," said Director Rubio.

"What a Christmas present Fradkov is giving to the world. So, we have less than two weeks. Do we have troops or equipment that can be diverted to shore up the EU positions until they can build up their own forces?" inquired Monty.

"We have 350,000 troops en route to Europe, but they were slated to head towards Greece and open a second front against the IR in Turkey," replied the general.

"If the Russians are going to invade, then opening a second front against the IR is a moot point. As those troops deploy to Europe, have them head to our bases in Germany, Poland, and Romania. Let's initiate Operation Reforger and get the gravy train of equipment headed towards England, France, and Germany," said the President.

Once again, America is going to have to save Europe from their own inability to protect themselves. Something has to change in this equation or saving Europe is not going to be worth it, the President thought to himself.

"Sir, we can reroute the troops and equipment, but we need to recognize that it will take us close to a month to get an Army group equipped and operationally ready to take on the Third Shock Army. We have 140,000 troops in Italy right now, but they're supposed to join General Gardner's Command. I recommend that we still send them. We obviously cannot fight on three fronts right now, so let's finish and secure one front while we can. Then we can move more of those forces to the other fronts. The main issue our forces in Europe will face is air power. Most of our air power is supporting our forces in Israel," the SecDef said.

"It's going to be tough, gentlemen, and perhaps we end up trading land for a time, but we need to help the EU hold Germany. It's their industrial center, and losing it will hurt the EU's ability to build up their forces. To your other point, Eric, you're right. We cannot fight on three fronts. I want our focus to be on securing Israel and removing the IR as a threat. In Europe, we need to focus on delaying action and plan to make a stand in Germany. For Asia, I want the focus to also be on delaying damage. Until our naval forces are able to take on the Chinese directly, we're not going to be able to do much against them."

"With all due respect, Mr. President, the EU has really shot themselves in the foot in this situation. Once again, it's America coming to their aid a third time with our military. I respect our EU military forces, but their people and politicians continue to rely on America to defend and save them. I know we can't let the Russians just take them, but there should be something in it for us." A few jaws dropped when National Security Advisor Mike Williams was finished. All eyes turned to the President.

Chuckling slightly, the President responded, "I spent several years working for the DoD in Europe during the 2010s. I couldn't agree with you more, Mike. The question is, what will make it worth it? We can't let Russia have all of Europe. We also can't continue to defend Europe when they should be able to defend themselves." Rubbing his eyes slightly, the President stood. "I appreciate everyone's hard work and effort. These are trying times for America, and we as a country are going to have to rise to meet this challenge. I don't have all the answers, and neither do any of you...what we do have is a will to win and a determination to make that happen. I'll think about what you said Mike, and tomorrow we can discuss it further. With that, I want to end this meeting. We will reconvene tomorrow."
****

19 December 2040
Kramim, Israel

Sergeant Joe Thornton's platoon had advanced steadily once the 4th Marines had hit the IR forces near Be'er Sheva the day before. Despite the numerical advantage the IR had, the American fighter drones had been pounding the IR for days. "Lieutenant Lee, are we going to advance with the 4th further into the Jordan Valley?" asked Sergeant Thornton.

"No, Sergeant. Our orders are to hold this location, so have the rest of the platoon dig in defensive positions. Word has it the IR is about to be pounded from the air, and then we move in and mop up what's left."

That afternoon, the 307th Bomber Wing, consisting of eighty-four B5 strategic bomber drones, flew over Jerusalem, the Jordan Valley, and the bulk of the IR army. The slow and relentless whistling of tens of thousands of bombs being dropped in a pattern designed to saturate every square foot of land below them was nothing short of sheer terror. The mixture of high-explosive and incendiary bombs was designed to not just destroy but incinerate everything in their path. The ground shook and rumbled as if a long and deep earthquake was happening. The Israeli and American forces watched the death and destruction being rained down throughout the valley in awe. A swath of the valley nearly twenty miles deep and sixty miles long was a burning cauldron of death that few, if any, could survive.

After nearly ninety minutes of continuous bombing, Private Thomas and the rest of his platoon stood up and surveyed the damage in the valley. "Do you think anyone lived through that?"

"Listen up, people," said Sergeant Thornton, "the lieutenant says the platoon will be moving out soon to see what's left of them after the bombardment, so get your gear ready. Remember the rules of engagement—if they are unharmed and they surrender, accept it. If they are wounded and need more medical assistance than what the corpsman can provide, shoot them. The higher-ups have said we don't have the medical supplies and support to treat both their wounded and ours. We're not going to sacrifice a wounded Marine for one of theirs—understood?"

"Yes, Sergeant," echoed the chorus of voices through the platoon.

Chapter 17
The Day America Changed Forever

19 December 2040
New York Harbor, New York

The Coast Guard boat was bouncing around as it sped through New York Harbor while the crew began their inspection shift. They were responsible for conducting boardings and inspections of ships as the higher headquarters or DHS directed. Since the start of the war, DHS had been directing the Coast Guard to conduct an increase in cargo ship inspections before ships were allowed to move up the Hudson River.

"I was watching the news before we left on the boat. Those videos they were showing of that air attack in Israel were unbelievable," Mike said while lighting a cigarette.

"I missed seeing it. I heard a few of the guys say they wiped out most of that Muslim army," said George as he sped the boat towards a group of freighters entering the harbor.

"Cut the chatter, guys. Take us towards that freighter near Ellis Island. It's not answering the harbor master's hails, and DHS wants us to investigate before it enters the Hudson River," said Petty Officer Ed Phillips.

While the small Coast Guard boat headed towards the freighter, they could see it pick up speed as it moved past Ellis Island, heading into the Hudson River. "That freighter is moving a bit fast into the Hudson, don't you think, George?"

"Ed, that ship looks like its speeding up, not slowing down," George warned.

Boom!

As the new sun expanded into lower Manhattan and Jersey City, it rapidly gained in speed and temperature, quickly rising to 20 million degrees Fahrenheit, vaporizing everything—buildings, trees, cars, and people—in a mile-and-a-half radius. In an instant, nearly one million people were killed, and four million people received fatal doses of radiation and deadly burns. As the wind swept through the city and surrounding boroughs at several hundred miles an hour, it blew out windows, pushed cars into each other and threw tens of thousands of people on the streets of New York to the ground and into buildings like rag dolls.

Within seconds of the blast wave dissipating, thousands of taxis, delivery trucks, and other vehicles that traveled the busy streets of New York began to explode as the firestorm from the blast created thousands of secondary explosions. Gas and water mains also exploded, further adding to the chaos and destruction being wrought on Manhattan and the surrounding boroughs.

Battery Park, Ellis Island and the Statue of Liberty were obliterated in the blast, destroying one of the most recognizable symbols of America. As the Statue of Liberty fell apart, so too did any restraint President Stein or the military were using in the war with the Islamic Republic. More Americans had died in this single act of aggression than any other in American history. The Islamic Republic was showing no restraint in their war against Israel and the US. It was time for not just the muzzle to come off the American military, but the leash as well.

From the Authors

Miranda and I hope you've enjoyed this book. We always have more books in production; we are currently working on another riveting military thriller series, The Monroe Doctrine. If you'd like to order Volume One of this action-packed page-turner, please visit Amazon.

If you would like to stay up to date on new releases and receive emails about any special pricing deals we may make available, please sign up for our email distribution list. Simply go to https://www.frontlinepublishinginc.com/ and sign up.

If you enjoy audiobooks, we have a great selection that has been created for your listening pleasure. Our entire Red Storm series and our Falling Empire series have been recorded, and several books in our Rise of the Republic series and our Monroe Doctrine series are now available. Please see below for a complete listing.

As independent authors, reviews are very important to us and make a huge difference to other prospective readers. If you enjoyed this book, we humbly ask you to write up a positive review on Amazon and Goodreads. We sincerely appreciate each person that takes the time to write one.

We have really valued connecting with our readers via social media, especially on our Facebook page https://www.facebook.com/RosoneandWatson/. Sometimes we ask for help from our readers as we write future books—we love to draw upon all your different areas of expertise. We also have a group of beta readers who get to look at the books before they are officially published and help us fine-tune last-minute adjustments. If you would like to be a part of this team, please go to our author website, and send us a message through the "Contact" tab.

You may also enjoy some of our other works. A full list can be found below:

Nonfiction:
Iraq Memoir 2006–2007 Troop Surge
Interview with a Terrorist (audiobook available)

Fiction:

The Monroe Doctrine Series
Volume One (audiobook available)
Volume Two (audiobook available)
Volume Three (audiobook available)
Volume Four (audiobook still in production)
Volume Five (available for preorder)

Rise of the Republic Series
Into the Stars (audiobook available)
Into the Battle (audiobook available)
Into the War (audiobook available)
Into the Chaos (audiobook available)
Into the Fire (audiobook still in production)
Into the Calm (available for preorder)

Apollo's Arrows Series (co-authored with T.C. Manning)
Cherubim's Call (available for preorder)

Crisis in the Desert Series (co-authored with Matt Jackson)
Project 19 (audiobook available)
Desert Shield
Desert Storm

Falling Empires Series
Rigged (audiobook available)
Peacekeepers (audiobook available)
Invasion (audiobook available)
Vengeance (audiobook available)
Retribution (audiobook available)

Red Storm Series
Battlefield Ukraine (audiobook available)
Battlefield Korea (audiobook available)
Battlefield Taiwan (audiobook available)
Battlefield Pacific (audiobook available)
Battlefield Russia (audiobook available)
Battlefield China (audiobook available)

Michael Stone Series
Traitors Within (audiobook available)

World War III Series
Prelude to World War III: The Rise of the Islamic Republic and the Rebirth of America (audiobook available)
Operation Red Dragon and the Unthinkable (audiobook available)
Operation Red Dawn and the Siege of Europe (audiobook available)
Cyber Warfare and the New World Order (audiobook available)

Children's Books:
My Daddy has PTSD
My Mommy has PTSD

Abbreviation Key

ACLU	American Civil Liberties Union
AFC	America First Corporation
AG	Attorney General
AIR	Advanced Infantry Rifle
AT	Antitank
BCT	Brigade Combat Team
CAG	Commander, Air Group
CAP	Combat Air Patrol
CENTCOM	Central Command
CIC	Combat Information Center
CIO	Chief Information Officer
CMC	Central Military Commission
DHS	Department of Homeland Security
DIA	Defense Intelligence Agency
DoD	Department of Defense
DOE	Department of Energy
DOJ	Department of Justice
EMP	Electromagnetic Pulse
EO	Executive Order
EU	European Union
EUCOM	European Command
FP	Freedom Party
FSB	Russia's version of the CIA (Federalnaya Sluzhba Bezopasnosti)
GC	Grain Consortium
GDP	Gross Domestic Product
GRU	Main Intelligence Directorate of the General Staff of the Russian armed forces, Russia's equivalent to America's Defense Intelligence Agency (DIA)
HEAT	High Explosive Antitank
HUD	Heads Up Display
HUMINT	Human Intelligence (information gained through spy craft, interrogations, and source operations)
ID	Infantry Division
IDF	Israeli Defense Force
IED	Improvised Explosive Device

IR	Islamic Republic
ISI	Pakistani Inter-Services Intelligence Agency
ISR	Intelligence Surveillance and Reconnaissance
J2	Joint Intelligence Directorate
JDF	Japanese Defense Force
JSOC	Joint Special Operations Command
KIA	Killed in Action
LNG	Liquid Natural Gas
MANPADS	Man-Portable Air-Defense Systems
MIA	Missing in Action
MEF	Marine Expeditionary Force
MLRS	Multiple-Launch Rocket System
MRE	Meal Ready to Eat (packages of meals that are shelf stable for a long time and used by the military)
NAD	New American Dollar
NCO	Noncommissioned Officer
NIC	National Identity Cards (biometrically enabled cards for identification and tracking)
OPEC	Organization for Petroleum Exporting Countries
PACOM	Pacific Command
PGA	Provisional Governing Authority (temporary government set up by the US)
PLA	People's Liberation Army (Chinese Army)
PLAN	People's Liberation Army Navy (Chinese Navy)
PLAAF	People's Liberation Army Air Force (Chinese Air Force)
PM	Prime Minister
POW	Prisoner of War
RPG	Rocket-Propelled Grenade
SecDef	Secretary of Defense
TDF	Taiwanese Defense Force
WIA	Wounded in Action
WMD	Weapons of Mass Destruction

Made in United States
North Haven, CT
16 January 2024